THE QUEEN BEE WANTED HONEY

To the devoted followers of POWERESSENCE, Dr. Rubin Dolomo was their all-wise, all-powerful supreme leader. The truth was somewhat different. The truth was that Rubin Dolomo was putty in the hands of his wife Beatrice. He—and everyone else.

Now Beatrice looked hungrily at the newest converts to their cause. An old Oriental named Chiun and a tasty young American named Remo.

Actually, it was just Remo she was looking at.

"You're mine, young man," said Beatrice, trying to put her hand on Remo's arm. The arm kept escaping her.

"Tell him to be still," she ordered Chiun. "I'm Queen, and I can have anyone in my kingdom."

"She doesn't really care about your body," Chiun told Remo in Korean. "It's hers she's interested in. Satisfy it."

Remo had taken many orders from Chiun—but this one was too much. He refused.

Chiun sighed . . . then he prepared to show Remo . . .

The Destroyer

LOST YESTERDAY

WARREN MURPHY & RICHARD SAPIR

A SIGNET BOOK

NAL PENGUIN INC.

PUBLISHER'S NOTE

This book is a work of fiction. Names, characters, places, and incidents
either are the product of the author's imagination or are used fictitiously,
and any resemblance to actual persons, living or dead, events,
or locales is entirely coincidental.

SIGNET, SIGNET CLASSIC, MENTOR, ONYX, PLUME, MERIDIAN
and NAL BOOKS are published by NAL Penguin Inc., 1633 Broadway,
New York, New York 10019

First Printing, July, 1986

3   4   5   6   7   8   9   10   11

PRINTED IN THE UNITED STATES OF AMERICA

*For the Wonderful Webbs
of Marlborough Street,
Justin, Brandon, Whitney,
Nancy and Jack*

AUTHOR'S NOTE

This Destroyer novel is based upon the original Remo legend, not the one used for the movie. It makes a difference if you remember from one book to the other, a feat that sometimes eludes the authors.

1

Mankind had lost its power because it allowed itself to reciprocate negative energy. The only reason anyone had a headache or couldn't lose weight was negative energy. If you knew you wanted to lose weight and knew how to lose weight, then why didn't you lose weight? If you didn't want a headache and you got a headache, then why did you get it? It was your head to control, right?

Wilbur Smot asked these questions earnestly and was earnestly ignored.

"I'm not joining Poweressence, Wilbur," said the secretary to the chief chemist of Brisbane Pharmaceuticals of Toledo, Ohio. To any unenlightened man, the secretary seemed attractive, but Dr. Wilbur Smot had learned that true attractiveness was harmony with the forces of the universe. Those who resisted could only exude a spiritual homeliness. That was why a Poweressence soul could only be happy with another Poweressence soul.

The secretary's perfect breasts and cupid mouth were only empty temptations unless she had Poweressence. Her sparkling eyes and dimples were really snares. He was attracted to all the wrong things, he had been taught. That was the reason so many marriages failed. People went for the deceptions, not the truths.

The truth was that once Wilbur attained spiritual oneness, he would be able to commune perfectly with another person fortunate enough to be freed from self-destruction by Poweressence. That would be paradise.

Unfortunately, breasts, dimples, and smiles still held

their allure for the young chemist. He didn't care that his boss's secretary was still hopelessly caught in the big "No" of the pitiful little planet Earth.

"Wilbur, you'd better stop talking that nirvana stuff. Brisbane Pharmaceuticals is a scientific institution," she said.

"Scientific as nail polish and headache formulas," said Wilbur. He was twenty-three years old, presentable in a thin sort of way, almost, but not quite, athletic. Almost, but not quite, dark and handsome. Almost, but not quite, one of the better chemists.

The best thing about being a chemist for Brisbane was that one did not have to be as well-dressed as the salesmen or look as solidly prosperous as the executives. Barring obscene dress, the chemists could wear just about anything that fell out of the closet. Even the lowliest secretary could tell the chemists at a glance. They were the ones who looked comfortable.

Wilbur customarily wore a white shirt and chinos. He ate candy bars and, in those rare moments when he wasn't extolling Poweressence as the salvation of the world, he complained that he wasn't doing important things for mankind through chemistry.

And that was the one freedom Brisbane did not allow its chemists. As the foremost manufacturer of women's hair colorings and over-the-counter symptom suppressants for headaches, sniffles, sleeplessness, and other nuisances of life, Brisbane demanded that its hardworking chemists never doubt the importance of their jobs. They were all in pursuit of scientific excellence. Period.

"Wilbur, don't knock it," said the secretary with all the ensnarements the negatives of the world could muster.

"It's so," said Wilbur.

"So what?" said the secretary.

"The truth will set you free," said Wilbur.

"Well, the truth is that Poweressence is a phony religion run by hucksters who are under indictment. It was made up by some writer who was broke. It's a fraud."

"You have to say that," said Wilbur. "Otherwise you

couldn't live your miserable little life, knowing you could be freed from your slavery to the negative rejection of all that is positive.''

"If I'm so negative, why do you keep hanging around me?"

"I want to help you."

"You want to help yourself into my pants."

"You see? That's the negative way to look at love. Your whole life is devoted to love of the big 'No.' "

With that, Wilbur left, telling himself he was leaving her to mull over his brilliant analysis of her character flaws. What he could not know was that he was really leaving to threaten to return all mankind to the intellectual dark ages. For Wilbur Smot was about to unleash on an unsuspecting world the most dangerous chemical compound ever created, a potion that could rob the human race of its past, and therefore, its future.

In a way, old Hiram Brisbane's "brain regenerator" had already robbed Brisbane Pharmaceuticals of a proud past. Its very existence was a problem because it hinted that the modern pharmaceutical company was founded by a snake-oil salesman. Which it was, much to the chagrin of its public-relations department.

As a teenager, Hiram Brisbane had toured the Midwest with a wagon, two good horses, and case upon case of his father's homemade snake-oil medicine. The snake oil, he said, would cure everything from rheumatism to male impotence. He peddled women's solutions, as well; especially potions reputed to reduce the pains of the "monthlies." Like most of the tonics of the time, Brisbane's elixir contained a good dose of opium. As a result, his following was very large and extremely loyal.

Brisbane was a natural businessman and before long, he had turned his wagonload of home brew into a pharmaceutical company. He had to give up traveling, of course. He also had to give up his huckster past, which meant giving up his father's snake oil for more refined compounds. Last but not least, he had to give up hawking his potions from a wagon and learn to hawk them in print.

But the one snake-oil throwback old Hiram Brisbane refused to give up on, although he never tried to sell it, was his father's prized "brain regenerator."

"Indians used to give it to their worst criminals. I thought it was poison. I was a boy at the time, traveling with my father," old Hiram would say.

"Well, they would single out the most horrible outlaw of their tribe, but they wouldn't hang him by the neck like civilized people. Hell, no. They wouldn't even cut off the balls of a rapist like good Christian folk. They'd just give him a shot of this potion. And you know what happened?" old Hiram would say, waiting for his college-educated chemists to ask, "What?"

"Nothing would happen," he would answer. "Worst damned criminal in the world would just grin from ear to ear, then wait to be taken back to his teepee. He'd just smile. Now, is that a fitting punishment?"

Old Hiram would shake his head. And he would wait of course for his college-educated chemists to shake their heads also.

"Criminal looked so happy, my father wanted to try it. But the old medicine men wouldn't let him. Said it was the greatest curse on earth. Now, how could being struck that happy be a curse?"

The college-educated chemists were shrewd enough to appear puzzled.

"How, Mr. Brisbane?" someone would have to ask.

"Medicine man wouldn't say. But since he was grateful to my father for providing elixir on short notice, or at least the opium part, he gave my father a batch. Warned him not to try it on any living soul. So my father gave a teaspoon to a nigger. Nigger swallowed the damned thing and became ornery as hell. Wouldn't say 'sir' or 'ma'am.' The man just stood there grinning. Wouldn't fetch. Wouldn't haul. Wasn't good for anything for the rest of his life, but he never had no headaches, neither. Nosiree— that nigger's headaches were gone forever.

"My father tried it again on a man in West Newton, Wyoming, named Mean Nathan Cruet. Old Cruet was one mean-looking SOB—never did hurt nobody, though. He just went around mumbling. Mumble in the morning. Mumble in the afternoon. Finally my father asked what he was mumbling about, the old Cruet answered he had this headache. Had a headache from the first bejesus day he could remember.

"My father warned him about the potion, but said it might help in a small, small dose. Mean Nathan Cruet took just a little bitty tongue touch from the jug my father was saving, and a smile crossed his face. A big, benign smile."

Hiram's voice would become mellow with that statement, his hands marking the path of a big smooth smile.

"And my father said:

" 'Nathan, how is your headache?'

"And Mean Nathan Cruet, who had been suffering from headaches since as long as he could remember, answered, clear as a bell:

" 'What headache?'

"Gentlemen, I don't know what they teach you in your fancy colleges, but I don't need no slide rule to recognize a headache remedy. What we're selling now is a headache remedy in spruce water. Pure spruce water. But figure out what's in that Indian potion and Brisbane will be the biggest drug company in the world. We'll call it the 'brain regenerator', just like my daddy did. God rest his soul."

With that, in the presence of the first generation of Brisbane chemists, the old man ordered the big safe in his office to be opened. And for the first time ever, out came the wood-stoppered jug. One chemist actually tried to analyze a small portion of it. Some said he merely tasted it. Others said he took a big drink. In any case, he wandered away from the lab and never returned, his mind so addled he didn't even recognize his wife.

To Brisbane's first chemist, the "brain regenerator" had proven itself to be as cursed and "ungodly" as Darwinian theory, but in the 1950's, when no scientist believed in curses and the faith of reason ruled the land, another chemist decided to analyze the potion. This was a time of splitting the atom, of mass spectrometers, of the absolute certainty that all things were matter, and all matter could be understood. It was a faith so firm it would have made a pope envious.

The chemist announced that with only one gram of the potion, he would quantify to the last molecule every ingredient in the "cursed brain regenerator."

He uncorked the jug with a smile. He was still smiling when he asked what time of day it was. He was told it was three-thirty.

"Oh," he said, beaming with enlightenment. "That means the little hand is on the three, and the big hand is on the six. That is the six, isn't it, the one with the handle and the little circle on the bottom?"

In the progressive fifties, crazy people were helped, not ignored. So the chemist was helped into a straitjacket, then into a quiet hospital. Within a few days he was well again. But he could not remember one iota of what had gone wrong. The last thing he could recall was spilling a drop, and trying to wipe it up.

When, decades later, Wilbur Smot happened over the company threshold, Brisbane Pharmaceuticals was on the corporate forefront. Their nursery provided day care for under-paid female employees. Their Enlightened Employment program introduced "blacks" both into the vocabulary and the lab. A minority quota was hired, and that quota met visiting government officials at the door and toured them around the lab. In fact, the "enlightened" employers knew there were no more blacks in the laboratory now than there were during old Hiram's days, but now everyone knew not to call them insulting words. And they had learned something else—something about the "mind regenerator." It could actually be absorbed through skin.

Thus when Wilbur Smot walked into the lab, it didn't surprise him to see the senior chemist wearing rubber gloves and a rubber mask. He knew he was trying to crack the chemical code of the "mind regurgitator," as the chemists jokingly called it.

Wilbur sidled over to the senior chemist. He had to make him understand that the real power of the mind could be unlocked only by eliminating resistance to natural power.

"I've got it," said the senior chemist, seeing a pale cloudy reaction in a beaker. "Of course. Do you know what it is?"

"No," said Wilbur Smot. He knew the senior chemist had discovered a component because it had reacted to an element in the beaker, a common chemical test. But he had no idea what great secret the senior chemist had discovered.

"This supposedly cursed formula doesn't regenerate the brain at all. It is unique, no doubt about it. But it doesn't make the brain work better, although people might think it does."

"What is it?"

"It is the reverse of sodium pentothal. I've never seen anything like it."

"The truth serum?"

"No. Pentothal used in small doses will trigger the memory, free it up. It isn't so much truth you get with pentothal but memory. This 'brain regenerator' actually hardens the arteries in the brain, cutting off functions, not freeing them. It is like instant amnesia."

"So that was why the chemist in the fifties forgot how to read time?" said Wilbur. "Every Brisbane chemist knew the story of the old Indian secret the founder of the company had challenged his chemists to unlock, and how the years had yet to bring an answer."

"Exactly," said the senior chemist. "But his memory came back. Fifty years earlier he would have been allowed to wander out of town, like the previous one. Maybe the first chemist took too much. Powerful compound."

"And the black person," said Wilbur, understanding now, "forgot to be subservient. It eliminated all learned functions."

"So he became absolutely normal, and was called ornery."

"And the Indians gave criminals a large dose so that their negative adult behavior patterns reversed to those of infancy," said Wilbur, who had learned much about negative thoughts at Poweressence. But then he wondered why it would be called "cursed" by the Indians.

"Well, think about it, Wilbur," said the senior chemist. "If you forget enough, you forget who you are. You forget who you love or who loves you. You forget where you belong. And for an Indian to forget his traditions is to die a living death."

"That's awful," said Wilbur.

"Yeah. We should be able to sell this to mental hospitals," said the senior chemist, swirling the fluids in the beaker to better examine the reaction. He breathed deeply, satisfied with himself.

"But if it is so powerful, don't you think we should use it for all mankind?"

"Use what for all mankind?" said the senior chemist.

"The solution you're examining."

"What about the solution I'm examining?"

"It can harm people," said Wilbur.

"This?" said the senior chemist, holding up the vial.

"Yeah," said Wilbur.

"What is it?" said the senior chemist.

"The 'mind regenerator.' You have discovered it works in reverse of a memory jogger. You've broken the secret of the curse. You have discovered it induces amnesia."

"What induces amnesia?" asked the senior chemist.

"That," said Wilbur, pointing to the vial.

"Yes. What is it?" said the senior chemist.

"A memory supressant?"

"Thank you, no. I already forgot what the hell I am supposed to be doing today," said the senior chemist.

And in that instant, Wilbur realized his superior had inhaled the potion. He also realized it was too valuable to leave in the hands of the crudely commercial. It had to be taken from those people whose negativity was so strong they would inflict it on anyone just for profit.

This boon or curse to mankind belonged in the hands of

the only people who truly cared about human life; the people liberated by Poweressence, which was not a cult, not a religion, not a fraud, but as Wilbur Smot understood in the very marrow of his soul, the absolute truth.

Wilbur eased the older man back to his office and then, being very careful neither to breathe nor to touch the brownish potion, he discarded the tests in the beakers. He removed all the notes compiled by the Brisbane chemists throughout the years and stuffed them in his pockets. Wilbur would take both the vial and notes to the one place in the world that would know how to use it. He would get them to the place he trusted, the place he trusted so much he allowed them to take thirty percent of his pay every week.

It was an old brownstone building, bathed in the sharp light of a sunny winter day, snow caked on the roof, a big sign in front offering a free character test. Wilbur had taken one of those when, lonely and frightened, straight from college, he came to Brisbane Pharmaceuticals.

The first level of tests showed that he had suffered blockages that made him, in the words of the attractive female examiner, unsure of himself.

At first he thought anyone could have assumed that simply because he had taken the test at all. Wilbur was not stupid. But then their probing questions turned up areas of fear and anger that even he was surprised to see actually existed. And when the examiner gave him a simple mental exercise to do, among a group of people, and the fear was diminished, he signed up for Level One. He did not hesitate, especially since the course was going up in price the next week.

Level One gave him a sense of a grand goal in his life as well as the tools to help him achieve it. Level Two gave him a sense of strength and peace. Level Three, far more expensive, gave him the challenge of throwing off all the shackles that bound everyone outside Poweressence.

Level Four, he knew, would be far more expensive than Level Three, and he did not know how many more levels he had to pass to free himself totally. But he did know he had found the truth. Those who made accusations against this wonderful freedom-loving, human-enriching movement were really suffering; they were sunk in the mire of negativity right up to their eyeballs.

The truth always had enemies.

Dr. Rubin Dolomo, founder of this great freeing secret of mankind, was perhaps, like all the great truth givers, the most persecuted person of his time. And why?

People feared the truth. From governments to secretaries with nice breasts and dimples, the truth presented a danger to them. And why? Because if they knew the truth, they would have to give up their slavery to their negative meaningless lives.

Dr. Rubin Dolomo did not hate these people, he felt sorry for them, and Wilbur should also. They were in darkness and could not help the things they did.

Of course this didn't mean the group didn't have to defend itself. Indeed it did. A child driving a massive truck might be innocent of all wrongdoing because of its age, but still the truck would do horrible damage. Imagine it running into a crowd. Imagine how many people it would kill.

In that case would it be wrong to remove the child? Would it be criminal then, to save so many?

When Wilbur looked at it like that, the fact that an eight-foot alligator was deposited into the swimming pool of a newsman writing defamatory articles about Poweressence did not seem so terrible. Poweressence had no intention of killing the man; they only wanted to bring him to his senses. Not that Dr. Rubin Dolomo would ever do anything like that himself. But enthusiastic supporters, full of desire to free the writer's soul, had ventured what might seem too far in the eyes of the world at large.

"You mean you follow a man who sneaks alligators into people's pools because they say bad things about him?" Wilbur's mother had asked.

"You don't understand, Mom. Dr. Rubin Dolomo can free you from a life of pain and underachievement and loneliness. Someday I hope you will change your mind."

"I already have. I used to think he was a hustling fraud. Now I think he is a vicious hustling fraud. Wilbur, leave those people."

"Mom, get rid of your negative forces before they ruin you."

"I'll pray for you, Wilbur."

"I'll release my negative forces for you, Mom."

Wilbur remembered that sad conversation as he bowed to the portrait of Dr. Rubin Dolomo, founder of Poweressence, set above the entranceway to the second floor of the building. Only those who had passed the first level were allowed up here. Those walking in from the street for their free character test were kept downstairs in booths, away from pictures of Dr. Dolomo, even away from any mention of Poweressence. This was not deception.

The deception was all the lies people told about Poweressence. Therefore, to hide the fact that Poweressence was behind the tests was really giving the truth a chance, because then the person, after taking the test and seeing what was offered, would have a chance to judge fairly. Otherwise, bombarded by newspaper propaganda, a perfectly innocent person might logically be led to think this was all a come-on for a fraud, a hustle to part a victim from his money and his self-control.

Therefore, Dr. Rubin Dolomo's picture was kept only on the second floor, and only when a person reached this floor was he allowed to venerate the picture and understand, yes, indeed, in the secrecy of pure surroundings, that this was religion, and Dr. Dolomo was sent by the forces of the universe to help mankind.

Only when he saw the picture did the young chemist allow himself to think thoughts of religion. He kept the vial and the formula close to his body. He told one of the workers he had an urgent message.

His Level Three guide was unavailable, so a Level Four guide had to come and see him. The Level Four guide looked somewhat harried for someone who was supposed to be free of negative thoughts.

"I have discovered in my job an incredibly powerful

drug that will remove people's memory. It is so dangerous only we should have it.''

"Fantastic. What does it do?"

When Wilber explained the chemical formula, the Level Four guide decided it was above his power to make a decision and moved Wilbur up to a Level Five guide. The Level Five guide whistled at the thought of blocking memory with a whisper of a substance and he passed Wilbur along to the next level. The Level Six guide was working an adding machine and smoking a cigarette. Cigarette addiction was something Poweressence was supposed to cure.

Level Six did not seem at peace with the positive forces of existence, rather still a sufferer of negative input.

"Okay, what do you got? Whatya got?"

Wilbur explained.

"Okay, what do you want for it?"

"I want for it to be used for the positive power of mankind.''

"C'mon. You gonna do business or you gonna play in my pudding? How much you want? You sellin' the formula? You sellin' what? A dose? A quart?"

"I am not selling anything. I want to give back the many blessings I have received."

"Where did you come from?"

"From downstairs."

"What level are you?"

"I have, with the good help of my guides, broken through to Level Three."

"Ooooooh," said the man with the light of recognition on his face. "I see. This is not business. Good for you, kid. You're going to give it away, right? Explain it to me again."

And Wilbur tried to explain the formula.

"Look, kid. That's too big for this Toledo franchise. You had better go right to headquarters yourself. Right to Dr. Dolomo."

"I'm going to see the doctor?"

"You got to. This is national. But tell him that Toledo is

in for Toledo's share. Okay? He'll know what I'm talking about, and don't forget to tell him you're at Level Three. Right?" said the man, giving Wilbur's cheek a little pat.

"I'm only at Level Three. I don't know if I am qualified to talk to the good doctor myself."

"Yeah. Yeah. You are, kid. It's beautiful. You're a sweet boy. Just tell him what you told me."

"Do you think I should work on a rapid transcendence of the spirit before I enter his presence? I've heard it could be rushed with help."

"What's that, the $1,998.99 weekend in our Chillicothe temple?"

"No, I believe the offering is $900 and it's a day's intensive powering in the Columbus facility."

"Just pay for your own plane fare to headquarters. That's purifying enough. Okay, kid, anything else?"

"Yes. I thought you weren't supposed to smoke once you passed Level Three," said Wilbur, nodding to the burning cigarette.

"Right. Go downstairs; there are people paid to explain it all to you. Now get outta here, kid, and don't forget— tell Dolomo this is a Toledo find. He knows what I'm talking about."

Wilbur went right to the airport, not even bothering to inform Brisbane Pharmaceuticals he was taking a day off. He was troubled by the cigarette smoking at so high a level. But then he remembered what they had told him at Level Two, when he had paid for the $500 hard-bound step-by-step guide through the levels.

"Don't expect to get rid of a lifetime of wrong thinking just because you buy a set of books. It will take years. It will take courses. And most of all, it will take money. But don't feel that because you still worry, or want to smoke or drink or spend your money foolishly, that you have not progressed. Sometimes an isolated negative thought will strike even the most advanced of us."

This explained why someone at so high a level could still be smoking. Still, Wilbur worried about it, though his concerns turned to elation as his cab pulled up to the

famed "Tower of Poweressence." Dr. Dolomo lived on an
estate in California, facing the Pacific. It had more lawn
than most state parks. He had read about it in Poweressence literature.

Dr. Dolomo, having achieved the highest level of Poweressence, needed no sleep and worked twenty-four hours a
day for the good of mankind. And he worked his great
works from here. Wilbur pulled out his step-by-step guide
but he was too excited to cram. In a few minutes he'd be
face-to-face with the young man with incredibly blue eyes
who stared out of the book cover. This was a Level Two
book. There were rumors that people just sleeping on it
under their pillow had advanced in positive power. Wilbur
slid it between the seat of the car and the seat of his pants.

There were guards at the gates, but once inside, people
seemed to wander about at will. There were no prohibi-
tions. Wilbur Smot tried to absorb the positive vibrations
that must be coming from here. He felt the sun and the
grass and he knew again all was good.

A secretary downstairs brought him to an inner room
where a man who called himself the Midwest regional
director watched a taped football game while eating
chocolates.

"He's to see Dr. Dolomo. He's from Toledo."

"Upstairs," said the man.

"Don't you think you ought to go with him? He is sort
of new to everything."

"No. No. Leave me alone. What's there to climbing
stairs? Get out of here."

Wilbur looked to the secretary. That was definite negative behavior.

The secretary smiled.

"It's all right," she said. "Just go upstairs."

On the second floor a group of maids were in a frenzy.
Mrs. Dolomo, he heard, was screaming about something.
Mrs. Dolomo was using profane language. Mrs. Dolomo
didn't want to talk to him or any other jerk from Toledo,
Ohio. Mrs. Dolomo wanted her beige bathing suit and she

wanted it now, and if he didn't know where it was, would he kindly stay the bleeping hell out of the way.

Wilbur Smot found Dr. Dolomo dozing, his potbelly heaving with each breath, a large cigar stagnating in an ashtray.

"Dr. Dolomo?" Wilbur said, praying this was not the man who had found the force that had released Wilbur from so much personal pain.

"Who wha?" cried out the portly figure in panic. He jerked himself up to a sitting position, reached for his bifocals, and focused his eyes. "Get me the pills. Those pills."

Wilbur saw a pink plastic container on a table three steps away from the divan the man was lying on. He gave him the pills. The man's hands were shaking as he threw them into his mouth.

Wilbur perspired in his heavy Midwest winter clothes. Rays of beautiful California sunshine bathed the room as soft Pacific breezes played with a light curtain and made Wilbur's very breath a song of joy. The man cleared his throat.

"Are you trying to kill me? What do you mean coming into this room and waking me up? I don't know who you are. You could be the feds come to throw me in the slammer. You could be some disgruntled parent wanting his kid back come to kill me."

"Those are negative thoughts you are bringing on yourself. You should speak to Dr. Dolomo sometime. You would realize you yourself are bringing all the bad things of your life into your life. No one else does it."

"I don't need grief like that this early in the morning."

"It's the afternoon," said Wilbur.

"Whatever. Did Beatrice send you in here with that crap?"

"Beatrice?"

"Mrs. Dolomo. She resents anyone who thinks. I think. Therefore she resents me."

"I feel sorry for you in your suffering in negativity, but I have been sent here from Toledo to see Dr. Dolomo."

"All right, what do you want?"

Wilbur saw the eyes, the watery blue eyes. The whitish hair had been blond apparently. The face that sagged now had once been young. It was the man in the poster on the second floor of the Toledo Temple, the man that smiled out from the jacket of his Level Two book. Dr. Rubin Dolomo.

"No," said Wilbur. "I have made a terrible mistake."

"You already woke me up, so let's have it."

"I am not giving you anything."

"I didn't ask for anything, but now that you've ruined my day, I am sure as hell going to get what you came for."

"I would never give it to you."

"You've just realized this is a hustle and you're at Level One or something."

"Three," said Wilbur.

"All right. We'll give you your money back. I don't need this grief. But look, you didn't get in here without clearance. And you obviously have something for me. Right?"

Wilbur did not answer. He wondered if he could make the gate running full out. He wondered if he could climb over the gate at the far end of the expanse of lawns. He knew he shouldn't tell what he had.

"I was just reporting from the Toledo Temple. They said they are going to give you an extra payment this month."

"Look," said Dr. Rubin Dolomo with weariness in his voice. "I know you are here with something else. But worse for both of us, Beatrice will know you are here with something else. She'll know. And she'll get it. Me, I would just as soon fly away and not bother with any of this. Personally, I am sorry it all went this far. But you have not yet had the pleasure of meeting Mrs. Dolomo. May you never have to endure that pleasure. So what is it?"

"I won't tell you."

"I'm going to call her."

"No," said Wilbur.

'Before I call her, I want you to know, sonny, that I had nothing against you. And by the way, her name is Beatrice and never, ever call her Betty. Gets her nose out of joint.''

"I'm leaving."

Beatrice!'' screamed Dr. Rubin Dolomo, and the woman who had been cursing in the hallway came into the room still cursing, cursing that she was being bothered.

"I knew you'd find out sooner or later. But there is some kind of good news from Toledo and this kid here is a believer and he won't talk.''

"I am leaving," said Wilbur.

Wilbur found out that Mrs. Dolomo did not believe in arguments. She believed in radiators. Two large strong men with hands like steel vises tied Wilbur to a radiator. Even though the day was warm, there was still steam in the system. It was used to heat water.

Wilbur, understanding what the drug might mean in the wrong hands, held out until he was crying in pain. And then, mentally begging forgiveness, he told the Dolomos about the mind drug that could wipe out memory.

But he warned them how dangerous it was. He begged them not to use it, even as Dr. Dolomo talked of using Level Two people as guinea pigs, of selling small doses of it, or better yet, using it as a teaching booster at the first level. The possibilities were endless: give a group dose to the entire second level and then, as the dose wore off, make the members believe Poweressence had returned their memory. Of course, they would have to give the Toledo franchise its cut. Or better yet, a dose of the drug. They would forget they owned a piece of the potion.

"I was thinking about getting it into the food of the witnesses against us," said Dr. Dolomo. He lit the end of the cigar.

"The witnesses against you, Rubin," said Beatrice Dolomo.

"I am your husband."

"Please," cried Wilbur.

"What do we do with him?" asked Dolomo.

"I am not going to have someone with an assault charge

in his pocket against me running around the streets," huffed Beatrice.

"I told you, kid," said Dr. Dolomo, shrugging.

"Please," sobbed Wilbur. "Please let me up."

The woman nodded for him to be untied.

"We don't have to kill him," said Dolomo. "He already told us everything it did. Give him a good swallow like the Indians used. He'll forget everything."

"No," said Wilbur.

"Young man," said Beatrice Dolomo. "Do you know how alligators eat their dinner? Well, either you take a swig out of that vial you just showed us, or you will become very familiar with the dental pattern of the American alligator. They rip their food rather than chew it, you know. Thrash it about, so to speak. Not much of a choice, is it, dear?"

Wilbur looked at the brown liquid. He wondered what he would feel like not remembering anything, not remembering who he was, who his parents were, or how he lived, and he understood in that last mature moment of his life what the Indians meant by a punishment. When he swallowed the little vial, he said good-bye to himself.

The liquid was surprisingly sweet and pleasant. Wilbur thought that he would make a mental note of how long it took before the potion took hold and what the last moments of memory would be like.

He did not harbor this thought long. He was standing in a room with people looking at him and had something sweet in his mouth. He did not know whether they were kind people or bad people. He did not know he was in California. He knew the sun was shining and someone, some nice person, was telling him they were going to fix the boo-boo on his backside. He had been burned. But Wilbur Smot did not quite understand those words. He did not know what burn was. He did not know what boo-boo was.

He was on the floor, because he had not yet learned to walk.

2

His name was Remo and he was learning again. But it seemed slower this time, the wall did not seem as exciting this time. His body did not seem as alive this time.

The beach sands blew on the stone walk around the luxury high-rise building, collecting around bushes and posts and his bare ankles. Behind him, the sun rose red over the dark Atlantic. Miami Beach was quiet but for the distant scratching of rats in the garbage cans. He felt the salt sea air on his skin, moist and warm and fertile as the things of the sea. His lips tasted faintly of salt and white brick wall loomed up above him, straight up above him fifty stories into the last of the night sky.

It had been so easy for so long, and now he was doing it again. The first time, so many years before, he had started at the top and descended. But that was a test of fear, that was a test of controlling the one thing that stopped the body from moving at its optimum.

He touched his open palm to the brick and felt the mortar joints, concrete crumbling under his fingerpads. His body moved into the wall so that there was a true pressure against it, from his spine, from his breathing, from the human form that so rarely in all history was used to its full. His toes felt the moisture on the brick, and set themselves ever so precisely to balance his body against the wall with an even force. And then fingerpads against mortar, toes against brick, the body moved upward into the building, so that Remo could feel with his cheek the very vibrations of the foundation sunk into the supporting rock of Miami Beach.

The brick brushed the cheek, and the hands, as though swimming, pressed down against the wall as his toes pushed upward. And the trunk rose, smooth as a yawn, hands up and down, feet together, toes pushing down, hands up, toes down, hands down, toes up, faster and faster until the yawn became a rapid whisper up the walls. As he moved past windows and ceilings, as the brick went by and the roof came down to the rising figure, it was all the same again. Smooth again. Perfect again. As he had been told it would be.

If someone had been watching he would have seen a man swim up a wall. That was how it would have seemed. But the miraculous thing about it would have been that it would not have seemed miraculous at all, because the way this man moved his body was in unity with all living things. Someone seeing it would have seen the most natural thing in the world.

"Not jerky," came the high-pitched voice from the roof. Remo topped like a diver at the apex of his jump, and landed on the roof. He was thin but with thick wrists. He had dark eyes and high cheekbones and thin lips. He wore dark slacks and a dark shirt.

"Maybe," he said, "I am feeling at one with myself again."

"That is not the one to be at one with, yourself. I am the one to be at one with. That's why you got into trouble. That's why we are relearning. What will happen when I am not here anymore?"

"I'll probably have a moment's peace, little father," said Remo.

"Death is the most relaxing experience of all," came the squeaky voice from the shadows. The breeze on the roof rustled the dark robes of the old man who had just spoken. The wisps of hair around his ears floated like pennants, but the body was centered with more firmness than the very foundation of the building. He raised a single finger, its nail like a curving quill, long and smooth. "Death," said Chiun, "is the easiest thing of all."

"Well then, little father," Remo said. "It's my death."

"No," said Chiun. "Not anymore. You do not have a right to die, any more than I did before I found a Master to take my place, a Master of Sinanju."

Remo did not answer. He knew the old man was right. He had endangered himself by exposing his highly sensitive nervous system to radioactive materials. Normally he would have noticed, sensed it. But Remo had been desensitized by anger. Chiun had declared that the substance was cursed, and Remo did not believe in curses, especially not the curses recorded in the histories of the House of Sinanju. Therefore he did not listen to his body, which would have warned him about the radioactivity. After he had been weakened by it, he could sense it even less.

Chiun had nursed him back to health, but had never let him forget that the histories of Sinanju would have saved him. Remo's problems with the histories of Sinanju began with Chiun, because he read what Chiun wrote, and he knew the reports were highly shaded. For one, Chiun avoided mentioning that he had trained not only the first nonresident of the village of Sinanju, but also the first non-Korean to be a Master, and the first non-Oriental to boot. A white man.

To read a current history of Chiun and the new world, America, "A happy but nervous people, quick to anger and even quicker to do nothing about it," one could imagine that Remo could be a Korean. There were many references to Remo feeling an attachment to the waters of the West Korean Bay, when actually Remo had been to Sinanju only once, and then for a fight. Almost every time Chiun mentioned Remo he stressed how different his high cheekbones were from those of the normal white.

And the fact that Remo was an orphan meant to Chiun that he could not definitely say his mother or father wasn't Korean.

"I can and I do. I'm white," Remo had repeated. So

Chiun had taught Remo everything, but not how to make an entry into the histories of Sinanju. And Remo still did not believe the histories of Sinanju, even though as he relearned the wall ascent Chiun commented:

"The great Wang perfected that. We owe all ascents to the great Wang. If I were not here, you could have read the histories and known how to do it again."

"If you were not here, little father, I probably would never read the histories of Sinanju. I don't read them now, come to think of it."

"You must again," said Chiun.

There was a banging on the door to the roof of the Miami high-rise.

"You out there, how did you get up there?"

Remo went to the door where the voice was coming from. It was locked. He enfolded the handle lightly in his palm and then, making sure the lock was tight against the handle, snapped it up. Metal parts flew like shrapnel and the door opened slowly.

A security guard stepped up onto the roof.

"Breaking and entering," he said, noticing the lock was no longer on the door.

"I only broke it to let you out here," said Remo.

"Then how did you get up?"

"You wouldn't understand," said Remo.

"Notice his low cheekbones," said Chiun to the guard. "That is a common ordinary white. Of course he wouldn't understand."

"Who are you jokers calling common?" said the security guard.

"He doesn't mean what you think he means," said Remo.

"Low cheekbones. Look at yours, buddy. You look like the old man, like a gook."

The guard stood ready for a fight. He had his hand on a billy club. He weighed as much as Remo and Chiun put together. He was sure one blow would do it.

When the old one moved toward him, he raised his club, prepared to bring down all its force right into the flowing robes of the old Oriental. His arm was coming down when he felt something against his cheek. Two lips. Then he heard a smack. The Oriental had given him a kiss on his cheek as he was trying to hit him. And then, more smoothly than the guard's eyes could believe, the Oriental was behind him.

"A Western custom of thanks," said Chiun, explaining the kiss, the first kiss he had ever given, much less to a white. In Sinanju there were tendernesses, but never delivered in this Western form. But the joy in Chiun's heart had demanded that he offer thanksgiving to the big white man in the guard's uniform of blue and the square badge of silver.

The guard somehow had missed the old man, but he wasn't going to miss the younger one. He swung the club at his midsection, swung it with the anger of a man who had tried to kill and been dismissed by a buss on the cheek. Remo caught the billy club in his palm and pushed it back like a turnstile.

He had to catch up to Chiun. While the counterforce meant little to one whose every cell moved in unison, to the guard it was like swinging his body into an oncoming truck. The jolt of his body moving into Remo's shattered his pelvis, separated spinal disks, shredded the cartilege at the shoulders, and took a good half-hour out of his life as he waited unconscious on the roof.

Remo, on the other hand, did not miss a pace. He followed Chiun.

"That guard didn't see that well at night," said Remo.

"He was white. He saw as whites see."

"You yourself said whites have funny eyes, that they can't see well because round things never focus as sharply as pointed ones."

"His could see well enough," said Chiun. He was picking up speed. Remo followed. Down one flight after another to the tenth floor with the kimono whipping behind him, Chiun moved, faster than an elevator, faster than a sprinter on a dead run, but never without grace and flow in his movement. Into their temporary apartment he moved, right to the ink and scroll he moved, and then upon the rugged floor of this Miami condominium did Chiun, Master of Sinanju, write what he had beheld this very evening, even as Remo complained.

"Lo these many years, the Master of Sinanju had toiled with the new Master, Remo, as was his name, in the adopted country where Chiun had found him. And hence, he noticed the difference in him from his white surroundings," inscribed Chiun. Even with his awesome speed, each Korean character was perfect, aligned with greater accuracy than if on a grid. This dawn the Master was inspired. This dawn he wrote with joy.

"And lo, one night a simple white stationed to guard the environs of one of their minor castles for the common man, did set eyes upon Chiun and his pupil, Remo. And in that peculiar red light of the morning that allows round eyes to focus better than normal, he saw what Chiun had seen so many years ago. He saw it in the cheekbones and in the eyes. And what he saw was resemblance.

"Even the most common white could not miss the absolute Koreanness of Remo, humble though the white was. And he bespoke this fact to Chiun.

"This, then, raises the one question that had long haunted Chiun, discoverer of America, the nation (not the continent which was discovered in the first realm of the Maya by Master Can Wi). Which Korean had been ancestor to Remo?

"Was it the lost Master? Had he secreted his seed in the new nation so that later, Chiun might harvest? To which Sinanju parent could Remo trace his unknown ancestry?

Chiun had curved himself over to the paper as a flower bent above a white parchment pond. Now he straightened, and with satisfaction he handed the brush quill to Remo.

"You cannot say that this is not the truth. Write now your first sentences of the history."

Remo easily read the Korean. It was the old form, more influenced by Chinese than Japanese. But many of the characters—like the symbols for payment—were unique to Sinanju itself. Sinanju alone had brought the wealth of the

West in tributes to the House of Assassins to the East. Things that were never seen before in the Orient had come to Sinanju by boat and caravan. The old Sinanju Masters, then, had to create characters in order to catalog their treasures. It was a labor of love.

Remo remembered Chiun showing him the scroll marked with his own first entry; his writings followed Chiun's father's entry, and that of his father's father. Cousins from way back were chronicled, as were second cousins, and so was a very supple entertainer who was half from Sinanju and half from the notorious city of Pgyong-yang, home of loose women and looser men, not a fitting place for the upright of the little fishing village of Sinanju.

Remo had been referred to in the histories of this house of assassins as "the half-breed."

He took the quill in his hand and read again what Chiun had written. He knew the marks, and he knew future generations would judge his hand, if there were future generations. He wondered when he too would have to train a future Master. Originally he had learned Sinanju to serve his country, but now knowing Sinanju placed an obligation on him to teach it to someone else also. The tool had become at least equal to the purpose.

Remo read what Chiun had written yet again, then quickly drew the character he had been thinking of. It was a combination of the horns of a bull and the waste product of said bull. In America this phrase was a colloquialism for something that was untrue.

Chiun read the word and slowly nodded.

"Now that you have explained what white gratitude is worth, would you care to corroborate what you heard on the roof."

"He didn't mean what he said."

"Ah," said Chiun. "You have advanced in Sinanju to become a reader of minds. Please then, tell me what is on my mind."

"You don't want to admit you trained a white."

"If that is what you think, then you write that down here on the scroll," said Chiun, his voice as cold as the polar depths. "Go ahead. Write it down. Each Master must write the truth."

"Okay," said Remo. "I am going to write that I work for the organization, and you are my trainer. I will write that in the course of training I learned something else and that what I learned made me become someone else, but I am white. A white person has mastered Sinanju, and is Sinanju. That is what I am going to write."

Chiun waited, saying nothing. But when Remo was about to put the brush back to the scroll, Chiun quickly rolled it up.

"The histories of Sinanju are too important to write such nonsense. Without a history, man is nothing. The worst thing that you whites did when you enslaved the blacks was not to make them slaves. Was not to kill them. Was not to rob them of their lives, for others have done that throughout the ages. What you did most shamefully was to rob them of their past."

"I am glad you are admitting I'm white now," said Remo.

"Only the flaws. You couldn't help but adopt some of the flaws, having lived among them after birth."

"Where my mother suddenly flew from Sinanju to leave me in downtown Newark where I was found, looking very white. There are the orphanage records, you know."

"Believe what you will. I know what is true," said Chiun.

"Little father, what is so bad about admitting you gave Sinanju to a white? Does it not make you look better that you took a meat eater, cigarette smoker, whiskey drinker, punch-with-the-fist white man and found in him that which you could make Sinanju?"

"I thought of that," said Chiun.

"And?"

"And I dismissed it. For centuries, thousands of years, none but Sinanju has mastered Sinanju. We have all accepted that. And here you come along. What does that do to our histories? If this is not true, then what else is false?"

"Little father," said Remo, "I have left most of my ways to follow Sinanju. Granted I didn't have much. I wasn't married. I had a pretty crummy job, I was a cop. No steady girl. No real friends, I guess. I love my country and I still do. But I do find something that was absolutely true. It's Sinanju. And I bet my life on it. And so far I have won."

"You are too emotional," said Chiun, turning away, and Remo knew it was because Chiun did not wish for him to see how moved he was.

The phone rang three times and stopped. Then it rang once. Then it rang two times and stopped. Upstairs was calling with an assignment.

Remo answered the phone. He was feeling good again. He needed his country and he needed to serve, just as he did when he volunteered for the Marines the day after graduation from high school. As for Sinanju, that had become who he was, and it was strange being part of a house of assassins already famous in the Orient when Rome was a muddy village on an Etruscan river. On the one hand, he didn't know his mother or father. On the other hand, he knew his spiritual ancestors further back than Moses.

All of this he brought to the telephone and to his country as he punched in the numbered response. One multiplied each code right by two. Upstairs had said that would be simple. If he heard two rings, punch in the number four. If he heard four, punch in the number eight.

What, he had asked, if he heard a nine-ring code?

"Then it won't be us," said Harold W. Smith, the only American besides the President allowed to know of Remo's existence, the one who ran the organization once called America's hedge against disaster, more recently called in times of crises "our last hope."

Remo punched in the proper code. Then he punched in the proper code again.

So important was secrecy, because the organization was itself outside the law, that the phone was supposed to activate a scrambler system from anywhere. He didn't know how it worked but even on an extension phone no one could listen in on him.

Remo got an operator in Nebraska telling him that the local service was glad to help him. Then he got switched to a national service which was also glad to help him. Then he was told how much money he was saving with another national service, and then back to a Miami operator, who asked which system he was using.

"I don't know," said Remo. "Do you?"

"We are not allowed to give out that information," said the operator. "Would you like to speak to my supervisor?"

"You don't know who you work for?"

"Would you like to speak to my supervisor?"

"You mean you don't know who you work for?"

"It's just like your telephone bill, sir. I get fourteen pages of explanation for who pays me and I don't understand a word of it."

A sharp buzzing came over the phone, and a sharp lemony voice interrupted. It was Harold W. Smith, head of the organization.

"Sorry, Remo, we can't even scramble the phones without a hitch anymore."

"You mean I didn't mess up the code?" said Remo.

"No. Ever since AT&T broke up, nothing has worked well. It was the greatest communication system on earth at one time. We were the envy of the world. Unfortunately, the courts decided otherwise. All in all, I guess I'd rather have some law and order in the country, than phones that work perfectly. Given a choice, you know."

"I didn't know about the phone company breakup," said Remo.

"Don't you read the newspapers?"

"Not anymore, Smitty."

"What do you do?"

It was a good question.

"I breathe a lot," said Remo.

"Oh," Smith said. "I guess that means something. In

any case, we have a problem with a witness in a big racketeering case. Seems someone has reached him. We want you to see that he testifies honestly. This one witness could take down the entire mob west of the Rockies. Are you up to it? How are you feeling?''

''Not peak, but more than good enough for what we have to do.''

Chiun, realizing Remo was talking to Harold W. Smith, the man who secured proper gold delivery in tribute to Sinanju for Chiun's and now Remo's services, said in Korean:

''That is no way to talk. If an emperor thinks you are serving him despite injuries, allow it. Allow as to how every living breath serves his glory. Provided of course the tribute arrives on time.''

Remo didn't even bother to explain anymore that Smith was not an emperor. He had explained to Chiun too many times already that the organization served a democracy which decided its emperor by voting, not be an assassin's hand or marching army or accident of birth. This Chiun not only thought of as a foul abomination, but also impossible in the affairs of men, and Remo was only a fool to believe it, like our Western fairy tales such as Santa Claus, or that God decreed who would rule. The saying in Sinanju had always been, ''The divine right of all kings is crafted by the hand of the assassin.''

It had been a good selling point in the Ming and Chang Dynasties of China, and the court of Charlemagne.

''Is that Chiun there? Send him our regards and tell him the tribute shipment arrived on time,'' said Smith.

''He knows that, Smitty.''

''How? I only found out this morning.''

''I don't know how he knows. There was a problem once with a delivery and the accumulated treasure of the house, and ever since, he has kept an eye on the accounts.''

''He doesn't trust us anymore?''

''Sort of,'' said Remo. How could he explain it to Smith? Chiun didn't trust anyone beyond the suburbs of Sinanju proper and did not have all that much use for everyone inside those boundaries either. He trusted Remo because he knew Remo. He most certainly was not going to trust a client.

"We have a minor court reinforcement in California," said Smith. There wasn't too much more to be said, except for the name and place.

Remo had done it many times. Made sure witnesses didn't clam up. It was part of the original purpose of CURE, as the organization was called, to make sure the nation could survive within the Constitution. That meant making the courts work. But so many witnesses had been bought off or frightened off that in entire states the justice system barely creaked along. It was the one thing Remo could say CURE had actually improved. The rest of the work was keeping the world from falling apart, and he was fairly certain that in that area, CURE was losing.

"You're not ready yet," said Chiun.

"For you, no. For what I have to do, yes."

"The first step into eternity is a missed breath."

"I'm good enough."

"Good enough? Good enough?" said Chiun. "Good enough would be to hit someone over the head with a brick. Good enough would be to use a gun. You are Sinanju, not some . . . some white gangster in a uniform."

"I'm still white, little father."

"You sound it."

"Didn't you say that emperors couldn't tell perfection from duck dung? That all they cared about was putting a head on a wall?"

"Yes, but we care. That is who we are. Besides, in this country they do not put heads on walls. They are crazy. They are ashamed of their assassins."

"Right, little father. We're a secret organization."

"See. You are ashamed of what you do. And that is the fault of the mad Smith. In any civilized country he would have used me to openly declare himself emperor. He would hang all his enemies' heads on the palace wall to show his strength. But no, we must skulk around like criminals."

"Right, little father. Secret," said Remo pleasantly.

"Only a worm is pleased to live under a rock," said Chiun.

"No time to argue, little father. I've got to get going."

"To do what? To remove a rival for a great throne, adding honor to the history of Sinanju? What should I write down now that you do? Deliver packages? Watch over machinery like a slave at a water wheel? What new misuse for the talents of Sinanju?"

"I am going to make sure a witness testifies."

Chiun rolled up the scroll and capped the ink.

"You are all crazy. All crazy. If Emperor Smith wants a decision from a judge, why doesn't he buy the judge like in any civilized country?"

Remo had packed everything he needed for the trip. Everything was a wad of cash in his pocket.

"That's what we're fighting against," said Remo.

"Why?" said Chiun.

"It has to do with the Constitution, little father, and I don't have time to explain it now."

Chiun shrugged, folding his long delicate fingers underneath his robe. He would never be able to explain it in the histories of Sinanju. Here was a piece of paper Smith and Remo held sacred. The very existence of what they called the organization violated that piece of paper, but the organization was created to protect it. And therefore everyone had to be secret about what they did. Even for whites, this was puzzling. Remo denied Smith had plans for becoming the emperor, which they called the President here. But if that were not his real plan, what was it? It certainly could not be protecting a sacred piece of paper. There weren't even any jewels on it. He had seen it once in a glass case.

"That's it?" Chiun had asked, looking at the simple old parchment.

"That's it, little father," Remo had said proudly. "A lot of men died for that."

"Who killed them?"

"Lots of people. People who would destroy America mainly."

"You mean if that piece of paper burned up, America would no longer exist? It is magic then. The magic paper that holds America together."

"Yes. In a way. In a definite way, yes," said Remo. Chiun remembered how happy he had been when he said that. Actually happy. He wasn't lying either. Remo didn't lie. A frightening characteristic in a human being, like an inability to blink one's eyes, but nevertheless a characteristic of Remo.

And so there was Chiun standing before the glass case in a white man's building, listening to Remo happily explain a fairy tale about a piece of paper, claiming its words ran America.

But nowhere in the document was there any mention of king or emperor. Nowhere. All it talked about was what the government could not do to its subjects. Remo had read through about a half page of citizens' rights when Chiun had asked to be excused. He was going to vomit if he heard any more.

To the service of this nonsense was the awesome magnificence of the power of Sinanju now dedicated. Chiun thought about that as Remo, happy, left the apartment.

3

Gennaro "Drums" Drumola weighed four hundred and thirty pounds and when he laughed his stomach stayed still and the room shook.

It didn't help that he was in a small wood frame house. But the U.S. attorney wanted him there, wanted him miles away from downtown Los Angeles or any city. He wanted to make sure Drums's friends could not reach him. The best military guards were posted at the edges of the woodlands. Electronic sensors were hidden in a necklace of warning underneath the ground behind the human shield. And above them all, aircraft constantly patrolled. Gennaro Drumola by his testimony alone could bring down most of the narcotics trafficking and protection rackets operating in California.

Drums had been more than willing to do this for his government. Drums had an aversion to gas chambers, and his government had told him he could live, albeit in prison, if he would help them build their case against the people he used to work for.

"You mean break my oath of silence?" asked Drums.

"Mr. Drumola, we have ironclad evidence that will convict you of crushing three people to death for money. Have you ever seen anyone in a gas chamber? Have you ever seen how they die?"

"You ever see how people die who sing against the mob?"

"We'll put you in a camp protected by the military.

We'll have planes overhead. Your friends won't be able to reach you where we'll put you."

"Will I eat good?"

"Like a king, Mr. Drumola. And that's your choice: you can either choke to death in a gas chamber or eat like a king."

"You make it simple," said Drums. "Still, you got to get a conviction first."

"We have video film of you sitting on a little old lady. Do you know what you see on that film? Two little old arms and two little old legs and you on top. You see the legs move a lot, Mr. Drumola. Then you don't see the legs move at all."

"Ey. She was a deadbeat. A bum. She owed."

"She owed three thousand dollars on a two-hundred dollar loan, Mr. Drumola. The court is not going to look very favorably on your motives. They're allergic to loan-sharking."

"How'd they get the tape?"

"Some kids with a home video camera and a telephoto lens. Not even grainy. Maybe your friends will kill you if you testify against them, but with us there's no maybe. No lawyer is going to get you off when a jury sees this video-tape."

And so Gennaro Drumola began explaining to the U.S. attorney who did what and when in California and where the bodies were. Gennaro's testimony ran three hundred pages. It was so complete that all he had to do was appear in court and testify that he had said all those things he had said to the U.S. attorney, and the mob would be broken from Oregon to Tijuana.

And then one day, Drums looked at the pages and pages of testimony stacked on a table in the center of the cabin, and said:

"What's that?"

"Your ticket out of the gas chamber, Drums," a guard answered. He refused to call him Mr. Drumola.

"Yeah, what gas chamber?"

"The extra-strength gas chamber they'll build just for you if you forget to testify."

"Hey, no. I'll testify. What do you want me to say? What do you want me to talk about?"

"Me? Nothing. I just work here," said the guard. "But the U.S. attorney wants you to talk a lot."

"Sure," said Drums. "About what?"

When the U.S. attorney heard about Drums's new attitude, he came to the cabin himself and promised Gennaro Drumola that if it were the last thing he ever did on earth, he would make sure Drumola would die in the gas chamber.

"What are you talkin' about?" asked Drumola.

"You're going to die, Drumola."

"What for?"

"Murder one."

"Who?"

"The little old lady we have tapes of you killing."

"What tapes?"

The U.S. attorney stormed out of the little cabin. His case was over. Somehow, some way, someone had reached the turncoat, and now all they had was volumes of testimony that could not be backed up in court by the witness.

He did not know that others were watching the case or that when he filed his report about the sudden bad turn of events, it automatically would be picked up by computer terminals he was unaware of. He did not know that there was an organization specializing in making sure, among other things, that United States justice remained justice.

Remo arrived outside the holding tank and easily moved past the guards in those moments when their bodies said their minds were wandering. It was not the greatest trick to recognize the moment when attention flagged; the body fairly screamed it. There would be a stillness in the person, and then movement. That stillness was when the mind took over.

Remo could also sense distraction. Most people, at least

as children, could sense others, but they had been trained
out of it; Sinanju had rained this perception back into
Remo.

He moved through the forest, aware that the soil had
been disturbed and there were strange things in it. He did
not know that they were sensors, just that these alien
objects were to be avoided. The land told him that. He
spotted the cabin in a dense grove of trees. A guard sat in
front of the door with a carbine on his lap and a telephone
behind him.

Remo moved to the rear of the cabin and found a
window that he could open quietly by forcing the wood
evenly upward without the slightest jerk. A large man with
a belly that heaved with each breath slept on a cot.
Drumola.

Remo moved through the open window and across the
wood floor. He sat down next to Drumola.

"Good morning, Drums," he said. "I hear you have a
problem with your memory."

"Wha?" grunted Drumola.

"I'm here to help you remember," said Remo.

"Good," said Drums. "You know I just don't
remember nothin' anymore. It's like a page has been
ripped out of my life. Whack. Out."

"I'm going to reinsert it," said Remo. He took
Drumola's large hamlike fists and compressed the fingers
so that the nerves felt as though they were being pulled out
from his hand. Not to disturb the guard, he pressed shut
Drums's lips.

The huge body convulsed. The face reddened. The black
eyes grew wide with the scream that could not escape his
mouth.

"Well, sweetheart, does this remind you of anything?"
asked Remo.

Drums convulsed again.

"You may not know it, sweetheart, but we have this
down to a science. First the pain. Now the terror. I'd hang
you over the side of a building," said Remo, "but the

ground floor isn't that frightening. What about smothering as an alternative? You into that, Drums?''

Remo released the now reddened fingers and slid his own hand under the sweaty bulk of Drumola's back. Like a nurse with a hospital sheet, he turned Drumola, but unlike a nurse he did it in an instant, sending the man spinning upward and then landing on his face. The cabin shook.

"You all right, Drums?" called out the guard.

"Uh-huh," said Remo.

"Well, don't go flyin' around or nothin', okay?"

And that was it from the guard. Remo forced Drumola's rib cage up toward his chin, not hard enough to separate the ribs, which could puncture the lungs, but with enough force to make Drumola feel as though he were being crushed under a mountain.

"Just a little bit more, Drums, and you are no more," said Remo. Then he released everything.

Gennaro Drumola quivered and then began crying.

"Shh," said Remo. "Do you remember now?"

"Anything," said Drumola.

"What do you remember?"

"What do you want me to remember?"

"Your testimony."

"Yeah. Yeah," said Drums. "I did that. I did whatever. I remember whatever."

"Good. Because if you forget, I'll be back."

"I swear by my mother's grave, I remember," said Drums. His anal sphincter had released, so Remo left before the odor got to him.

But the next day, Smith was reaching out for Remo again.

"It didn't hold," he said. He had come down in person to the Miami Beach apartment. "Are you all right, Remo?"

"Yeah. I'm fine. I'm great."

"Chiun says you're not correct yet," said Smith. Chiun sat in a gray presentation kimono, one worn before emperors, a dull color to show that the assassin was there to glorify the emperor and not himself. Sometimes a presentation kimono was bright gold, and Remo asked why that wouldn't be a detraction. Chiun had said that was for the occasions when the assassin's glory added to that of the emperor. Remo always felt, however, that Sinanju Masters wore what they felt like and made up reasons for it afterward.

Smith wore his usual three-piece gray suit and lemon-faced frown.

"You don't understand. When Chiun says I am not ready, it means that I can't do things that a Master of Sinanju can do. It's got nothing to do with the needs of the organization."

"What can't you do, Remo?"

"I can't harmonize with cosmic forces on a level that is continuous and smooth."

Chiun nodded. There. Remo had said it. Openly admitted it. Of course, one should never admit anything in front of an emperor, but in this case it served Sinanju well. Remo needed more rest and more retraining.

Smith heard the answer and looked blank. Chiun was nodding and Remo was shrugging, each indicating that he had won an argument that Smith didn't even understand.

"I'm sorry, I don't understand," said Smith.

"I can move up and down walls. I can put my hand through solid objects, and I can take any dozen men who need to be taken."

"Not Masters of Sinanju."

"There's only one of you in the world, little father," said Remo.

"There was the evil Master. What if you should meet him again?"

"I'll call you."

"That is not being a Master of Sinanju. Our noble emperor Harold W. Smith has paid tribute for the services of a Master of Sinanju and you must perform as a Master. Otherwise you are robbing him. I will not allow it."

"How am I robbing him if I am working for him, for us, for the organization, instead of resting?"

"By giving insufficient measure."

"He doesn't even know what I'm talking about when I mention the cosmos."

"Well, it certainly has affected your performance, Remo, I am sorry to say," said Smith.

"How can it? When you harmonize with the cosmic forces it only means enhancing your source of energy and balance. If you have enough energy to move up and down buildings, you don't generally need more."

"Well, you certainly needed something more with that witness, Drumola."

"I turned him back."

"Well, he didn't remember a thing last night," said Smith, taking a sheet of paper out of a thin briefcase he had on his lap. It was a memo from a U.S. attorney regarding one Gennaro Drumola.

It read:

"This afternoon, subject had a sudden change of heart. As in so many of those cases where witnesses have turned against their testimony and then suddenly turn back, it was mysterious. We have been having many of these mysterious reversions in the last few years, and I saw no need to press an investigation of it at this time. But in the case of this subject, his reversion didn't seem to take hold. He seemed willing enough to cooperate, but when I pressed him for details he didn't remember anything about the testimony he now suddenly said he remembered. Moreover, a medical examination showed he was in a state of high anxiety."

Remo returned the copy of the memo.

"I don't know what happened to him. I know I had him. I know when I have someone."

"You see, little mistakes always lead to big ones. I am glad that you have decided to wait until Remo can glorify you instead of fail," said Chiun.

"I didn't fail. I know when someone has been turned. You, little father, know that I know."

"I understand. I, too, would be reluctant to admit that I failed before such a gracious emperor," said Chiun. He of course said this in English. Remo knew this was only for Smith's benefit. In Korean, Remo told Chiun he was full of the droppings of a diarrhetic duck.

Chiun, hearing this insult from Remo, took the injury to his heart, where he could nurture it and make it grow. One day he would use it profitably against the man who had become his child.

Smith only waited. More and more now, these two would drift into Korean that he didn't understand.

"I want another crack at that guy," said Remo.

"They've moved him," said Smith.

"I don't care where he is. I want him," said Remo.

Gennaro Drumola was eating a triple order of spare ribs in the penthouse suite of the San Francisco Forty-Niner Hotel when the thin man with the thick wrists dropped in on him again, this time through the window.

Drums did not know how he could have gotten through the guards, much less to the window. The guy had to climb walls.

Drums cleaned his dripping hands on his great mound of belly covered by a white T-shirt. Thick black hair sprouted from the shirt's every opening. Even his knuckles had hair. This time Drumola would be ready for him. He would not be caught napping. Drumola picked up a chair, cracked it in two with his bare hands, and was ready to put a sharp splinter into the skinny guy's face when he felt himself being dragged by an awesome force right through the window. Drums would have screamed but his lips were pressed together just like back at the camp when he felt a mountain had collapsed on him.

His lips were closed and he was being swung thirty stories above San Francisco by something that felt like a vise. Upside down, looking down at the street as he moved like a pendulum, he wished it were even tighter.

"Okay, sweetheart. What happened?"

Drums felt the man release his lips. He was supposed to talk. He talked.

"Nothin' happened. I did what you said. I said I remembered."

"But then you forgot."

"For Chrissakes. I wish I could remember. I don't remember."

"Well, try," said the man, and dropped him a story. It felt like it was going to be twenty-nine more of them, but something caught him again.

"Are we getting any better?"

"I don't know nothin'."

Drumola felt warm liquid run up his ears. He knew what it was. It was running from his pants, down his stomach and chest, and dripping out his shirt around his ears. His bladder had released in fear.

Remo swung Drumola back up to his penthouse suite. The man wasn't lying. He was tempted to let him drop all the way, but that would have let the world think the mob had killed him. Remo stuffed Drumola's face back into the spare ribs and left him there.

Remo had failed. It was the first time he had failed to persuade a witness. There was an instant before death, he had been taught by Chiun, when fear takes over the body. In that instant, the will to live became so strong that it grew into an overpowering fear of death. And at that moment, nothing else mattered—not greed, or love, or hate. All that mattered was the will to live.

Drumola had been in that state of fear. He could not lie. And yet Remo had failed to turn him back to his testimony.

"I am not losing it," he told Smith.

"I'm asking because we have what seems to be a sudden rash of forgetful witnesses."

"Then let's get 'em. I need the practice."

"I never heard you say that before."

"Well, I said it. But it doesn't mean I'm losing anything," said Remo into the telephone. He wondered if he should visit Smith and perhaps shred the steel gates of Folcroft over Smith's head. He hadn't been to the sanitarium headquarters of the organization for a long while now.

"All right," said Smith. The voice was weak.

"If you don't want me to do it, just say so. And I won't."

"Of course we need you, Remo. But I was wondering about Chiun."

"You don't even know Chiun," said Remo. He was at a telephone at the Portland, Oregon, airport. A woman at the phone next to him asked him to be quiet. He told her he wasn't yelling. She said he was. He said if he wanted to hear yelling, he could yell. She said he was yelling right now.

"No," said Remo, collecting power in his lungs, and then setting a high pitch to his voice. "This," he sang so that the very lights quivered in the ceiling, "is yelling."

The three floor-to-ceiling windows at gates seven, eight, and nine collapsed like a commercial for sound tape.

"Well," said the woman. "That certainly is yelling to me." And she hung up and walked away.

Smith was still on the phone saying shocks had somehow altered the scrambler system and he was getting warning signals that this might be an open line very soon. No protection for secrecy.

"I'm all right," said Remo. "I know I had my target in panic. That's what does it. Making the life force take over."

"Does that life force have anything to do with the cosmic relationship?"

"No. That's timing. That's me. Life force is them. No. The answer to your question is no."

"All right, Remo. All right."

"The life force is not me," he said.

"All right," said Smith.

"All right," said Remo.

"The name is Gladys Smith. She is twenty-nine years old, a secretary to one of the largest grain-trading companies in the world. She is testifying against her entire firm, which has been making secret deals with the Russians undercutting our entire agricultural policy. The government is keeping her in a Chicago apartment. She is not that heavily defended, but she is defended."

"So she's defended. Defenses aren't a problem for me," said Remo.

"I didn't say they were. Remo, you are more important to us than these cases. We've got to know we have you. America needs you. You're upset now."

"I'm always upset," said Remo. "Just give me her address."

When he left the little phone area, he saw workmen were cleaning up the barrier glass at the gates and people were staring at him. Someone was mumbling that Remo was the one whose voice had shattered the windows. But an airport maintenance director said that was impossible. A car could drive into that glass and it would not shatter.

Remo grabbed the next flight to Chicago and dozed in first class. Before they landed he did his breathing and felt the good leveling force of all power move through him, calming him. He realized then he had done what he should never do, let his mind take over, the mind where doubts lived and thrived on selected pieces of negative information culled from the universe of information. He knew he had done his job right. The witness had somehow truly forgotten. He decided not to use fear this time.

Gladys Smith had finished her fourteenth romance novel of the week and was wondering if she would ever get to have a man's arms around her again, when the finest romantic experience of her life walked through the door she thought had been locked.

He was thin, with thick wrists and a sharp handsome face with dark eyes that told her he knew her. Not from an earlier meeting, but in some other, deeper way.

He moved silently with a grace she had never seen in a man.

"Gladys?" he asked.

"Yes," she said.

"Gladys Smith?"

"Yes."

"I'm here for you."

"I know," she heard herself saying. He did not grab her like one of the boyfriends that haunted her past. He did not even caress her. His touch was gentler than that, as though his fingerpads were an extension of her own flesh.

She never knew her arms could feel so good. She sat down on the bed. She never knew she could feel so good about her body. It was becoming alive in ways she had never known. It was welcoming him, it was wanting him, and finally it was demanding him.

Her mind was like a passenger on a trip her body was taking. And just when she hovered at the edge of a climax that would satisfy every longing she had had as a woman, he asked for something so minor and trivial all she could do was sob, "Yes. Yes. Yes." And that sob became a scream of satisfaction and joy.

"Yes," she said quietly. "Yes, darling, anything. Of course I'll remember. What should I remember?"

"Your testimony," he said.

"Oh, that," she said. "Of course. What do you want me to remember?"

"Whatever your testimony was," he said. She put his hand back on her neck. She never wanted his hands away from her again.

"Sure. But I don't remember it. I don't remember anything that happened at the company. It's like almost everything after my twenty-first birthday never happened."

"Of course it happened."

"I know it happened. But I don't remember it, darling. I don't. When I look at the pages of testimony I gave, it's as though some stranger had said it. I don't even remember giving the testimony. I don't remember anything past four weeks ago."

"What happened four weeks ago?"

"Put your hand back where it was. Okay. There. Right where you had it before. People were looking at me. And they were asking me things, strange things about grain transfers. And I didn't know what they were talking about. They told me I had worked for a grain-trading company. They got very angry. I don't know why they got angry. They asked me who bought me off. I would never lie for money. I'm not that sort of person.''

"You really didn't lie," said the man with the dark eyes that knew her.

"Of course not, darling. I never lie."

"I was afraid of that. Good-bye."

"Wait. Where are you going? Take your clothes back off. Get back here. Wait. Wait!"

Gladys ran after him to the door.

"I'll lie. If you want me to lie, I'll lie. I'll memorize everything in the transcript. I'll remember it. I'll say it word for word. Just don't leave me. You can't leave me."

"Sorry. I've got work."

"When will I ever find someone else like you?"

"Not in this century," said Remo.

This time he did not phone in his failure. He insisted on a meeting with Smith.

"That won't be necessary, Remo. I know you didn't fail. As a test, one of our government agencies damned worried about this thing ran lie-detector tests on two witnesses who claimed to have forgotten their own stories. Both of them passed. They weren't lying. They really did forget their own testimony."

"Wonderful," said Remo.

"Wonderful? This is a disaster," said Smith. "Someone out there knows how to dismantle our entire justice system. This country is going to fall apart pretty soon."

"Pretty soon? When was the last time you made a phone call, Smitty? You want to watch falling apart in action, call a repairman."

"I mean there will be no way we can enforce any law if someone knows how to make witnesses forget. No law. Think about it. If you can make people forget, there will never be another witness. Never."

Remo thought about it. He thought about forgetting

things, forgetting his early life in the orphanage. If he could only forget selectively, he thought, it might be the best thing that ever happened.

"Remo, are you there?"

"I'm thinking about it, Smitty," he said.

4

Beatrice Pimser Dolomo was happy. Rubin Dolomo, the guiding genius of Poweressence, the spiritual force, was feeling almost good enough to get out of bed. Cutting his minimum daily requirement of Valium down to a single triple dose helped, but it was always easier getting out of bed when Beatrice was happy. Everything was easier when Beatrice was happy.

But the Dolomos' lawyer was not happy.

"I don't know what you two are giggling about, but the feds have got us nailed."

"If you would only renounce your failure mechanism you would reap success and power. The only thing between you and your new dynamic life is yourself," said Rubin.

"You want a Poweressence convert or you want to try to stay out of jail?" asked Barry Glidden, one of the foremost criminal lawyers in California. The Dolomos had hired him because he was known as a no-nonsense, no-holds-barred defender of clients, provided those clients had a no-holds-barred attitude toward payment.

Barry rested his arms on the table of the beautifully lit Dolomo day room, overlooking the magnificent Dolomo estate. He already had plans to buy it from them when they went to jail and turn it into a condominium development. There was enough prime land here to build an airport if he wanted.

"Let me tell you two happy people what they got on you, in case you think this hocus-pocus you make so much money on can work miracles. One, they got the alligators

55

you put in that columnist's pool. That's Exhibit A. They got a wonderful witness, one of your former devotees, who says that Exhibit A was what you, Beatrice, told her to put into the pool. Because you aren't going to pass that off as stocking of wildlife, and because no one is going to believe an alligator walked from Florida homing in on a columnists' negative forces, that leaves any reasonable jury only one option: attempted murder."

"That was Rubin's idea," said Beatrice, displaying her charms in a halter and slacks. She knew Glidden wanted the property. One of Rubin's Poweressence converts was a movie star who had already been approached to invest in the consortium Glidden was organizing to make the purchase. She did not tell him she knew this, however.

She had told him simply that if he lost this case his children would be boiled in oil, alive.

He had offered to resign the case. She had told him she was only joking. Mostly. She had laughed coquettishly when she had said that. Barry Glidden had not thought it a thing of mirth.

"In *Dance of the Alarkin Planet*, a creature very much like a crocodile kills people with negative vibrations," said Rubin. "Animals sense these things. Their instincts are a lot purer than the twisted products of the human brain."

"He's not interested in your short stories, Rubin. He's interested in money. Right?" said Beatrice.

"I'm interested in the law. You put an alligator in a person's swimming pool to kill him. I've told you a hundred times, Beatrice, that you can't threaten, maim, buy, destroy, and knife your way out of everything. There comes a time when the world catches up to you. You are going to do time on this alligator thing. That's it. We can cop a plea and with a little bit of finagling here and there, get it down to six months. That is a light sentence for attempted murder."

"No plea," said Beatrice.

"I cannot get anyone on a jury to believe that cockamamy negative-force nonsense. You're going to do serious time if you don't plead. Jurors do not read *Dance of the*

Alarkin Planet. And if they did, they wouldn't believe it."

"They have been programmed by failure not to believe," said Rubin.

"Rubin, you have not paid taxes for twenty years. No jury is going to accept that you owe your first allegiance to the universe. Not when they pay their taxes for sewer systems, national defense, police forces, and various other things that make a civilization."

"We're in religion," said Rubin. "They cannot tax religion. We have a right to be free of governmental oppression."

"This is not exactly a church here," said Glidden, pointing to the rolling California landscape of the Dolomo estate.

"Have you ever seen the Vatican?" said Beatrice.

"You are comparing yourself to the Roman Catholic Church?"

"So they have been here a bit longer," said Beatrice. "But they, too, were persecuted in their time."

"And we offer two more sacraments—the holy character analysis and blessed success on earth. Granted, they have been here longer," said Rubin. "But in a time warp a couple of thousand years is nothing."

"I don't know which one of you is crazier. The lady who thinks any threat to anyone will do, or you and your cockamamy fairy tales."

"Our money is not crazy," said Beatrice. "The checks are good."

"Listen. I am just a human being. I have weaknesses. Juries are made up of human beings. They have weaknesses too. But don't underestimate the strength of their beliefs. They may not believe in negative vibrations. Most of them will not believe that the planet Alarkin exists. But they do believe that the President of the United States exists. Now, do you want to tell me about that, Beatrice?"

Beatrice Dolomo adjusted her halter. She cleared her throat.

"No," she said.

"Some Americans might find it disturbing to hear that

you have threatened the President of the United States. Did you do that, Beatrice?"

"I take whatever actions I have to. If I let the world bully me, I would be bullied by everything. Rubin and I would be nowhere if I listened to people who said I should know when to quit. I never quit. If I listened to them I would be the wife of a nobody science-fiction writer, at a time when science fiction is not selling."

"So you threatened the President of the United States," said Glidden.

"We used to eat tuna fish for Sunday dinner. Rubin wore vinyl belts and polyester suits. We were intimately familiar with every tenant-protection law on the books. We learned how to delay evictions by months."

"So you threatened the President of the United States. You did," said Glidden.

"Diamonds? Hah. I had a glass ring. It cost two dollars and thirty-five cents. When Rubin proposed to me he promised he would buy me a ring as soon as he sold his next book. He said every penny he made from *Dromoids of Muir* would go toward getting me that ring. And do you want to know something?" said Beatrice, her temples throbbing, her face flushing with the heat of her anger. "Do you want to know something?"

"Beatrice, please let go of my face. I can't talk," said Glidden. His client had risen from her seat in fury. Her red-lacquered fingernails were now digging into his cheeks.

"You want to know something?" she yelled again.

"Yes, please. I certainly do," cried Barry, who wanted his cheeks back with as little puncturing as possible.

"He kept his word. Rubin wasn't lying. He spent the entire proceeds of *Dromoids of Muir* on that two-buck ring. And you're telling me to back off?"

Barry felt his cheeks go free, and quickly began dabbing at the blood with his handkerchief.

"Yes, Beatrice. I want you to back off. I will be no good to you if you get still another charge against you. I can't keep up with them."

"We didn't threaten," said Rubin.

"The attorney general of the United States phoned me last night to tell me one of your Poweressence nuts at a formal state dinner mentioned to the President that the only way he could save himself from death was to have all federal charges against you dropped. That is not a threat? It seems like a threat to me."

"You mean Kathy Bowen, that lovely, talented actress? That sweet girl who has seen her career blossom since she joined Poweressence? The Kathy Bowen we knew would be attending that state dinner? She did it on her own."

"With Kathy Bowen's boobs, I could have been Jayne Mansfield. Yes, that Kathy Bowen—the one who danced with the President and said he was going to die if he didn't lay off you. That lovely girl who will never be invited to the White House again. That one."

"She's a movie star," said Rubin. "Lots of movie stars understand Poweressence because they already receive positive vibrations from the universal force."

"I have movie stars as clients too. I know movie stars. They receive their vibrations from the universal farce. I got one movie star who believes he is the reincarnation of Genghis Khan. I got another star who bathes her duff in seaweed. I got another star who believes that blowing up children's hospitals will further the Marxist cause. I got more movie stars than I know what to do with, and I have yet to meet one with enough sound judgment to make it legitimately into junior high school."

"Not only are we not copping a plea but we are going to be found innocent," said Beatrice.

"She's right," said Rubin.

"Well, if you get nearly eternal terms, don't blame me."

"Of course I will," said Beatrice. "If you don't have a witness against us, then I certainly will blame you if we are found guilty."

"Don't count on that kind of luck," said Glidden. "Less than one percent of witnesses retract their testimony. The odds are a hundred to one against you."

"On the contrary," said Beatrice. "The odds are in our favor. Can I get you a bandage for your cheek wounds?"

"You might try letting the blood flow stem itself naturally," said Rubin. "In course number thirty-eight, we offer that technique for $1,285, but you can have it free. It's a general-health maintenance program."

"I'll take the bandage," said Glidden.

"I'll get it for you," said Beatrice. "Rubin has a lot to do."

Rubin Dolomo shuffled out of the room, a cigarette dangling from his lips. He wheezed his way down to the spacious basement and ground out his cigarette on the concrete floor. Neatly hung up on one wall were several dozen rubber suits. He got into one with great effort. He hated the way it stuck to him, hated the weight and heat it concentrated on his body. Normal breathing was hard enough for him, but the suit made it almost impossible. But Beatrice was right—he had a lot to do and no time to waste. He snapped on the rubber face mask and adjusted the goggles.

The founder of Poweressence, the hope of humanity, waddled to the rear of the basement, where an airtight door, like that of a submarine compartment, was set into the wall. He turned the wheel unlocking the door, and entered. The five herbs and three chemicals that made up the formula lay in separate barrels. As Rubin ground the herbs, his goggles began darkening, a sign he was going to pass out soon. But he knew he could make it. He'd made it before.

While the fresh potion dripped through a sieve and into a container, Rubin nearly collapsed into one of the large gray plastic barrels. He heard his heart beat in the suit, but did not hear the container close. He could smell the rubber, even taste it on his tongue.

He got out of the room just in time to make it to the shower. With his last ounce of energy, he kicked the large button on the floor and the room flooded with a harsh hot spray. Dolomo lay down to conserve his vanishing breath. When he felt the spray stop he put the container into a small vat and pushed the vat to a small conveyor belt set into one wall.

Rubin Dolomo cut himself free of the suit with an Xacto knife and a great deal of effort. When he regained his breath he met the little container again in another room, but this time he was separated from it by a glass wall fitted with protective rubber arms. The container had been jostled along the conveyor route and now it rested on its side. Rubin slipped his arms into the rubber sheaths set into a window and set it right atop a little table. On the table was a single sheet of pink stationery and a matching envelope addressed to a former Poweressence devotee, one who felt he had been robbed. With his rubber fingers, Rubin opened the container of fresh formula, then took a small cotton swab from underneath the table and dipped it into the vial. He dabbed a touch of the formula in the upper-left-hand corner of the pink sheet of paper. Then he put the swab back into the formula and resealed the container.

Now came the hard part. Rubin had to fold the paper and put it in the envelope. Using rubber hands, this simple task took twenty minutes. By the time he was finished Rubin was sweating.

He lit a cigarette, threw a Valium and a high-blood pressure pill into his mouth, and then wheezed his way to a reception room, where the messenger waited for the letter.

He was a middle-aged executive who credited his rise to the vice-presidency of his corporation to his new self-confidence, and he credited his confidence to Poweressence. He believed that the United States government was persecuting the one religion that could save the world. He had nurtured that belief in an Idaho chapter.

Rubin had paid the chapter chairman fifteen hundred dollars for this volunteer. But he was worth it.

"Let me get this straight. I make sure no one but the traitor touches the upper-left-hand corner of the letter inside this envelope. I go directly to the building he is being kept in, and I announce that I am a friend who has a message from his sweetheart. And that is it. Simple."

With that, the executive opened the letter just to make sure that his perception of an upper-left-hand corner jibed with Rubin Dolomo's. That determined, he shook hands with the man who had pulled his life back from the brink of wretchedness.

"Mr. Dolomo, you are one of the great minds of our time. And I am honored, deeply honored, to have this opportunity to serve Poweressence."

"Watch the letter. Your finger is touching the corner. Watch the letter."

"What letter?" asked the executive.

"The one in your hand," said Rubin.

The executive looked down at his hand and the pink paper, which he was gripping by the corner.

"Did you just give me this letter? Or am I supposed to give it to you? Who is it for?"

"All right," said Rubin wearily. "Put down that thing you have in your hand. We're going to the recovery rooms."

The executive handed the letter to Rubin. Rubin stepped back.

"Put it down. Down. On the floor. Down," said Rubin. Then he guided the man by an elbow to the rear of the mansion.

"Tell me," said Rubin. "If you had a choice of something to play with, would it be a rattle, a toy train, a video game, or a woman and fifth of bourbon?"

"A choice? Wonderful. Why are you so nice?"

"It helps us figure which room you go in."

"I'll take the bourbon," said the executive.

"Good," said Rubin. "You didn't get much. I'm getting pretty good with dosages."

They passed one room that was a din of screaming. The executive could not help peering in a small glass opening in the door. The inside was a horror. Grown men and women were rolling around on the floor, some wetting their pants, others pulling hair, still others were crying.

"I didn't know the dose then," said Rubin. "But we take care of them. We are a responsible religion."

"That's awful," said the executive. "There's a grown man there sucking his thumb."

"That's Wilbur Smot."

"He's smiling."

"A lot of them do," said Rubin. "How do you feel?"

"Not that good. Average, really. I just can't seem to recall what I'm doing here."

"Do you remember joining Poweressence?"

"I remember taking a character test back in Norfolk, Virginia. Did I join?"

"You'll be all right in a while," said Rubin.

They passed another room full of grown-ups but these were engrossed in electric trains and dolls. In the next room, a middle-aged woman with neon-blue hair and plastic jewelry played a video game. The final room was more to the executive's liking. It was a lounge, with soft music and a bar where he could help himself.

"You remember your address in Norfolk?" asked Rubin.

"Sure," said the executive.

"Then take yourself a drink, and go home."

"What is this? What is all this?"

"This is the latest scientific advancement created by one of the great minds of the Western world. And Eastern world, too. It is a gift to mankind from the great spiritual and scientific leader Rubin Dolomo," said Rubin.

"Doesn't he run Poweressence?"

"He has brought that enlightenment, yes," said Rubin.

"I remember seeing a picture of him. Yes. On a book cover, I think. Good book, too."

"Do you notice any resemblance?" asked Rubin, pushing back the thin remnants of his once full flowing hair.

"None."

"Well, then, forget the drink. Just get out of here," he said.

"Fine. I don't know what I'm doing here anyway."

Rubin went into the lounge and poured himself a stiff drink. He had the formula prepared, which was good. Now he needed another delivery person. This had cost them too much already. But the entertainment rooms were necessities. Because the formulas' effects could vary widely, Poweressence had to have a good test of the memory remission of someone affected by the formula. A fresh spill could send the deliverer back into childhood if he touched it with bare skin. Once the formula had dried, it could be counted on to shave a year or two off of the memory if touched within a week. Beyond that, somehow it got so powerful it was too dangerous to use. Rubin had spent a half-dozen lives finding out how to make the stuff and deliver it. Sometimes he thought he might slip a few drops into Beatrice's coffee and send her back to childhood. There was one horrible thought that stopped him. If Rubin should ever miss and Beatrice should find out, Rubin's life would be worth less than yesterday's garbage. Beatrice was ruthless.

A full-bodied woman sidled up to him.

"Hi," she said.

"Save it," said Rubin. "I run the place."

"Do you want some? You're paying for it."

Rubin looked longingly at the round rich curves, at the young curves, at the curves he wanted in his hands. But Beatrice meant more to him than a single wild exotic fling with a bar girl they had hired to work the recovery rooms. In her own way Beatrice had established a protocol for affection. She might, if she needed it to reaffirm her womanliness, take young men. Rubin might, if he needed other female companionship, face the loss of his sexual organs through the pounding of a frying pan upon those sensitive parts. Rubin, therefore, had been as faithful as a monk throughout the years.

"Thank you, no," said Rubin. He had to buy another Powie, another dedicated devotee of Poweressence. The problem with getting a good one, one who truly believed, was that the Powie was worth anywhere from three to five thousand dollars a year in Poweressence courses. If he lost one, like those now kept in the rehab rooms, he could safely multiply those figures by ten to cover all the years of lost revenues. Every chapter franchise could understand that. They would withhold a percentage of the Dolomo dues until that loss was recouped.

As a responsible religious leader, Dolomo had to inform the Norfolk chapter head that he had lost a tenth-level member. The chapter head was furious.

"I had him signed up for every course. I had him doing regressions to clear out his astral lives. Do you know what we are getting for that in Norfolk, Virginia? I was in his damned will. What about that?"

"We'll make it up to you," said Rubin.

"How? By getting convicted for attempted murder, fraud? Every time you two get nailed for something, Poweressence becomes a harder sell here."

"Beatrice is doing something about that."

"What is she going to do, put a cobra in the President's bed?"

"Don't talk about Beatrice like that."

"Why not?"

"She might be listening."

"Dolomo. We're in trouble, all around the country."

"Don't worry. We're not going to be convicted. I just phoned to let you know that your Level Ten might not be coming back. Of course, if he does come back, you get a bonus. Since he has forgotten everything, you might be able to work him through the whole thing again. In which case we don't owe you salt," said Dolomo.

"I'll never send you another."

"We don't need you. This is California. This is gold country for this sort of stuff."

"Then why did you call me in the first place?"

"I want to spread these things around the country. If you believe anything, believe we are going to beat this charge," said Rubin Dolomo.

"I believe we'll lose half our membership when you're convicted."

Rubin Dolomo hung up and had another Powie in the house within the hour, from a local chapter they still owned. The Powie was a problem, however. When she heard it was Rubin Dolomo himself she was talking to, she wanted him to take her through an astral regression.

"I get a sense that my planets are not organized within me. That I still retain negative memories," she said. She was twenty, with the trim build of a gymnast. She said she had almost made it to the Olympics. If she had had Power-essence then, as she had now, she would have won the gold medal. But because she still harbored violent tendencies from another life, she was not allowed to win.

"Look, girlie," said Rubin. "Take this pink letter. Do not touch the upper-left-hand corner, but deliver it. Do not tell who sent you because the evil forces will try to destroy your religion if you do. Do you understand?"

"Are you willing to risk using someone who hasn't totally cleared her memory of negative forces?"

"Have you been through Level One?"

"Yes."

"Then you're strong enough," said Rubin.

The Powie looked at the pink letter on the floor.

"What is it doing there? Why don't you pick it up?"

"I have a bad back," said Rubin. "And don't forget about the corner. Do not touch the upper-left-hand corner. The guards will probably want to read it. Let them, but you hold the letter. Only the witness touches the left-hand corner. Got it?"

"Upper left. Only the witness touches it."

"Right."

"I feel better already. Your power forces just reflected through my toes."

"Yeah. I am like that," said Rubin, who badly needed a Dexamyl, two aspirins, a Valium, and six cups of coffee to give him enough strength to get to bed for an afternoon nap.

"And don't forget. Be pleasant and open and they won't stop the letter."

"I'll use my positive essence."

She picked up the letter by the lower-right-hand corner and walked out of the Dolomo mansion refreshed. How true was Poweressence. How profound were the lessons she'd learned. When she smiled she felt better. When she smiled at others, they treated her better. All this from only a first-level course discount-priced at $325.

Ordinarily the U.S. attorney would have the witness secreted in a safe location where only prescreened mail could reach him. But since that didn't seem to protect all the witnesses lately and since this witness wanted to go home even more badly than most, the U.S. attorney relented. He allowed the witness to live in his own home. There was a special advantage in that. That hysterical pair, the Dolomos, seemed very likely to attempt some trick. And some government agency was going to lay a trap for them.

The reasoning was that anyone who would put an alligator in a columnist's swimming pool would try anything. And this might lead to finding out how witnesses were being turned. It was so secret the U.S. attorney was not sure which department was involved in the ambush, but when a thin man with dark eyes and thick wrists arrived outside the witness's home, the attorney knew not to question him. He just called off the normal guards.

The home was in a middle-class neighborhood of Palo Alto; needless to say, it was a neighborhood in which no middle-class worker could afford to live anymore.

Remo sat on the steps to avoid questions from the witness inside. The man wanted to know what his badge number was and where the guards were. He wanted to know how one lone unarmed person could protect him. Remo locked him in a closet for twenty minutes until he stopped yelling. Then he let the man out.

The man did not question him anymore but Remo had been put in a foul temper. He knew that anger could kill him, for it was the one emotion that blocked strength, turning it into unfocused energy. He had just decided to breathe himself out of it when a sweet young thing came up the walk to the house carrying a pink envelope.

"Hi. I've got a letter for the occupant of the house."

"No," said Remo.

The girl smiled, very broad, very bright. Continuously.

"I understand he is part of the government witness program and I understand that his mail has to be screened because it might contain a threat to him."

"No letters."

"Why not?"

"Because that means I'll have to open the door and hand him the letter. He'll expect me to speak to him and I don't like him. I don't like you either, to be honest."

"You have a lot of negativity, you know. May I ask you if it is doing you any good? Because it isn't, you know. I can help you be as happy and free as me. Would you like that?"

"No," said Remo.

"May I read you the letter, then, and then slip it under the door?"

"Nope."

"It's a beautiful love letter," said the Powie. She knew what she was up against: guard types were chosen just because of their unflagging slavery to negative forces. And what could be more negative than force that wanted to limit the freedom of Poweressence?

" 'My dearest Ralph, my love forever,' signed 'Angela,' " said the Powie.

"Not good enough. Rewrite it."

"But it's his love letter."

"I don't like it. I don't like Angela. And I don't think I like you," said Remo.

"How can you be so negative?"

"Easy. I like it."

The Powie stepped back and yelled at the house.

"Ralph. Ralph. I have a letter for you. It's from Angela, but your guard won't let me give it to you."

Remo opened the door.

"Want the letter, Ralph?"

"You going to throw me back in the closet?"

"No," said Remo.

"Then I don't want the letter. Angela was a dumb Powie I used to sleep with."

"Powies are not dumb," said the young girl.

"They're all dumb," said Ralph. "And I was the dumbest of them all. I stole the alligator for them."

"Ralph, don't you even want to read your letter?"

"That's just what I don't want," yelled back Ralph. Remo shut the door. The next day Ralph testified that under the instructions of Beatrice Dolomo, he did upon a certain night at a certain time purchase one alligator, Exhibit A, now sloshing around in a large glass pool brought into the courtroom for the viewing of the jury. The jury, watching the alligator's teeth chomp around for a day and a half, convicted the Dolomos of attempted murder.

At Folcroft Sanitarium, Harold W. Smith heard the verdict and despaired. This had seemed like the perfect witness to be attacked by a loss of memory. And he was not attacked. They had nailed two petty crooks for national fraud, and the American justice system still hung vulnerable to a strange new force. On the same day the head of the California rackets was acquitted when his chief accuser, a former strong-arm man, could not remember enough to validate notebooks full of testimony.

That same day, Angelo Muscamente thanked the justice system of the United States, his lawyer, his mother, a statue of the Virgin Mary, and the proud new force that had brought success to his life. He joined the famous actress Kathy Bowen and other celebrities in saying, for the benefit of the press, that the saddest day for American freedom was the day the Dolomos were convicted of a crime.

"It will shame America, the way Jesus' death shamed the Roman empire, the way Joan of Arc's death shamed the French, the way Moses' death shamed someone or other," Angelo announced on the courthouse steps. "I am free but these good people now are in jail."

"They're out on a million dollars bail," a television reporter told Muscamente.

"Yeah? A million dollars bail?"

"They put it up in cash."

"Well, they got the dough," said Muscamente, who went back to his well-guarded home to confront his astral negativity and rid himself of a little more of it. And why shouldn't he? he thought. He had paid a half-million to reach Level Twenty, and at that spiritual apex no court case could ever harm him. It was guaranteed, money back if not delighted. As he explained to his bodyguards, "Don't knock what fuckin' works."

5

The trap had failed. Smith told Remo he did not blame him. Chiun apologized for the failure anyhow.

"Let us stop him from embarrassing you further, O great Emperor Smith," said Chiun into his end of a three-way telephone hookup in the Miami condo.

"It's not his fault, Chiun," said Smith. "It's mine."

"Never," said Chiun. "Thy radiant wisdom is a success the moment it leaves your magnificent lips."

"Things don't work sometimes," said Smith.

"Smitty, stop reasoning with him. You're not in the right century for that. The operation failed. What do we do now?" asked Remo.

"We stop blaming our gracious emperor," said Chiun. "We stop right now. How can we blame our emperor when we are not at correctness?"

"What do we do now, Smitty?"

"Why don't you take a look at the people who got off. Find out how they're doing it. Who are they paying? And try not to leave bodies, all right? We're not a revenge outfit."

"Right, Smitty."

"No revenge?" said Chiun.

"No. No. We're not here for revenge."

"You have another plan?"

"We have many plans, Chiun, but revenge is never one of them."

"Begging your gracious pardon, why?" asked Chiun.

"We don't believe in it."

Chiun was silent. Remo glanced into the other room, where Chiun was holding the telephone, dumbfounded. Remo got the information and then hung up. Chiun stood stunned, clutching the receiver in his hands. Remo hung it up for him. Chiun did not move.

"Did I hear correctly? Did Emperor Smith say he did not believe in revenge?"

"That's what he said. He's not here for revenge."

"An emperor known not to seek revenge is one who is dead by the morning. Revenge, known public revenge, is what keeps civilization from chaos."

"Well, he's doing something else."

"It is a disgrace to work for an emperor who will not use revenge. How can he employ the premier house of assassins of all time and not use revenge? Would you buy a car and not drive it? Marry a woman and not make love to her? Walk through a rose garden and not breathe? How can he say he will not use revenge when the House of Sinanju stands ready to glorify him?"

"Good questions, little father," said Remo.

"That means you're not going to answer me," said Chiun.

"You're catching on," said Remo.

William Hawlings Jameson celebrated the court's verdict of innocence in grain-market manipulation with a party so lavish it consumed almost ten percent of his illegal profits from those manipulations. At the party he was beaming. Everyone could understand that. He had just escaped ten to fifteen years in the federal penitentiary.

But his wife said he had been feeling that way for weeks before the trial. She told this to a very attractive dark-eyed man with high cheekbones. He was very interested in Bill. No, he didn't work for Bill, but he wanted to speak to her husband.

"He is so high on life, I don't think he could speak to one person alone. It would be a downer to him—like having only one bank account. Wasn't that court decision wonderful? Isn't it miraculous?"

Mrs. Jameson was one of those women of advanced middle age whose wrinkles could be formed into something attractive only with the massive amount of cosmetic talent that lots of money could buy. She smiled a lot to keep the wrinkles up. Remo estimated she had had two face lifts already. Her teeth, of course, gave her away. Teeth aged in almost everyone, everyone he knew except Chiun. And now, of course, himself. He did not know why this was so about him and Chiun, but he did know that the greater truths, the more basic reasons for things, were just as much a mystery as the far side of the universe.

"Is there something caught in my teeth?" Mrs. Jameson asked.

"You're sixty-two, right?"

"I beg your pardon?"

"Maybe sixty-three."

"That's rude," said Mrs. Jameson.

"I'm right, then," said Remo.

"Young man, that was uncalled for."

"You're right," said Remo. "I'm really in a foul mood."

"Well, you certainly know how to ruin a party," she said.

"You ain't seen nothing yet, sweetheart," said Remo. Somehow that made him feel a little bit better. Mrs. Jameson called the butler. He would politely ask the gentleman to leave, and if he did not leave, the butler should use whatever force was required.

"Whatever force," she repeated.

She did not see her butler again that evening, but she did see the rude young man. He seemed enraptured with Bill's explanation of his new religion.

"Yes, I know there's a lot of stories about cult hustles and Poweressence, but the proof of anything for me is in the pudding," said Bill Jameson, a portly man with the sharp executive face of success. He didn't have to wear a tuxedo and a gold Rolex to show he had money and power. Wealth was reflected in his eyes and the sure set of his head. His smile was the smile of a man who gave approval and didn't need it for himself.

"Bill, isn't Poweressence that thing founded by a science-fiction writer? If it's so successful, how come he and his wife were just convicted of attempted murder? They also have three counts of mail fraud and conspiracy to extort. This doesn't sound like Billy Graham or the pope to me," a guest said.

"You've got to understand Poweressence. A force so good has to attract evil. The evil the Dolomos attract keeps it away from the followers. They are really suffering for us, so to speak. That's the way it was explained to me, and damnit if it didn't work out that way."

"Maybe you had a good lawyer."

"I had the best, but he couldn't shake my secretary's testimony. They had me. I was gonzo. And then I believed."

"What did it cost you?"

"He who has, does," said Jameson with a knowing smile.

"A half-million?"

Jameson laughed again. "That's the initiation fee. But look, they said they would give it back if my life didn't improve. If I weren't found innocent. You don't knock success."

"I do," said the young man in his early thirties with dark eyes and high cheekbones. "I knock it a lot."

"Who are you?"

"The success knocker, Jameson. I want to talk to you," said Remo.

"I am busy talking to friends."

The young man put a friendly arm around his shoulder but the shoulder didn't feel a friendly arm. The shoulder felt like it had been connected to a wall outlet. He couldn't even scream. He could only nod. He would go wherever that hand wanted him to go, in this case a study off the main ballroom. The door shut behind them and the tinkling noise of his freedom party was shut out.

The room was filled with rich dark wood shelves and

warm yellow lighting and solid polished wood chairs. It smelled faintly of rich cigars and old brandy.

"Excuse me, I don't know many important corporate executives so I've got to use my own humble working-class ways to speak with you," said Remo.

"What did you do to me?" Jameson gasped, trying to shake life back into the shoulder the young man had seemed to electrify with just a touch.

"That's nothing. Will you listen?"

"There isn't much else I can do."

"Good," said Remo. Then he slapped the president of International Grains, Carbides, and Chemicals on the cheek hard enough to move him two feet to the side. Then he slapped him again.

"That's hello," said Remo.

Jameson emitted a pitiful grunt, then quickly emptied his pockets of cash, took off his watch and held it toward Remo.

"I'm not the crook. You are."

"The court found me innocent," said Jameson.

"Bring your lawyer in. I'll work him over too," said Remo.

"What do you want?"

"Now we're talking. Who turned the witness for you? Remember Gladys? Your secretary. Told the world all the nasty things you were doing, and you thought because you paid her so much she would keep quiet. Wno's the one who made her forget?"

"What do you mean?"

"This party isn't for your birthday," said Remo.

"It was the positive forces of the universe which were unlocked for me. That's what got me freed."

Remo slapped him again. "That's my positive force."

"I didn't bribe anyone. I didn't reach anyone. I just joined Poweressence when everything else seemed to fail. And then my life became positive again. It became good again."

Remo put Jameson's right wrist between his fingers and turned so that the arm would turn at the socket. It was not like turning a solid iron knob. The wrist and elbows were weak joints and they could snap at any moment.

Jameson wept in pain.

"Tell me how good your life is, Jameson," said Remo. "I want to hear about the good forces of the universe."

"You wouldn't understand."

"Wouldn't understand? I am the force of the universe, jerk."

"Please . . . "

"Forget it. You're not lying."

Jameson cradled his damaged arm in the other as he leaned forward, crying.

"Are you the agent of darkness?"

"What's this agent-of-darkness stuff?"

"The stronger the forces of good are, the stronger positive forces are, the more they bring out negative forces. If you join Poweressence and people see you are happy, they begin to knock Poweressence. They can't live with your happiness. So they have to call Poweressence a fraud. It takes the form of jealousy. Good things always attract bad."

"Are you saying I'm bad?"

"No. No. It's just that you're so powerful. And you have turned that power against me, against my positive forces."

"I'm a good person," said Remo.

"Yes," said Jameson immediately. He shielded his face with his good arm. "You are a good person. A good person."

"Sometimes I have to use methods you might not like," said Remo.

"Right," said Jameson.

"But I am a good person."

"Right," said Jameson.

"Now, are you going to sit there and tell me you're innocent? You robbed America. You robbed every American farmer. You robbed every citizen in the country who depends on the farmers you robbed. It is not a good thing that you got off scot-free. So why don't you and I work out a deal?"

"Sounds fair," said Jameson. He sat very rigid in the chair, with his backbone as far away from the young man with the horror-dealing hands as he could.

"You did commit crimes, correct?"

"I did. True."

"You got off free."

"I've donated to charity, to religions."

"That thing with the Mickey Mouse forces of the universe won't do. You don't even understand the forces of the universe. They're not in some cult. They're in the universe. No, I'm thinking of an agreed-upon punishment for you, so you don't quite enjoy your life knowing you escaped. Because that's what you did, Jameson."

"What do you suggest?"

"How about not walking again?"

"No."

"One of your arms is damaged already."

"No, not my arms."

"Tell you what. One night, maybe sooner, maybe later, I'm going to come back and make you pay for your crimes," said Remo.

"What are you going to do?"

"I'll just have to decide when I get to it. But wait for me. I'm coming back," said Remo, and he walked out of the room into the party, thanked Mrs. Jameson for inviting him, and asked her again if he weren't absolutely correct about her age.

Remo thought it was a fitting punishment, tormenting the executive with the fear that Remo would return to inflict damage upon his body. Of course, he wasn't going to come back, but the executive didn't know that. The constant terror would be the best punishment of all. It was enough, and Remo hadn't done it so much for the country as for himself. It was just too wrong for someone that bad to escape so freely to a life that good.

And besides, Remo was in a foul mood.

* * *

The second lucky recipient of an acquittal lived very well
also. He had an estate that covered miles of Oklahoma
prairie land, a magnificent home more like a castle than a
house. He had servants and he had bodyguards, range
riders, tough men with carbines and Bronco land cruisers,
ten-gallon hats, and weathered faces.

When Remo unweathered a few of the faces, they
brought him right to their employer, a man who had
swindled thousands of people out of their savings in a
diamond-investment scheme. It was as old as fraud itself.
He paid the first investors back handsomely with the
profits from ensuing investors, and when he had enough
people pouring their nest eggs into his bank accounts, he
stopped paying everyone and headed toward Brazil, which
had no extradition treaty with America. He didn't make it
and was charged with fraud. His accountant, whom he had
planned on leaving behind, prepared the entire case for the
government. In fact, he was glad to help because his
employer, Diamond Bill Pollenberg, had arranged it so the
accountant signed all the incriminating documents.

It was an airtight case and the accountant, happily
anticipating his revenge, could not be reached. Until that
day when he forgot everything after his first college course
in double ledger entries.

And then Diamond Bill Pollenberg went free. He went
back to his vast rangelands to enjoy nature. And he
enjoyed it right up until a thin man with thick wrists told
him that if he didn't explain some things right now, he was
going to embed a horse's hoof in Mr. Pollenberg's rectum,
and he was going to leave the horse attached.

Bill Pollenberg knew the time to use reason when he saw
it. What he saw this day was two of his toughest range
hands with their wrinkles rearranged on their faces, and
tears of pain in their eyes.

"Howdy, podner," said Pollenberg, offering the
stranger a pot of coffee off the campfire. Pollenberg wore
a ten-gallon hat, Levi's, and boots, which offset his

$200,000 diamond pinkie ring perfectly. It was the only real diamond he had ever owned.

"Where'd you pick up this 'podner' stuff? I got you down as having been born on Mosholu Parkway in the Bronx."

"I am a reasonable man. Let us reason together."

"How'd you turn the witness?"

"I didn't do anything, friend. Have some coffee. Get with the positive forces. Unleash yourself. Become your real self."

"What did you do to the witness?"

"The forces of the universe did it for me," said Bill Pollenberg with a smile. Shortly thereafter, smiling Bill was found minus his diamond ring and serving as a cushion for his favorite horse's right rear hoof. Every time the horse used his hoof, Bill Pollenberg's stomach met part of his vast rangeland. The diamond ring was recovered from a little girl in downtown Oklahoma City who said a nice man gave it to her because she had such a pretty smile.

On a yacht cruising the Pacific along the California coast, Angelo Muscamente met his underbosses, his oily courtesy coating the ever-present malevolence that made his organization one of the smoothest-running in the country. They all had survived what had been the greatest threat to their freedom in a decade and they had gotten their reprieve when a minor enforcer, a witness, suddenly forgot everything.

No one who knew Mr. Muscamente believed for one moment he had not stretched his long powerful arms out to reach Gennaro "Drums" Drumola. Everyone knew that crossing Mr. Muscamente meant pain at least, and death at most. Those offenses that brought the death penalty were those jobs that cost Mr. Muscamente anything over $5,000. Because the boss was unreasonable and unbendable about the arbitrary line, only petty thievery could flourish in his mob. As his lieutenants boarded his yacht, each kissed his offered hand.

"Mr. Muscamente, it is a pleasure to be here," said one after another.

"Yeah. Okay," said Mr. Muscamente, receiving the homage with boredom. There were fourteen, all told, who were finally assembled on the rear deck of his oceangoing yacht *Mama*. They sat on small chairs, each with a small table in front of him. Whatever they wanted to drink or eat was set before them so that they would not have to call for anything. When Mr. Muscamente spoke, he did not like interruptions. Several of the underbosses made sure they used the head before he began. The yacht's crewmen were told they were not appreciated at the stern, but should go forward.

But these were not exactly the words Mr. Muscamente's bodyguards used.

"Ey! Youse guys. Get outta here. Go to the front. I don't want to see none of youse here no more. You hear? Now beat it."

When the decks were cleared of outsiders, Mr. Muscamente cleared his throat. He sat on a slightly higher chair near the rear railing. He wore his yachtsman's double-breasted blue blazer and white slacks with Top-Siders. Mr. Muscamente had seen others wear this uniform, and he had ordered it by having two of his men muscle a fellow yachtsman into a clothing store and find out what the clothes were called by saying:

"What's dis guy wearing?"

Then he ordered it for himself. And so from his high seat on his yacht *Mama,* perfectly attired in his seafaring regalia, Angelo Muscamente spoke now to his underbosses about a wonderful revelation.

"You see in me a new person," said Mr. Muscamente. Everyone agreed.

"But it is not new. Not new at all," said Mr. Muscamente. He waited for everyone to agree with his contradiction.

"Now, how can this be, you may ask yourselves."

"Good question, boss," said Santino "Big Jelly" Jellino.

"There is within all of us a positive power we fight against."

"We'll beat the shit out of it, boss," said Big Jelly.

"Shut up," said Mr. Muscamente kindly.

"Right, boss. Everyone shut up," said Big Jelly.

"Mostly you, Big Jelly," said Mr. Muscamente. "Now, how can there be another good person locked inside a struggling negative person?"

Only the sound of the engine purring belowdecks could be heard. No one was going to answer the question. Everyone avoided the eyes of everyone else. No one wanted it to be known that he didn't have the slightest idea what the boss was talking about.

Mr. Muscamente talked of the forces of the universe being good. He talked of astral power. He talked of a far distant planet that all mankind came from, which was what made them different from animals. They all waited for the pitch. When Joey "Fingers" Phalange heard the name Poweressence mentioned, he suddenly thought he understood what it was all about.

"Yeah. I could have bought one of those franchises from the Dolomos back in seventy-eight, real cheap. I know a guy that got stuck with one, though. What with all the bad publicity, alligators in swimming pools and everything, those franchises ain't gonna be worth salt in a year or two. I say we stay out of them."

"That alligator was attracted to that columnist's pool because alligators are negative astral creatures that respond to negative astral forces. That columnist drew the alligator to himself. No one put it in his pool," said Mr. Muscamente.

"No, boss. They got the guy that bought Exhibit A for the Dolomos. They got him in court. He nailed 'em. That appeal they got won't do business. The Dolomos are goin' to the slammer."

"Not if we can help it."

"What are we going to do?"

"We are going to do a hit on that turncoat traitor."

"Because we're takin' over Poweressence. We buy in on

the franchise low now, remove the witness, then we got somethin' that's worth somethin'. I see," said Big Jelly. Everyone nodded. Mr. Muscamente ruled almost as much through his brains as he did through terror.

"We are not touching one positive center. We are protecting it," said Mr. Muscamente.

"We sell the Dolomos protection," said Fingers.

"We sell nothing. We buy. I am entering you all at Level One. I don't want no negative consciousness around me. You are going to release your blocks. You are going to function with the forces of good, namely us. Anyone against us is evil. Got it?"

There were many yesses. The only thing they didn't understand was why Mr. Muscamente needed Poweressence to think everyone against them was evil. They had thought like that since childhood.

On the bridge, the captain noticed something moving toward the *Mama*. He brought his binoculars to bear, focused, then refocused.

Finally he asked the first mate to verify what he saw.

"Are my eyes going?" he asked.

The first mate focused, then he too refocused.

"I don't know what it is either. It looks like a man in a dark T-shirt and gray pants, swimming toward us."

"At twenty knots? Fourteen miles out in the Pacific?"

"It must be a small boat," said the first mate.

The captain took back the binoculars. He looked out toward the object.

"Right—a boat. With arms and legs that move. How can he swim that fast?"

The first mate got his own set of binoculars.

"You're right. He is swimming fast, and he hardly seems to be making an effort. Not like any swimmers I've seen. They splash a lot. Boy, is he smooth. Do you think we should tell Mr. Muscamente?"

"Those animals back there would tear us apart. He's having one of his meetings."

"Then what should we do?"

"Maybe that guy isn't heading toward us."

"Looks like it to me."

"If he's a man overboard, we have to pick him up," said the captain.

"Doesn't look like a man overboard to me," said the first mate.

"We'll all find out pretty soon."

One of Mr. Muscamente's guests spotted the man overboard soon after. The captain knew this because the guest fired a small pistol at the figure. The figure disappeared under the water. The figure came up at the rear of the yacht and began talking to Mr. Muscamente.

The first thing he did was to convince Fingers to let go of his gun. He did this by separating Fingers from the wrist that held the gun. Big Jelly went overboard like a bucket of chum. Then everyone sat back down quietly, including Mr. Muscamente.

It was a day that would be remembered forever in the annals of the California mob. It was a day that brought tears to the eyes of Mr. Muscamente. These tears came when he could not explain why the witness, "Drums" Drumola, failed to remember testimony.

Mr. Muscamente explained it as forces of the universe, while his underbosses listened politely. The guest who swam aboard had a strong tendency to respond with slaps and twists of arms.

Within a few minutes Mr. Muscamente was a helpless ball of flesh, his double-breasted blue blazer in shreds, his Top-Sider deck shoes kicking helplessly in the air. At that point, the guest who had swum aboard threw Mr. Muscamente over the stern. Every time Mr. Muscamente came up for breath, the guest asked how Mr. Muscamente made Drums forget his testimony. On the third and last time Mr. Muscamente surfaced, everyone on board realized he was telling the truth. He believed he had unlocked the forces of good on his side.

Everyone on board agreed on something else. They certainly didn't want to tamper with government witnesses if this man was protecting them, because they believed, as Mr. Muscamente had shouted, that indeed this man was the supreme force of negativity. And if that were the case, none of them wanted to be on the side of the positive.

Remo sailed back sullenly with the remnants of the California mob and a very impressed captain and first mate. He was quiet, even as his clothes dried. He had failed again.

Several of the underbosses wanted to know who he worked for, not that they were curious, Remo should understand. But they would be totally delighted to employ him. They saw in him the sort of person who shared their most basic convictions. They saw in him someone who would fit perfectly into the California rackets.

"No," said Remo. "I happen to be the good guy."

And since he said this as he threw someone overboard, there wasn't a soul to disagree with him as the *Mama* docked at the Los Angeles marina. They all allowed him to leave first.

When he phoned in to headquarters, he knew he had to be slipping somehow, because Smith was now conciliatory, telling him it was not his fault.

"I would say go at the Poweressence people because that's the only common thread we have here. But if they were behind this, why didn't they use this power to turn witnesses for themselves? It doesn't make sense. The only thing we know is that the whole justice system seems to be coming apart in California."

"Yeah, and if it happens in California, the whole nation catches it soon thereafter," said Remo.

"Are you trying to make me feel good?" asked Smith.

"I don't feel so hot myself."

"Why don't you take a look at that organization? Take Chiun."

"You don't think I can handle things anymore."

"Take Chiun."

"Are you telling me I can't do the job?" asked Remo.

"I am telling you I don't understand how you and Chiun work, and if he tells me you are out of synch with the cosmos, then that means there is something wrong. And you are for some reason not coming up with results.''

''You just told me it wasn't my fault.''

''I just told you I had no reason to believe it was your fault. I can't be sure.''

Remo pulverized the receiver of the pay telephone. It was so much more satisfying than hanging up.

6

Lawyer Barry Glidden sent his children off to Switzerland, telling them to use another name for a while. He would contact them when the situation improved.

"Have you done something wrong, Daddy?" asked his daughter.

"No," said Glidden. "I have a very difficult client who is very mad now."

"They won't pay you?"

"No. That's the least of my worries. There is a client I have who thinks the only wrong thing in the world is if something bad happens to her. And she does bad things."

"Like what, Daddy?"

"Like anything, honey. Absolutely anything. Anything, sweetheart. Do you understand?" Barry held the girl's head in his hands. He shuddered. "There is nothing beyond this sick, sick lady's imagination. Nothing that she won't do. To anyone. So that is why you have to leave. She is mad at me now."

"Couldn't you get policemen to protect you?"

"Doesn't work like that, sweetheart. Not with those two."

"Then why do you defend them?"

"Well, she paid a lot of money. Lots. And I didn't . . . couldn't believe they were as bad as they turned out."

"Oh, Daddy. You have had some absolutely horrid clients."

"She puts alligators in swimming pools of people she doesn't like. She threatens the President. And she promised to boil someone alive in oil if she lost a lawsuit. If I lost a lawsuit. Get on the plane, honey.''

"Did you lose the lawsuit?"

"Not yet, just the first round. But we don't stand a chance."

"She's going to boil you alive in oil, Daddy?"

"No, honey, someone I love."

"Good-bye, Daddy. Don't phone until it's over. They can trace phone calls."

"Good-bye, honey," said Barry Glidden, who despite his sense of terror was not too terrified to do some good business before he saw the Dolomos. He brought two more investors into the city complex he had planned for the Dolomo estate. Then he went out to see Beatrice and her husband. Gingerly he drove over one of her moats. He wondered if there were alligators in there. He wondered if she would throw him in before he got the chance to fit two hundred duplex units on the south lawn.

Glidden knew Beatrice was on a rampage because Rubin was hiding. He stood in the middle of the pink marble foyer and looked for clues as to Rubin's whereabouts. From the rear of the house echoed a sound—a gurgling, happy sound. He knew that couldn't be Rubin, but the sounds intrigued him. Glidden would investigate. He walked past a few of the bodyguards the Dolomos had stationed strategically around the estate since the parents of a Powie attempted to kill them for stealing their daughter.

Of course, they hadn't really stolen the daughter. They had only sold her some courses. She was working in Australia for the rest of her life to pay them off.

Glidden saw a row of doors with glass windows. The gurgling came from one of them. He peeked in. What he saw was grown people in diapers. First he wondered if it were a new form of California sex, but no one was touching except for occasional hair pulls. He looked into the next door. There were grown-ups playing with trains. Well, some grown-ups played with trains. But he had never seen them make the sounds of the whistles, at least, not with such abandon. In the next room a woman with grotesquely dyed hair pummeled a video machine. And in the final room was a bar with an available lady hanging around.

Barry let her give him a drink. Barry let her put a hand on his neck. Barry removed his own hands from his lap in case there was something she wanted to get to. She did.

He did not resist. He wondered if there was a little room around, some private place.

"Nobody comes in here," said the woman. He could smell her perfume, a foul cheap nostril-wrenching odor. However, when it came with an absolutely bare body, a beautiful body, a full body, a body waiting for him, Barry Glidden couldn't care less about the welfare of his nostrils.

A moment later, a roller-coaster would have been private enough for Barry Glidden.

Just before his moment of glory, Barry Glidden felt a shoe heel in his back.

"Barry. Where's Rubin? I'm looking for Rubin."

"In a moment, Beatrice," said her lawyer. "Just a moment."

"I don't have a moment," said Beatrice.

"Just one. Just one."

"Do you have to do that in here?"

"Yes. Oh, yes. I have to do it and I'm doing it."

"Well, where's Rubin? I want Rubin. Do you hear? I want Rubin. You two stop that."

Barry didn't want to stop. If a gun were pointed at his head at this moment he would have wondered if he could finish before he was dead.

He heard Beatrice doing something at the bar, and then with an earthquake size shock he felt the splash of a pail of cold water on his back.

"C'mon upstairs," said Beatrice. "We have work to do."

"Rubin says she's very forceful," said the woman.

"Yeah," said Barry. Sometimes a thousand condo units wasn't worth the price of working for the Dolomos.

In the large south meeting room where the Dolomos

often planned strategy with franchise owners, Beatrice seemed almost happy.

Barry blotted himself with paper towels.

"I want the truth now. On a scale of one to ten, what are our chances of winning an appeal?"

"We can still cop a plea on the charges of mail fraud."

"I didn't ask for that."

"No chance."

"Then," said Beatrice Dolomo, "we are going to start playing dirty."

"What are alligators in pools and threats to the President? Playing clean?"

"I mean we're going to play hardball, Barry."

"They put people in gas chambers for that sort of hardball, Beatrice. Why not cut your losses and run? You'll still have plenty of money, especially if you sell this estate you won't be needing. Considering the appreciation of your money—if you sell the estate you'll come out of jail set for life. No more cult business, just beautiful peaceful wealthy retirement."

"For the two to three years we would have left to live, Barry? No deal. I didn't crawl up from a stinking attic dragging Rubin with me because I am a quitter. You think Rubin is some great genius? He was just another hack science-fiction writer. He believed Poweressence. He was trying to help people when it began. Do you realize that? He actually believed people could cure headaches by finding the moment in their lives they couldn't let go of. I had to stop him from treating cancer patients before they sued us into penury. No, Mr. Glidden, I am not copping a plea."

"Then what are you going to do?"

"Escalate."

"You already tried to kill one columnist and have threatened the President. Where do you go from there?"

"If you don't make good on your threats, no one will believe you," said Beatrice. Today she wore purple lipstick with purple eyeshadow. She wore a white peasant blouse embroidered with flowers. She looked like a middle-age woman who had lost her own clothes and was borrowing those of a twelve-year-old daughter.

It was obvious to Barry why Beatrice always seemed to dress so inappropriately. There was no one brave enough to tell her she did not look good.

Beatrice glanced at her watch.

"We can't wait forever," she said. She went to the door and screamed out into the hallway.

"Get Rubin. We're tired of looking for Rubin."

"He's writing the founder's day speech for the faithful," came a man's voice. It was one of her bodyguards.

"Use last year's. Tell him to use last year's," yelled back Mrs. Dolomo.

"He says he can't. It's a new speech about the persecution of the righteous."

"Persecute his duff up here to the south meeting room," screamed Mrs. Dolomo, and then she returned to the table where Barry Glidden was desperately figuring out ways to sever relations with this client. He knew what was coming.

"Barry, we're going to make the President pay for this. We are going to make America pay for this. That guilty verdict was kangaroo justice inflicted upon us from the very top. All my life, I have respected the top too much. Well, Barry, I'm not taking it anymore. The President goes. Off with the top."

"Mrs. Dolomo, as an officer of the court, I am not allowed to hear this without reporting you. I am a lawyer, I have taken an oath. So I would suggest you keep whatever plans you have to yourself. Leave me out."

"You're in, Barry," said Mrs. Dolomo.

"I'm not good at these things. I'm just a lawyer."

"You'll learn. Rubin!"

"He's coming, Mrs. Dolomo," came the bodyguard's voice.

Someone was shuffling down the hall. It was Rubin. He came into the room with a cigarette dangling from his mouth at just the right angle to make his eyes water. He had not shaved for two days and he wore a bathrobe. From the bathrobe came a light tinkling, the sound of plastic rubbing together. It was Rubin's pills. He put them on the table, his hands shaking.

"Do you want to hear the message to the enlightened? It's truly beautiful," said Rubin.

"No," said Beatrice.

"Not really," said Barry.

"It's about religious persecution. I think it's the best thing I have ever written."

"We have business, Rubin," said Beatrice.

"It's especially meaningful in the light of our convictions, and appeals. The franchises will like it."

"No," said Beatrice.

"Legally I shouldn't be here," said Barry. "I wish you luck in what you're going to do."

"Enlightened ones," Rubin began to read as he put a hand on Barry Glidden's shoulder, seating him back down. "Times of trial are nothing new. Each of us has faced them in daily life. They are but small obstacles in the path of enlightenment, only pebbles under the feet if you are going somewhere, but boulders if you are not. Your faith has made you free. Never let your new strength fail before some minor tribulation. Know that all blocks are only temporary and that you are the children of the good forces of all being. You will prevail. Let power be in you."

Rubin rubbed a tear from his left eye with his bathrobe sleeve.

"You done?" asked Beatrice.

Rubin nodded, swallowing hard. He was deeply moved.

"Very nice, Rubin, and I will be sending you both my bill. I have to go now," said Barry.

"We haven't planned on how we are going to get the President yet," said Beatrice. "Sit down, Rubin, the President is not taking us seriously. What shall we do about it?"

"I don't know how we can get an alligator into the White House. We're going to have to do something else. What did you think of the speech? Do you think it was better than the Larkin king saying good-bye to the Dromoid mercenaries who had come to love him?"

"It's wonderful, Rubin."

"As an officer of the court I will be forced to report anything I hear of a criminal nature."

"Don't worry, Barry. There won't be any problem with that. You help us now and I guarantee you will have no problem with telling everything you know to the authorities."

"You said that the alligator witness would turn also."

"A little mistake. The President's. Now, how do we get the bum?"

"You don't," said Glidden. "He is always surrounded by bodyguards. They are called the Secret Service, and they are prepared for everything."

"Not everything. There's been one President killed and one wounded in my lifetime alone," said Beatrice.

"They have electronic sensors. They have men who will shield him with their bodies. They have everything they need to catch you. And then they're going to put you in jail for a very long, long, long time. Longer than the alligator thing, Beatrice Dolomo."

Barry Glidden felt the rage rise in him. His hands tapped the table. She had gone too far, and he knew what he would do to stop her. As soon as he got out of here, this responsible officer of the court would report this plan to harm the President of the United States. And he would forgo any fee. He would, for the first time in his glorious career, live up to that precious oath he had taken years before when he graduated from UCLA Law School. Then, once the Dolomos were safely in the slammer, he would make his move for the rolling lands of the estate and bring his children back from Switzerland.

The estate might be held against uncollected taxes. It might even be a steal.

"The President can't be reached through any girlfriends. He's faithful to his wife. You can't poison him," said Barry, "because he's got tasters. Those cobras you snuck into someone's bed won't work, and boiling oil could never get near him. You might try to plant a sniper on a roof with a rifle, but the Secret Service would spot him. I guarantee it."

"Does the President read letters?" asked Beatrice.

"Of course he does," said Barry.

"Then we'll send him a letter. Meanwhile, we want you to speak to the Vice-President. He, after all, is going to be in charge, after the current President is lost. Tell him to lay off Poweressence."

Beatrice nodded at the reasonableness of her own suggestion.

Barry gave only a polite smile. He wondered if he should drive directly to the Federal Bureau of Investigation or run. As Rubin escorted him to the door, Beatrice issued a particularly strange good-bye:

"Give him just enough for now," said Beatrice.

"What is she talking about?" said Barry.

"Nothing," said Rubin. He invited him to the lounge bar downstairs.

"No thanks, I was interrupted down there by your wife."

"Beatrice does not like to see anyone but her making love."

"It wasn't love."

"Whatever," said Rubin. He needed two Motrin and a Demerol to make it down the stairs. He asked Glidden if he would deliver a letter for him.

"Sure," said Barry.

Apparently Rubin was going to write the letter while Barry waited. In order to rush Rubin, Barry followed him through the door he'd exited. It led to a cellar, a cellar where many rubber suits hung against the walls. A cellar with several doors so that Barry couldn't quite be sure which he'd used to get in. So he picked one door at random and burst through. He found himself staring at Rubin. Rubin was sweaty-faced, wide-eyed, and on the other side of a piece of glass, and his hands were stuffed into rubber-coated arms protruding into Barry's room.

"Get out of there. Go back," yelled Rubin. The voice

was muffled by the glass. One rubber hand held a cotton swab and the other a pink letter.

"What are you doing with that letter?"

"Go back."

"You're doing something funny with the letter," said Barry.

"I'm not doing anything with the letter. Get out of here. Go back."

"That's the letter you want me to deliver?"

"Get back. For your own good. Get back. I control forces you know nothing about, forces beyond your understanding."

"That's the letter you wanted me to deliver. What are you doing to it?" Barry went over to the small table the rubber arms worked over. There was a jar of something on the table. The swab was wet with something. Barry leaned over the little jar. He sniffed. It smelled strangely like a root cellar he once had made love in. He had gone to a client's house to help her with a divorce. Her husband had accused her of adultery. He was very suspicious, she had said. Life was hell, she had said. Perhaps they had better talk about it in the root cellar, she had said. It was the first time Barry Glidden had ever accepted an alternate form of legal fee.

So Barry Glidden basked in the fond memories of this odor.

"Get back," said Rubin.

"What's wrong here? What are you doing, Rubin?"

"It's too intricate for you to understand."

"What if I were to take this jar and bring it to the police, Rubin? What would happen then?"

"You'd only hurt yourself," said Rubin. "Don't touch it, please."

"I'm not so sure," said Glidden.

"It's dangerous. What do you think I am doing on the other side of the glass shield with my hands in rubber gloves?"

"You tell me," said Glidden. He did not move. He liked the aroma of the liquid in the jar.

Beside the steel jar was a steel cap. If he could protect his own hands with his own jacket, Barry reasoned, he could cap the jar, put it in his briefcase, and drive it to some chemist to get it analyzed. It could be good evidence in the government case against the Dolomos, good enough to cut six months off the projected time when all this land would be sold.

Glidden removed his suit jacket, taking out the wallet and the keys and stuffing them in his pants. Then, very carefully, he used it like a giant potholder to move the steel jar top over the container of the pleasant-smelling liquid. One of the rubber gloves tried to push him away. It held the letter. Barry ignored it. Then the letter touched the back of his hand.

He looked down at his suit jacket. For some reason it was bunched up in his hand. Inside it was a jar top. He was holding a jar top with his suit jacket. He put the lid on the table and began to brush out his suit. As he did so, he knocked over the jar. A sense of panic seized him as the dark stain spread over his shirt and jacket and pants. Someone was going to tell his mommy.

Barry Glidden began to cry and he only stopped crying when the nice man brought him into a room with toys and other children, nice little boys and little girls. But they were not really that nice. They kept all the toys to themselves and would not share with Barry. Nobody would share with Barry. He cried even harder. Then a nice lady gave him the yellow boat, and he stopped crying. Barry Glidden, after twenty tough competitive years before the California bar, was happy at last.

Rubin Dolomo left Glidden in the first playroom and began his assault on the President of the United States. He was not sure whether he should cast legions in a wild charge such as in *Invaders from Dromoid,* or send in a single lone deliverer. Like in *Defenders of Larkin.*

Beatrice had a simpler plan.

"Do both and do it now. If we wait around for you to get things right, we'll die of old age," she said. She now blamed him for failing to turn the witness.

The problem had been that they couldn't get through. A man of such negativity as to be totally unreasonable had been responsible for keeping the love note from the President.

In his own way, Rubin Dolomo had more than a little shrewdness, and Beatrice, despite her haranguing, appreciated that. She knew that though he often failed once, he rarely failed twice, if one kept after him. So when he said he had a new and better plan to reach the President of the United States, she did not question him.

"I am only asking for one thing. Get the SOB. Get the President of the United States. Is that too much to ask?"

"No, dear," said Rubin. For this assault he was going to have to use Powies who didn't know him, or who couldn't trace him. This was not altogether impossible, because his photograph in the back of all Poweressence books was one taken of him in his twenties and then touched up by a comic-book artist, so that a powerful, benign, eternally young presence radiated from the picture. It wouldn't even pass muster now for his passport.

He created for this sacred mission the Servants of Zor, and then from franchises around the country he bought the names of seven Powies who had reached Level Seven. By Level Seven everyone had paid in at least eight thousand dollars. Anyone who had paid that much for Poweressence courses could be counted on for almost anything.

But Rubin Dolomo did not ask for just anything. From his hiding place in a darkened room lit only with candles, from behind a screen emblazoned with the sign of the eternal warmth of this galaxy, the sun, he addressed his band of housewives, executives, aspiring actresses, and a real-estate salesman from Poughkeepsie.

"You are a select group. You are the ones who have been given much—therefore, you must give much in return. You will save this country from religious persecution, from religious intolerance. You will guide the leadership of this land into the ways of righteousness. And future generations will call you blessed."

Thus spake Rubin from behind the magnificent partition

that was his shield in case his plan did not work, which seemed unlikely anyhow.

The real-estate salesman from Poughkeepsie felt a chill go up his spine. The housewife gasped—suddenly she was important in the world, important beyond her wildest expectations. The aspiring actress had a vision—a religious experience in which her name was up in lights, just like Kathy Bowen's. Kathy Bowen was a Powie. If she had gotten where she was by doing this stuff, so would she. And then she would do anything she pleased, from Shakespearean drama to Johnny Carson.

So when the man the actress could not see began talking about enlightening the President of the United States, about touching him with goodness, she had few questions. Fewer still when the speaker assured her that if there was any trouble, any fear, anyone questioning her, all she had to do was break a small glass vial and she would be invulnerable to the evil forces of the world.

But there was a warning.

"You must only break this glass vial when you are in trouble. Otherwise trouble will come to you," said Rubin from behind the screen.

"Isn't this wonderful?" said the housewife. "It's just like *Defenders of Alarkin*."

"Is that a book or what?"

"It's a book."

"Sounds like junk," said the actress.

"Whoever said that will be the first to save America," said Rubin Dolomo.

For the Secret Service, entrusted with protecting the President of the United States, the nightmare began somewhat harmlessly in the main mailroom of the White House. It was nothing great, but anything out of the ordinary had to be investigated. Several clerks now had failed to show up for work.

"As you know," said the supervisor, "we have five routings for mail. All of it is opened here after being checked for cookies, bombs, anything like that. Personal gifts go to the Courtesy Center, where thank-you notes are composed. If the gifts are worth more than a certain amount, our Courtesy Hostesses send them to the Smithsonian for display. Letters criticizing the President or the First Lady are routed to the Beige Room, where benign responses are written. Threats are sent to you for investigation. Letters that have to be answered by the President's staff of secretaries are sent to another department, and personal letters, ones that seem as though they actually come from people who know him, are handled by another. It was in this last category that we had the problem.''

"You mean the clerks who open the President's personal correspondence?''

"Oh, no. Machines open his letters. It was the clerks who handled them. They'd be working a regular shift and then they would just stare out into space. Just stare—gape, gawk, like they were in a void.''

"So you had no way to differentiate them from any other worker,'' said the Secret Service man. "Just a joke.''

"We earn our money here,'' said the supervisor, looking wounded.

"Sorry. Go on.''

"Well, they would entertain themselves for a while—play with stamps, trade lunches, that sort of thing, but then they would wander off. And when we phoned them at home, a few of them were gone.''

"What do you mean, gone?''

"They never returned home that day. Or any day thereafter.''

"Give me the names of those who didn't wander off,'' said the Secret Service man.

There were two of them. Both of them seemed unaccountably listless. And they were incapable of answering any questions about their jobs or why they left—in fact, they hardly remembered ever working there at all.

Then came the real problems. The President would be making a Midwestern road trip to speak to farmers. As usual, the Secret Service had to sanitize the route, making sure that no bombs were set in roads. All hiding places and potential sniper sites had Secret Service men stationed at them, and all the roads that could be used as avenues of escape along the motorcade route were barricaded.

Halls where the President would speak had to be examined with metal detectors. The local hospitals had to stock his blood type, more than enough for any major operation.

Airplane traffic had to be rerouted because no airplane could overfly the presidential caravan. And then, as though he was going out for a pleasant ride to meet the people of Wisconsin, the President rode through the suburbs of Racine, waving to everyone as though he didn't have a care in the world. And he didn't. The Secret Service did.

It was the usual crowd at the fairground. Ninety-nine percent of the people were there to cheer their President this sunny autumn day. Then there were the hostile sign holders, those who lived for the opportunity to tell the Commander-in-Chief to get out of South America, the Middle East, the Far East, Africa, Europe, and Racine. The television cameras zoomed in on the one percent as the President began to speak.

What looked, to the untrained eye, like randomly placed Secret Service men was in actuality three zones of protection strategically placed in the crowd. The second formed a barrier between the crowd and the President. The third zone was what was called the "body" grid. This group was never more than an arm's length from their charge. These were the men who would crowd around the President at any sign of trouble.

On this day in Racine, a very sweet-looking housewife who was extremely polite got through the second grid. She simply excused herself and squeezed past the agents; and because the metal detectors at the perimeter of the second grid picked up nothing on her body, no one would suspect that the demure lady wanted anything more than a better view. Until she actually reached the podium.

"You cannot shut out the light of the universe. Your negativity will fail," she shrieked. The cameras moved from the President, who was explaining how the nation was going to feed itself with an alteration in farm policy, to the woman's flailing arms. The body grid pulled closer to the podium. Within seconds the Secret Service wrestled her into an empty room for questioning.

"You can never harm me," she said, relaxed and smiling sweetly at everyone. But when she began urinating a doctor was called to put her into an ambulance. The woman's identification said she was a housewife, but she could not remember her married name. Nor could she recall where she lived, or how she had gotten to Racine. She didn't care about religious freedom; she only cared about one issue:

When was she going to get ice cream?

Even stranger, the agent who stopped her was found later that night wandering around Racine, thrilled that he had fifty dollars in his pocket. With that money, he was telling everyone, he could see twenty-five movies in a row if he didn't buy candy.

At every stop in the Midwest that week, similar incidents occurred. Once, one of the loonies almost reached the President.

Finally the Secret Service had to tell him, quite sadly, that they could not protect him anymore if he left the White House. Something was coming at him, and they had no idea yet what it was.

The President listened stoically, and then, when they were gone, went himself to his bedroom, where the previous President had pointed out the red phone, the special phone to reach the special people. He had used it often in his presidency and now he would use it again. All he had to do was pick up the receiver and two of the most powerful bodyguards in the world would be put at his disposal.

"Smith here, sir," came the voice.

"Smith, I have a problem that I am not sure would come under your jurisdiction. Somebody, or something, is attacking me. And my Secret Service says sooner or later they're going to succeed."

7

The Poweressence temple in Miami Beach was an elegant Spanish villa with spacious verandas. But Remo and Chiun met their first Powies several blocks away. They were trying to encourage them to take a character test. Much to Chiun's disgust, Remo accepted for both of them.

Outside the villa on its magnificent black metal gates a crude sign was posted:

"Free Character Test."

"This I cannot even imagine why you are doing," said Chiun.

"Some people are attacking the President. They are doing it with a strange phenomenon. And somehow the attackers forget what they've done, how they've done it, and even who they are. But there are too many Poweressence people involved not to investigate them."

"I'm sorry I asked," said Chiun. He wore a plain gray traveling kimono because he had been thinking about moving from Miami Beach. He was considering finding a more permanent home in America, which saddened him. If they bought a more permanent home here, that meant they would live here longer, and the longer they worked for Smith, the less chance of ever adding to the glory of Sinanju. Mad Emperor Smith not only insisted that everything be secret but also apparently was never going to seize this country's throne. The horror of it was that these whites were actually telling the truth when they talked about the people selecting a leader, instead of inheriting a traditional and more stable monarch by birth or even the more reasonable hand of the professional assassin, the traditional assassin, the house of assassins that had given the world more leaders than any royal line. This house of assassins that Remo refused to honor by doing something that would enhance its histories. Instead, he continued to serve a country which never taught him anything and an emperor so mad he openly admitted now he did not believe in vengeance.

"I guess this is it," said Remo.

"What is it? We are going to be priests now? What are we doing here?"

"I just explained to you," said Remo. "If you don't like it, go back to the condo. I don't need you. You know I don't need you."

"You do need me. But not for these silly things Emperor Smith sends you to do. Will you do his shopping next?"

"We may be saving the life of the President of the United States," said Remo.

"Why? We don't work for him. We work for Smith. We should be removing the President of the United States. We should be making Smith president."

"He wouldn't be president if we killed the President. The Vice-President would become president."

"Then him too. I remember the histories of the Lesser Wang. A shaman, a priest and distant relative to the king, called upon Sinanju with a great problem. Between him and the throne were fourteen heirs, from princes to princesses to royal lords. The Lesser Wang promised that within one year the shaman would be king. And he was. A vice-president has no more eternal life than a president."

"But after that comes the Secretary of State, I believe."

"When does Smith become emperor?"

"He never becomes emperor. Don't you understand?"

"If he never becomes emperor, what is he doing with the finest assassins in the history of the world? Why is he wasting Sinanju?"

"We're not wasting Sinanju. We're helping to save a country I love. Don't you understand? You don't want to understand."

"No. I do not wish to understand that you love thousands of square miles of waste and pollution and two hundred and twenty million people you have never met. Not when you give nothing to the one who gives you your powers. That's all right. I am used to this, Remo. I am used to your ingratitude. At least I should be by this time."

"It doesn't mean I don't love you."

"If you loved me, really loved me, we would be working for an emperor. You would not waste your talents and skills on this . . . this whatever-we're-doing."

"We're doing it," said Remo, and they were at the gate, where a young man in glasses and a white shirt handed them a piece of paper offering a free character test.

"That's what we're here for. We want to join."

"You're supposed to get the free character test and then you join."

"We want to join," said Remo.

"Could you take the test first?"

"We have characters. Why do we need character tests?" asked Chiun.

"I don't know," said Remo. "He wants us to take a test. We'll take a test."

"I don't want to take a test," said Chiun.

"Then don't."

"Are you going to take the test?"

"Yes."

"Then I'll take the test," said Chiun. "We will see whose character is superior or . . ."

"Or what?" said Remo.

"We will see if it is a bad test."

"You can't stand to lose, little father," said Remo.

"When I can lose, we're dead."

The test was given in a large room divided by small movable walls. Chiun tore down the wall between Remo and himself so he could see Remo's answers.

"You can't do that!" said a young woman with a loose-leaf folder.

"I just did," said Chiun. "I could do that all day."

"They mean you shouldn't, little father."

"Then they should express themselves more clearly."

The young woman looked to the other men in the room. They confirmed that these two were indeed hers.

"Hello," she said. "My name is Daphne Bloom. I am a counselor here at Poweressence. We are not trying to sell you anything, but rather to see if you might need what we have to offer."

Daphne was attractive, with a pert smile and a bouncy body to match. But every time the smile disappeared, she appeared desperately intense. The smile was only an external interruption.

"We don't normally test two people at once, but since you have removed the screen, I guess that's the way we'll do it. Who will go first?"

"Me," said Remo.

"I will go first," said Chiun.

"Go ahead," said Remo.

"No, you go. I want to hear your answers, so that I can show the correct answers."

"This is a character test, little father. No one wins."

"Someone wins in every test."

"You both can win," said Daphne, "if you find out what you need in life."

Remo glanced around the room. There were no curtains, no pictures, just the little cubicles placed in the center of what probably had been a vast dance floor. It seemed like a desecration, turning elegance into office space.

The room smelled of old cigarette smoke and floor cleaner. The chairs were hard metal folding devices, the table of the cubicle some synthetic composite designed by an accountant somewhere who thought low cost was the object.

"The first question is: Are you happy mostly, somewhat, or not at all?" asked Daphne.

"I can be happy knowing Remo is doing the right thing," said Chiun.

"Which means?"

"I am never happy," said Chiun.

"You're always happy, little father. You're happy when you're bitching."

"Put down 'never happy, ever,' " said Chiun. "Would you be happy, beautiful young lady, if you had a son who talked to you like that?"

"I don't think I would," said Daphne. "He's your son? You don't look white."

"I am Korean."

"Oh, he's Korean?"

"See?" said Chiun.

"Get on with the questioning. I'm white," said Remo.

"Even this beautiful intelligent young woman knows," said Chiun. "Thank you, miss."

"All right, Remo, are you happy mostly, sometimes, rarely?"

"All the time," snapped Remo.

"You don't look happy."

"I'm happy. Get on with it."

"I am the one who is unhappy," said Chiun.

"You look happy," said Daphne.

"One must bestow joy on his surroundings. Through joy, we have joy," said Chiun.

"That's beautiful," said Daphne.

"Wait until he tells you about heads on the wall," said Remo.

"Are you some Oriental religion? I love Oriental religions."

"I am Sinanju," said Chiun.

"That's beautiful," said Daphne. "I love the sound."

"Then you'd better like dead bodies," said Remo.

"How can you be so negative?" said Daphne. "I'm putting you down for negative."

"It's the truth," said Remo. "Okay, when do we join? I got the money right here."

Daphne put down the loose-leaf book. Her eyes narrowed and her back straightened. Her voice rang with conviction.

"Some people may be in this for money, but they're

losing the true strength of Poweressence. I have been in est, Sedona, Scientology, Intensive Reunification, but only now have I found the one thing that has turned my life around.''

"From what?'' asked Remo.

"Leave this good and beautiful girl alone,'' said Chiun. "She is trying to help.''

"Thank you, sir,'' said Daphne.

"Am I winning?'' asked Chiun.

"With me you are, sir.''

"She is not only beautiful, she is wise.''

"Okay, is the test over? We'd like to join.''

"There are more questions,'' said Daphne. "Are you ever bothered by something you can't seem to forget, something that just won't go away, some pain that recurs and you don't know why?''

"No. Can I join now?'' said Remo.

"And you, sir?'' Daphne asked Chiun.

Chiun nodded to Remo. "You are looking at that pain.''

"In love relationships, do things seem to go well for a while and then suddenly the person seems to be someone you don't like or who does hurtful things?''

"Ah,'' said Chiun. "Wisdom and beauty are one in you, my child.''

"No,'' said Remo. "Can I join now?''

"Do good opportunities seem to vanish from you when others enjoy them?''

"We can serve anyone in the world but are being held down in this madhouse going nowhere,'' said Chiun.

"And you, Remo, I imagine, 'No'?''

"Right. Can we join?''

"In a minute,'' snapped Daphne.

"Do you feel sometimes that the world is not a nice place to live? You, Remo, never, right? And you, Mr. Chiun?''

"To meet someone as wise as you enlightens and brightens the entire world for everyone,'' said Chiun.

Daphne trembled. Her eyes watered. "That's beautiful," she said. "We don't usually have winners and losers, Mr. Chiun, but you win. And you . . . you lose, Remo."

Chiun beamed. Remo shrugged and asked if they could join now.

"You are eligible for entrance level, the adjustment to your world and how to be happier, richer, more content and powerful in ten steps. Do you want that?"

"Not really," said Remo. "I want to join."

"Three hundred dollars for each of you."

Remo had it in cash. He had brought a large bankroll at Smith's suggestion. He peeled off six one-hundred-dollar bills and then asked to take the next course.

"You haven't taken the first one yet."

"That's all right," said Remo.

"I won't take the money," said Daphne.

"Is there a manager?"

"He won't take it either. You have got to take the course. You have got to expand your astral relationships. You have got to get your past lives in order so that you can move on through this one unencumbered by ancient sins."

"You speak great wisdom, child," Chiun said in English, and then in Korean said, "Only whites would believe something this stupid."

"A lot of Orientals believe stuff like that," Remo answered in Korean.

"Not quite that stupid. That stupid is white," said Chiun, and then switched back to English to tell Daphne Bloom how excited he was about taking the first level.

Remo asked if they could take the first level in ten minutes because he wanted to get on to the second level before lunch. Twelve thousand dollars later, they were at Level Seven, with Daphne Bloom suddenly discovering that she was elevated to spiritual director because of her success with these two clients.

"But I haven't coordinated all my past lives," she told the manager.

"That's okay, honey. You're a real winner. We got live ones now. Push it over the top. You can have free courses for life and a commission."

"I don't want commissions. I want my self-unity to unleash my power," said Daphne.

"Better yet. You got it. You got all the past lives you can handle, honey," said the manager of the Poweressence Miami Beach temple. "Could I interest you in some real estate too?"

Near the end of the day, Remo allowed as how he wanted to take more and more courses, hundreds of thousands of dollars' worth of courses, but he and his friend had a problem.

"We might have to go to jail. You see, there is this troublesome little court case against me and my friend and we'll have to stop now. Can't study this stuff in prison."

"We'll mail it," said the manager.

"No. I just really have to be out of prison to enjoy this. I hear that once you get this stuff into your system, everything works out well for you."

"Who told you that?" asked the manager.

"A businessman I know," said Remo, "and a rancher. And a mobster. They have a lot of faith in you."

"Big stuff has to move through upstairs. Maybe I can arrange something."

"That would be nice," said Remo.

"But you've got to tell them I sent you. You've got to tell them you belong to the Miami Beach temple of Poweressence."

"You can count on it," said Remo.

"Do you want to join the crusade also?" asked the manager.

"What crusade?"

"The crusade for freedom of religion in America."

"I thought anyone could believe what they wanted."

"Not if you don't please the powers that be. Not if you are fearless in your defense of truth. Not if you are positive."

"Are those the people who hold up signs and run at

the President whenever he makes a speech?'' asked Remo.

"I don't know those people but I do know our famous Kathy Bowen, who is leading the crusade. You can contribute to that.''

"Who's Kathy Bowen?''

"Famous Kathy Bowen?'' asked the manager.

"Yeah. Her,'' said Remo.

"She's the hostess on *Amazing Humanity,*'' said the manager.

"I don't know what that is either.''

"It's people doing fantastic things. Fantastic. They eat frogs, run through fire, build homes out of bottle caps, run races after they've suffered horrible operations,'' said the manager.

"I don't watch it. Where can I reach Kathy Bowen?''

"At crusade headquarters in California.''

"What does it take to join?'' asked Remo.

"A commitment to truth, freedom of worship, and the American way, plus five thousand dollars.''

"Why do I feel I could join the crusade for free?''

"You can, but the five thousand is a donation to help fight religious persecution in America.''

"I like religious persecution,'' said Remo.

The manager sat beneath a picture of clear-eyed, forward-looking Rubin Dolomo. On his desk was a stack of mimeographed bulletins called "Truth Grams.'' The manager kept looking at Remo's wrists. He stared at the eyes, not into them. Remo could tell where the man's pupils focused because they always reflected the level they operated from.

"Well, religious persecution is fine. Whatever. Whatever the force of power gives to you. Thank you and good day,'' said the manager.

When the especially wealthy new student and his Oriental friend left with their counselor, Ms. Bloom, a low-budget convert to Poweressence, the manager phoned the Dolomo estate.

"Hey, Rubin, I think I saw him.''

"Who? The negative one?''

"Well, you said there was this guy with thick wrists and dark eyes who was the force of negativity. I thought it was just hype, you know. Like course number fourteen, when you ran out of astral planes to clear in course thirteen and you had to come up with a 'Reversion Protection' course. I thought that was brilliant."

"It wasn't hype. People do revert to unhappiness."

"Sure, sure, Rubin, but I think I actually seen this guy."

"He's there?"

"Just left."

"Where's he heading?"

"Straight for you and our star performer, Ms. Kathy Bowen."

"Why did you do that?"

"He's been taking courses like there's no end to money. And he says he's got a problem with a jail thing. I thought you could help, you know. You told us to solicit those."

"But he's the negative counterforce of our positive power."

"Hey, Rubin. I'm a franchiser. I sell this stuff. Don't try to give it to me."

"It's true. How do you think we got so big, so fast? I uncovered the truth in the Alarkin planet chronicles."

"You got so big so fast because Beatrice knows how to make a buck. Look, Rubin, if you have problems with these people, why don't you take care of them in some sane way. And I don't mean some Powie nut with an alligator stuffing it in some pool somewhere."

"What do you mean?"

"There are professionals who do things right."

"You mean a professional hit man?"

"You can buy the best right here in Miami. This is the home of the cocaine trade. The best killers in the world are in Miami today. The best, Rubin."

"We don't have any contacts in Miami except you."

"What is your safety worth to you and Beatrice?"

"Thousands."

"You can do better than that, Rubin. You clear fifteen thousand a week from my franchise alone."

"Tens of thousands."

"Come on, Rubin."

"A million dollars. I can't go any higher, Beatrice will kill me."

"No problem. Now, no more of this Alarkin planet good-force stuff. We buy the best. The absolute best."

"They don't cost a million."

"I do. If you want me to get them. I'm here, Rubin. I know everyone."

"And you'll get the best."

"The forces of negativity will have more bullets in him than a firing-range target before he leaves Miami."

"I'll mail you the million."

"No. Wire it. I always like it in my hands before I do real business. We don't pay these people in reducing astral negativity, Rubin."

The hit was not complicated, the manager knew. The target would be coming to the airport, and once you knew where someone was coming, you really had a lock on the whole business. That is why of the million dollars, he only had to pay twenty-five thousand dollars to four pistoleros who promised they would empty two magazines apiece into the man and his elderly Oriental friend.

"They'll be going to California. And they'll be with this woman," said the manager, who happened to have Daphne Bloom's picture on a counselor-evaluation application. It showed her main ambition was to be one with the positive forces of the universe.

"What do you want done with her?"

The manager, seeing that she only earned credits by teaching and was not a major donor, said that whatever was convenient for the pistoleros was fine with him.

"But you got to get the guy with the thick wrists."

By the time Remo and Chiun reached the airport, Daphne had told them her life story. She was an especially sensitive person. By age seven she realized that five thousand years of Judaism was not the answer for her. By age fourteen she had joined three cults, all proving to lack the answer to her problems. So did Scientology, est,

Sedona, Personality Reunification, and the Hare Krishnas.

"In Poweressence I found the answer to the question."

"What's the question?" asked Remo. He looked for the shortest line at a major airline. This airport seemed to be a collection of forty airports, none of them really doing business with the other. It was strange. Chiun was being bothered by a woman who wanted to know where he bought that absolutely lovely kimono.

"It was made for me," said Chiun.

"By whom?"

"The mother of Genghis Khan."

"He must be beautifully clothed."

"He's dead. And so is his mother. Many centuries now. But the Mongol women were for a while great weavers of animal hair."

Daphne pinched Remo's arm. She pulled back her hand, startled. She could have sworn the arm pinched back.

"You weren't listening when I told you Poweressence solved the basic question of my life. The basic question of my life is who am I and where do I fit in the world scheme of things."

"I don't know of anyone who cares about that," said Remo. The two men in white suits were so obvious that they should have carried signs. While other people walked or strolled, these two were stalking. Their footsteps were stiffer, their backbones more rigid, and their hands never far from the bulges in their pockets. The question was, who were these two looking for? Remo knew Chiun saw them too, but Chiun was busy discussing fabric with a woman who loved his kimono.

The two were looking for something, as though they weren't ready to find it yet. Then unmistakably they made contact with someone across the airport corridor. It wasn't a nod. It was more silent than that. It was a purposeful way of not noticing someone, a smoother move of the head while they scanned. This could not be hidden.

Across the airport were two more men who just as obviously were stalking someone. One of them was looking at Daphne Bloom.

"Do you have any enemies?" asked Remo.

"No. People who truly establish their inner peace don't make enemies."

"Well, there are four men who want to kill someone and they're looking at you."

"They couldn't want to kill me," said Daphne. "I offer no negative threat to anyone. You see, that was my problem before. I would send out all the negativity of my past planetary lives and create enemies. But now I don't."

Daphne was still smiling when the first bullet rang out and Remo pushed her under the counter. Screams filled the airport. People looked for cover, and the four men advanced toward the ticket counter.

As in all crisis situations, almost everyone concentrated solely on saving his own life, and therefore any observation was secondary. So when the police put it together, they got something they had to attribute to hysteria.

There were several men firing pistols. Everyone agreed on that. Then one man or twenty men—no one could agree —began moving at the four men. Some said he moved quickly, so fast they couldn't see him. Others said his movements were strangely slow, as though he actually slowed down the whole world he was in. The gunmen seemed suddenly to become unable to fire accurately, shooting at the ceiling and the floor.

But some witnesses said that was where the quick- (or slow-) moving man was.

In any case, four narcotics enforcers were blotted up from the normally well-polished floor of the airport after the fracas. One man, who was traveling to Los Angeles with his elderly Oriental father, was the only one who said he saw absolutely nothing, and that he hid all the time. Which was just another contradiction in this strangest of all cases for the Dade County sheriff's office. Because he was the one a few people thought was doing the attacking of the gunmen.

"You were sloppy," said Chiun. "You have not been so sloppy for years, and you say you are good enough."

"They're dead. I'm not," said Remo.

"And I suppose that's good enough for you," said Chiun.

"The other way around is no bargain."

"Just to succeed at something is not enough. You must succeed correctly," said Daphne.

Chiun smiled. "She is correct. Listen. Even she knows what I am talking about."

"That's Poweressence," said Daphne.

"That is the truth," said Chiun.

"I'm going up front," said Remo.

"You don't have tickets for up front," said Daphne.

"I'll reason with someone," said Remo.

In a few moments a harried accountant begged to take the seat in the rear of the plane instead of his first-class assignment. He had traded with a gentleman with an absolutely foul personality.

"He's met Remo," said Daphne.

"I have had to live with him many years now," said Chiun.

"You poor wonderful man."

"I do not complain," said Chiun.

"You're so decent and sweet."

"I only do what is right," said Chiun. "I have trained him through the years to do what is right, but he does not listen. He takes this wonderful training and gives it away to madmen."

"That's awful," said Daphne.

"I do not complain," said Chiun. "We have a fine family tradition, but he ignores it."

"That's awful," said Daphne.

"I do not complain," said Chiun.

"You are the most wonderful decent splendid human being I have ever met," said Daphne.

"And you are the most perfect person ever to give a character test," said Chiun. "You are so good at judging them."

At the Dolomo estate, Rubin heard the good news and the bad news. The good news was that the Miami franchise was sending back the million dollars. The bad news was that the money would be returned because it hadn't been earned.

"They killed four of the best hit men in the city, Rubin, and they are coming right for you."

Rubin Dolomo barely had enough energy to get to the Motrin bottle. He emptied it into his mouth and rested against a stack of Level Nine books called *Inner Peace Through Peace Power*.

Then he went to Beatrice's room and waited outside until the grunts and groans were over. Beatrice was testing out a new bodyguard. Rubin did not like the fact that she cheated on him. But it did have its rewards. When Beatrice had a new attractive man to service her, she did not bother Rubin.

Beatrice was as seductive as a freight train and just as unreasoning. Her foreplay consisted of two English sentences.

"Okay. Now."

When the young man came out of her room, Rubin grabbed him and asked:

"Is she done? Did you satisfy her?"

"You're her husband. How can you ask that?"

"If you aren't enough, she'll want me."

"She's done," said the new bodyguard.

Ever so discreetly Rubin opened the door and entered his wife's boudoir. Apparently the sex had done something for her, because now she had an absolutely foolproof plan to kill the President of the United States and "get them off our backs forever."

8

She was eighteen. She didn't know if that were old enough for someone so distinguished.

"Hell, honey, that's old enough. You're not too young. I'm just too married."

She laughed. She thought that was the smartest thing she had ever heard anyone say. She never knew anyone who could think of answers like that. Just right out of their head like that.

The Air Force colonel would have dismissed these remarks as absurd flattery except that they came from a strawberry blond. And she had just the sort of body he dreamed about. She came up to his shoulder and had breasts like cantaloupes. Colonel Dale Armbruster remembered using that word in describing just those kinds of breasts. It was in a character test he had taken at some kook place. He forgot the place. But Armbruster did remember it was free. And one of the questions was what his ideal sexual fantasy would be. He had described the woman. Very young, a fawning personality . . . And her looks. Strawberry hair, short, just up to his shoulder, and breasts like cantaloupes.

"And what negative forces keep you from enjoying this?" the young questioner had asked.

"My wife and her attorney, who could draw blood from bone."

"So you are afraid of your wife? Would you like to live free from that sort of fear?"

"Sure. Wouldn't you?"

"I do," the questioner had told him.

"Yeah, but you're eighteen, and I am fifty-three."

"Do you feel that age hinders you?"

"No. There are just some limitations, that's all."

"In your job?"

"No. I like my job."

"What positive forces are at work that make you like your job?"

"I really can't go into it."

"Does your job bother you?"

"No. I just can't go into it."

"Do you feel some negative blocks stopping you from going into your job? You see, in Poweressence we know that what a person does is what a person is, not what he eats, but what he does. Do you know what I mean by that?"

"It's part of my job not to talk about what I do. No block on my part."

"Let's get back to your romantic blocks. Tell us exactly what you dream, because anything you dream you can have. All you have to do is think it. This world is not made for you to fail in. This world, the universe, is made for you to enjoy your full power."

The colonel went on for twenty minutes describing an affair he would like to have, and was surprised at how understanding his interviewer was. He got to like his interviewer. He even wanted to join because these people promised so much that if they delivered on only part of it, he would be getting more than his money's worth.

"Look, I'm sorry," he said at the end. "I can't join you or anything like you without endangering my job. I've got to be cleared for everything. I shouldn't even tell you what I do, but you give off such a nice positive feeling that I feel I have to give you some reason."

"All reasons can be overcome. Reasons are just other words for fear, as the greatest mind in the Western world, Rubin Dolomo, has said. Have you ever read any of Dolomo's books?"

"I don't read. I fly planes."

"Then why can't you join, and free yourself from letdowns, unhappiness, and doubt. Let us take all the worry out of your life."

"Because of the plane I fly."

"What can be so important about a plane that it can deny you the full use of your own life?"

"It's not the plane that's different. It's what's in it."

"If you carry atomic weapons, you are carrying the greatest negative force for mankind. Did you know that? Did you know that Rubin Dolomo says it is a prime example of power being destroyed by its negative implementation? Did you know that he was the first to understand atomic energy and what it meant to mankind?"

"It's not an atomic bomb. It's more important," Colonel Armbruster had said. And then he had leaned over and whispered:

"I fly *Air Force One.*"

"The President!"

"Shhh," said Colonel Armbruster.

"I won't tell a soul. I will forget it now. I believe in nothing but goodness."

What the interviewer did not tell Colonel Armbruster was that the essence of goodness was Poweressence, therefore anything he did to enhance Poweressence enhanced goodness. That rendered a promise made to someone who was not part of Poweressence, and therefore no part of goodness, completely invalid. She also didn't mention that the Washington temple of Poweressence collected all such information from the tests.

What the interviewer herself did not know was that these bits of information, if valuable enough, were sold by the local temple to California headquarters, where Beatrice had them filed for future reference.

And what Colonel Armbruster did not know was that two years later it all was going to be used on him, that this perfect little dream who was playing up to him at his favorite lounge in Washington, D.C., had been taken from his favorite fantasy. Cantaloupe-sized breasts and straw-berry-blond hair and adoration. All of it.

"I do have to get home to my wife," said Armbruster. The lounge was dark. The drink was good, the music was mellow, and Dale Armbruster smelled her perfume.

"Is that lilac?" he asked.

"For you," she said.

"What's your name?" he asked.

"I never give my name with my clothes on," she said.

Dale Armbruster looked to the doorway. If he ran out now, ran right out of the lounge, he could make it home safely and stay faithful to his wife and her vengeful lawyer. Of course, if he ran now, he would never forgive himself. He would always remember what he passed by.

"I'd like to hear your name," he said with a choking voice.

"I'd like to give it," she said.

"You really think I'm distinguished and not old?"

She nodded.

"And I want to hear your name more than anything else in the world. More than I want to wake up tomorrow."

Dale Armbruster heard her name in a small motel room he rented for the night. He saw the perfection of an eighteen-year-old body with breasts like fruit and smooth-skinned thighs, and that incredibly willing smile framed by the strawberry-blond hair he had always dreamed of.

She said her name was Joan.

"What a great set of names," he said, staring directly between her shoulders.

Like all dreams, the reality was not quite as grand. But even seventh place was better than anything Colonel Arm-bruster had ever enjoyed in his life. Within a half-hour he knew that he never wanted Joan out of his life, knew that he would do almost anything to keep her near him.

But miraculously, she didn't want anything extra-ordinary.

"I've always dreamed of a man like you. I've dreamed of a man like you treating me special, Dale."

"You are special, Joan," he said.

"I'd like to think so," she said. "I'd like to think you think of me at special times. Not just here in bed. Not just for my body."

"Not just your body," he lied. "You."

"No, really?" she said.

"Really," Colonel Armbruster said, feeling like a famine victim let loose in the fruit stalls of a gourmet store.

"Then would you read a love note I wrote at a very special time?"

"Certainly," he said. "Absolutely."

The girl called Joan left the bed momentarily with Armbruster reaching out after her.

"I'll be back, silly," she said. She reached under her skirt, which lay in a pile on the motel-room chair, and took out a pink letter, holding it by one end. She also had a Ziploc plastic bag.

"What's that? What's the bag for?"

"Well, Dale, I want you to read it where you work. And it's scented with perfume, perfume I rubbed all over my body, Dale, perfume that was on me in very tender places. That letter was in those places too, Dale."

"If we just met tonight, where did you get time to write a letter?"

"It wasn't to you by name. It was to the man who fulfilled my dreams. It tells that in the letter."

"Your dream too?" said Armbruster. He couldn't believe it. "You're my dream."

"You see. I knew that," said the girl called Joan. "I knew I would be someone's dream. It's all in the letter. But you've got to read it where you work."

"Why where I work? Where I work isn't that romantic."

"That's just it. I want to be more than just a single night in a motel room. I want to see you again. I want us to have something. I want you to think about me, think about me not just here but other times."

"Sure I will," said Colonel Armbruster, reaching out for the luscious young woman.

But she backed away.

"I don't know if I can believe you. You'll see in the letter what I want. I don't want to take away your marriage. I don't want your money. I want you. I've had a dream, and if you are not part of that dream, I don't want you. It's that simple."

Colonel Armbruster watched her cover up that luscious body with clothes; watched the cantaloupe-shaped bosom disappear into a bra, leaving only the outlines of what he still wanted to hold; he watched the skirt go up over the smooth young thighs.

"I will know if you read the letter anywhere else. I will know," she said. "I will know if you even open it anywhere else. And then you'll never see me again."

"How will you know? There's no way you can know," said Armbruster.

"I'll know," she said, leaning forward as though to kiss him, but dropping the plastic bag that contained the envelope onto the bed instead. She retreated quickly, taking her body with her.

"Good-bye," she said.

"You don't even know where I work," he said, laughing.

"I don't have to," she said. "It's not part of my dream."

It was enough logic for Armbruster to think about. If she were part of his dream, then why couldn't he be part of hers?

But how would she know where he opened the letter? He didn't want to bring the letter home because his wife might find it. And he certainly didn't want to read a perfumy letter in the cockpit of *Air Force One.* The President's pilot had to be above reproach.

Ambruster tried to think of the one place his wife would not spot the incriminating little plastic bag. At home there was none. Instead he chose his special locker at Andrews Air Force Base, home of *Air Force One,* the President's plane. Armbruster, the President's favorite pilot, was not scheduled to fly for a week, but he moved himself up in the rotation just to get a chance at being alone in the cockpit with the letter. He still didn't know how Joan would know where he read the letter, but everything had been so gloriously perfect with his dream that he decided not to take even that small chance.

The mission of the day was Cheyenne, Wyoming. The letter was safely sealed in the plastic bag inside his jacket.

Flying the plane that was called *Air Force One* when the President was aboard was easier than any other flight duty a pilot could have, even easier than commercial air. In commercial air, pilots always had to look out for other aircraft. But for this special jet, there was no real alertness required in that respect. An air corridor was cleared for miles around. And if any planes even got close to that corridor, Air Force jets would intercept and turn them away.

Once they were outside the Washington air space, the copilot and engineer took off their jackets and enjoyed a cup of coffee.

"Dale, can I take your jacket?" asked the flight engineer.

"No, I think I'll wear it," said Armbruster. He wondered if it mattered to the luscious Joan whether he read it anywhere at work or whether it had to be read from behind the controls. He could go into the lavatory and read it there. But he felt there was something so mystical about this chance meeting that the lavatory would not do it justice. Besides, he wanted to be able to tell her the next time they met that he was in the cockpit at the controls when he saw her words. He would describe everything to her.

Colonel Armbruster waited until they were over Ohio before he sent the copilot back to the main cabin to speak to another member of the crew, and then gave the engineer a task that would keep him intent at his charts for ten minutes.

He put the controls on automatic pilot and settled back in the seat to read his letter. The bag opened easily but the letter had some oily substance on it. He wondered how heavy the perfume on that wonderful body had been. He opened the envelope and then saw a blank page. He didn't know why it was blank. He didn't quite know why it was in his hand. He put it down.

The sky was incredibly blue up here. Not a cloud, like the purest blue glass. There were lots of dials in front of him. Pretty dials. He turned around. No one was looking at him. He saw a red switch. He wondered what it would do. Would it make the plane bounce and hop? Would it do fun things? Could he change the color of the sky? Would anyone spank him?

These questions passed through what was left of the mind of Colonel Dale Armbruster as he flicked the red switch. Then he pushed the wheel in front of him. The plane went down. He pulled back the wheel. The plane went up. He turned the wheel. The plane pitched and banked.

Whee, thought Colonel Armbruster.

"Turbulence, Dale?" asked the engineer.

"No," said Dale. He wondered how long he could do this before someone took him away and told him not to play with the plane anymore. He pushed the wheel forward, and the plane went down toward the clouds.

He went through the clouds. Everyone went through the clouds. And no one was stopping him. There was a lever to his right. He pushed it forward. The plane went faster. Whee.

"Dale, what the hell's goin' on there?" asked the flight engineer.

"Nothing," said Colonel Armbruster. "Leave me alone."

"I'm not bothering you. What's going on?"

"Nothing's going on. I'm not doing anything wrong."

"Nobody said you were. We're in a power dive. Why are we in a power dive?"

"It's nice."

"Dale? What the hell's going on?"

"My plane," said Colonel Armbruster.

At a thousand feet the copilot came sliding back into the

cabin, trying to get to the control. The last thing he heard
before the shattering crash was the captain fighting him
away, with a childlike scream. "Mine!"

The jet called *Air Force One* plowed into an Ohio
parking lot at five hundred miles an hour. There wasn't ten
feet of anything left connected. What had once been
human life had to be collected in little plastic bags no
bigger than the one that was now burned up along with the
letter in the explosion.

Remo, Chiun, and Daphne Bloom arrived in Los
Angeles an hour before the crash. Daphne was enthralled.

"We're here. In the home of the founder of Poweressence. Don't you feel the positiveness of it? The force of
the great 'yes' transcending all?"

"No," said Remo.

"You are most wise, child," said Chiun in English, and
then in Korean:

"Even in India there aren't people that stupid. And
India has got more gods than rice."

"This is California, little father. They have more gods
than rice also," said Remo in Korean.

"I love the beauty of your language. Is that the Sinanju
religion you were talking of?"

"No," said Remo.

"Yes," said Chiun.

"What a beautiful dichotomy," said Daphne.

"Have you ever met Dolomo or Kathy Bowen?" asked
Remo.

"We saw recordings of Himself several times. But Kathy
regularly visits the temples. And she has one in her own
home. She attributes her success to Poweressence unlocking her life forces."

"Is she high up in the organization?"

"She knows the Dolomos personally. She has dinner
with them. She is a personal friend of Rubin Dolomo
himself. Can anyone help but be successful being near
them?"

"Does she help people who are going to be tried? Ever hear anything about that?" asked Remo.

"Oh yes. She was the one who announced on her show *Amazing Humanity* that people who have suffered hopeless cases have suddenly with the help of Power-essence been freed of evil and negative forces. And it was so. The people were freed. They escaped the persecution of the government."

"Not all," said Remo.

"Every one," said Daphne.

"What about the Dolomos themselves?"

"Because they are closer to the forces of goodness, they have to face the greatest forces of evil. The United States government has to persecute them, because the government is evil."

"How did you come to that conclusion?"

"If the government weren't evil, why would they persecute the Dolomos?"

"Maybe they don't think that an alligator in a swimming pool is nearly as proper as a letter to the editor."

"Oh, that."

"You think alligators are good?"

"You don't understand. You just believe the partial story from a slanted media. That alligator was attracted by the evil of the columnist. But I suppose you don't have enough understanding to see that."

"I hope I never do," said Remo. "Where does Kathy Bowen live?"

"California, right near here," said Daphne.

"Where else," said Remo.

Daphne Bloom assured Remo and Chiun that she knew Kathy Bowen personally. She had met her three times and had gotten her autographed picture twice. She had never missed a show of *Amazing Humanity*.

Kathy Bowen personally interviewed all the people who wanted to be on the show. Anyone could get on if they could do something no one else could do, said Daphne.

It took a half-hour to get out of the airport traffic of Los

Angeles airport and ten minutes to get to the Poweressence
temple-studio of Kathy Bowen. Her ice-blond looks and
clear blue eyes with delicate features stared out of every
window of the temple-studio.

To the left of the entranceway, like a gospel reading of
the day in front of a church, was a large billboard. It had a
message from Kathy Bowen herself. It read:

"Love, Light, Compassion, and death to the President
of the United States."

Inside was a line of people waiting to be interviewed at a
desk. At the head of the line someone was saying that Ms.
Bowen would see everyone in their turn. Ms. Bowen loved
humanity. Ms. Bowen felt truly in touch with humanity.
But the humanity had to stay in line. And the humanity
should not make noise or eat anything in the temple-studio
itself.

"Her presence is truly positive," said Daphne Bloom,
glowing.

Ahead of Remo and Chiun and Daphne Bloom was a
boy who talked to frogs, a quadriplegic who could spit his
name in ink against a bedpan, and a grandmother who
liked to sit on ice with no clothes on.

Only the grandmother was rejected from *Amazing
Humanity* because no one could figure out a way to
dramatize nudity on ice gracefully. And besides, sitting
lacked the kind of action the producers of *Amazing
Humanity* liked. Everyone selected, of course, would get
to meet Ms. Bowen and sign, in her presence, the release
guaranteeing that the guest would not sue on grounds of
public ridicule or injury.

When Remo, Chiun, and Daphne Bloom reached the
producer's desk, they were asked what they did.

"I don't know what she does," said Remo, nodding to
Daphne, "but we do everything."

"Better than anyone else," said Chiun.

The producer wore a white robe and a dash of pink silk
around her neck. Every bit of the world appeared an insult
to his magnificently perfect sense of taste. His wavy hair
was dyed blue and hung down the back of his neck.

He liked California because he could go unnoticed here.

"We can't show everything. You've got to do something specific," he said.

"Name it," said Remo.

"For a price," said Chiun.

"Can you spit ink into a bedpan?"

"We can spit it through the bedpan. And you too," said Remo.

"That's hostile," gasped Daphne. "You've got to work out your hostile elements. That's hostile."

"I like hostile," said Remo.

"Spitting ink through a bedpan sounds absolutely perfect. How long have you been doing it?"

"Since I wanted to meet Kathy Bowen," said Remo.

"Will this be on television?" asked Chiun.

"National prime-time television, with Kathy Bowen as host and moderator and dynamic force."

"I have a little poem about a flower opening. It is in the Tang form, an ancient Korean dialect. It can be edited for television."

"Poetry doesn't go. Could you recite it underwater?"

"I suppose," said Chiun.

"Could you do it underwater while eating lasagna?" said the producer of *Amazing Humanity*.

"Not lasagna," said Chiun. "It has bad meat and cheese, does it not?"

"Eating anything you like?" asked the producer.

"I suppose," said Chiun.

"While being attacked by sharks?" asked the producer.

"A shark is not an invincible weapon," said Chiun.

"You can beat a shark?"

Chiun looked to Remo, puzzled. "Why not?" he asked.

"Yeah, he can do sharks. I can do sharks. We both do sharks. We could do a whale if we had to. When do we meet Kathy Bowen?"

"They're Level Ten Powies," said Daphne helpfully.

"I like that. I like the whole scene, but do we need the poem?" asked the producer.

"Absolutely," said Chiun. "I will wear my recital

kimono. What you see now is ordinary traveling gray, with speckled bluebird wings. Not suitable for prime-time television."

"Okay, do the poem for ten, may twelve seconds and then we'll bring on the sharks while you're eating your favorite meal underwater."

"I can cut the Tang to its barest lean form," said Chiun.

"Perfect," said the producer.

"Ten hours."

"Nothing runs ten hours," said the producer.

"True Tang poems run to fifty," said Chiun.

"Can't use more than ten seconds," said the producer.

"How do you know? How do you know unless you have heard a Tang poem?"

"I don't want to hear ten hours of anything."

"Then your ears need readjusting," said Chiun.

Helpfully he massaged the producer's ears until enlightenment filled his fair Western face. The producer agreed to ten hours of anything if Chiun would only stop.

He did.

Kathy Bowen was preparing the press conference of her life, as she called it, when one of her producers insisted she meet the odd trio. The old one recited poems while eating underwater and fighting sharks, the young one just fought sharks, and the girl did nothing.

"Maybe we can put her in a costume or feed her to the sharks," said Kathy. She wore an elegant light print dress with sunflowers, signifying her bright positive attitude toward the world.

"Can't feed a performer to the sharks. It will never get past the screening committee. No real blood around," said her lawyer.

"Can the sharks eat her without blood?"

"I've seen it done."

"Wouldn't be a bad attraction. I could look distressed, we could have some attendants desperately try to fish her out, no pun intended, and then cut to a commercial until we come back. No one would leave their sets."

"Death doesn't go on national television."

"I see it on the news all the time."

"You have more leeway with news."

"They get away with everything," said Kathy. "All right. Show them in. But I don't have much time. I absolutely want to be in front of the press as soon as possible. I have a warning for America."

Kathy was given the release forms and the performers were told to enter her presence. Kathy Bowen Enterprises had found out long ago that if she herself handed performers the documents, they would put up less fuss in signing away all their rights.

She would give her famous perfect white-toothed smile and her perfect upbeat handshake and then slip the suckers a pen. It rarely failed.

It failed this day.

The old Oriental wanted ten hours of air time. To her horror, Kathy saw that one producer already had promised it. The younger man, an attractive dark-eyed specimen who did not seem impressed or amused by *Amazing Humanity*, wanted to talk about Poweressence.

"I've got a problem. I am facing a stiff court fight and it looks as though I am going to lose. There is a witness against me who has me all but convicted. I hear Poweressence can help people like that."

"Poweressence helps everything."

"But I want that," said Remo.

"You can get that. But you've got to make it to the thirtieth level."

"I've never heard of the thirtieth level," said Daphne. "That must be ecstasy. Do you remember me? We met at the Miami temple. You gave me an autographed picture. I was at Level Three at the time. I couldn't afford more."

"And how much does it take to make it to the thirtieth level?" Remo asked, undistracted.

"Well, the thirtieth is a major spiritual threshold, so there is a major contribution required."

"So it's a strict cash deal then."

"No. You have got to embark on all the courses. You have got to believe. If you don't believe, it won't do you any good."

"And what happens if I am convicted?"

"You get your money back."

"And who gets this money?"

"You can leave it here or send it to the Dolomos. For me that doesn't matter."

"What I want to know is how you make witnesses forget."

"I don't do anything. The Dolomos don't do anything. The forces of the universe can do everything and will do everything."

Remo handed back the paper. Televison cameras were being brought into the room. Remo stepped out of the way. He did not want to be recorded. Chiun kept himself between Kathy and the cameras as he began the first two-hour ode to the essence of the purity of the flower petal which marked the traditional Tang opening stanzas.

"We have business, little father. Step back," Remo said in Korean. Remo stepped way back. He didn't want to be on national film. Chiun reluctantly joined him, complaining of Remo ruining his chance to make America aware of true art and of the true artist that Chiun was.

"Why is it that when I offer something as beautiful as the Tang, Americans want to see sharks? You are just like Rome at the beginning of your calendar."

"Glad to see you're admitting I'm American and not Korean."

"Shh," said Daphne. "She's going to speak. Isn't this wonderful?"

Kathy called the television reporters to the front and told the print media, newspapermen mostly, to take the rear seats.

"I am glad all of you could come during what must be a busy, busy day for all of you. But you all must know why the President of the United States died. Why he had to die. Not even the President of the United States can defy the forces of the universe. In pressing to convict two innocent bearers of beauty and light, our President criminally has brought death on himself. As a hope for all Americans, I can only express my deepest sympathies for all of us and beg the new president not to follow such a course of folly. Had the President listened to my advice in the White House before I was forcibly removed, he would be alive today.''

"But, Ms. Bowen," said a television reporter in the front row, "the President of the United States isn't dead."

"What about his plane crash?"

All the newsmen looked puzzled.

Kathy Bowen looked at her watch. "What day is this?"

"Wednesday," she was told.

'Damn,'' she said.

Twenty minutes later, when the plane crashed, the Federal Bureau of Investigation arrested Kathy Bowen on the charge of attempted murder, and their case was augmented by the testimony of another Powie who told a tale of seduction and intrigue that she never knew would end in death. All she had to do was hand the man an envelope and tell him not to open it until he was at work. She didn't know he flew the President's plane. All she knew was that she could get to Level Four of Poweressence if she did this one little thing for them.

And she had needed it for her acting career, wanting to become as famous as Kathy Bowen herself.

9

"I didn't say Wednesday," hissed Rubin Dolomo. "I said don't be surprised if the President's plane crashes Wednesday."

"You said Wednesday," said Kathy Bowen. "You told me Wednesday. You said Beatrice said Wednesday." Kathy Bowen looked around. Her voice was hushed. A glass-and-wire screen separated her from Rubin Dolomo. "I heard you say Wednesday."

"Even so, why did you call a press conference for Wednesday?"

Rubin glanced to his right. A guard was sitting supposedly too far away to hear. But Rubin did not trust distances. He did not trust guards of any kind. He shivered at the thought of his being in a place like this.

"Beatrice says we will get you out. We have things under way, big things that are going to turn this whole business around. We're not taking it anymore," said Rubin proudly.

Kathy's face looked like a collapsed balloon. All the energy and verve that had made her smile look like a lit billboard had vanished.

"I can't hold onto my positive course anymore. I'm losing my power. You've got to clear me, you have got to do a clearing of my mind."

"That's what Beatrice sent me for."

"I owe everything to the enlightment. Now I feel I have lost it. I'll lose everything."

"You own your own temple franchise. You should know how to go through the mind clearances yourself."

"This is too much. I look around and all I see are bars on one side of my cell and cement on the other. I have a single open bowl for a toilet and a sink. I wouldn't have a closet this small. You've got to help me."

"All right, what's the feeling you have?"

"I feel I am in jail."

"In what part of your body is that feeling?"

"It's all over me. I feel trapped. I feel I can't move around."

"In what part of your body is it strongest?"

"Everywhere."

"Good. Now how strongly do you feel this?"

"Totally."

"Is there any part of you that doesn't feel it?"

"My ring. My ring doesn't feel it."

"Any part of your body?"

"My ears. Yes. My ears. My ears don't feel trapped."

"Concentrate on your ears. What is the feeling?"

"Freedom. Light. Power."

"You see, you still have your freedom. It is only your negative mind that tells you you are trapped. Move your arms. Are they free?"

Kathy wiggled her arms. She smiled broadly. She nodded.

"Move your head. Is that free?"

Kathy shook her hair and was almost laughing.

"Free," she said.

"Your body," said Rubin.

Kathy jumped up from her seat and shook her body. She was laughing now.

"I've never felt so free. I'm free." She reached toward Rubin and hit the screen.

"Ignore that," ordered Rubin quickly. "Ignore it. It's not your wall. Don't make it your wall. Don't make it your prison. It's their wall."

"Their wall," said Kathy.

"Their prison," said Rubin.

"Their prison," said Kathy.

"They built it. They paid for it. It is their prison."

"Their prison," said Kathy.

"Not yours."

"Not mine."

"You are free. Your ears understand what the rest of your body forgot. Their problems are theirs. You had made their problems your problems. You had bought into their negativity."

"Their negativity," said Kathy.

"You are always free. As long as you can make contact with your ears that remembered your freedom and power, you will always be free. It is they who are in jail."

"Poor people. I know what it feels like. I feel sorry for them."

"Them. Right. As long as you know it is they who are in jail and not you, you will be free."

In her joy, Kathy reached out for Rubin but remembered they were separated by walls that kept the guards and officials prisoners of their own negativity.

She blew him a kiss and as an afterthought added her own observations.

"Do you remember how we learned that there are people who are consumed by negativity and how they bring negative life forces to others? Well, just before my press conference the most negative person I have ever met came as a contestant. Very negative. He was even arguing with the two others. One was one of us, a Powie. Yes, let me transmigrate my mind back to the scene."

Kathy closed her eyes and pressed fingers to her temples.

"Yes, he was with an Oriental. The Oriental was nice. The girl was nice. He was negative. Yes. And I should have known not to have that press conference with him around. I should have delayed it."

"You've found the negative force that put you here."

"Yes," said Kathy. "He exuded negativity. And I ignored it, and paid the price."

"Did he have dark eyes?"

"Yes. Yes. I see them. Handsome. High cheekbones."

"And wrists. What did the wrists look like?"

"Thick. Very thick wrists, almost as though the forearm went right into the hand."

"Oh," said Rubin, reaching into his pants for one of the pill packs. He didn't even look. He took two. He took three. He kept taking them until numbness released the panic in his body.

"He wanted to know about help with a witness. He said he had a court case against him."

"You didn't send him to us, did you?"

"No. The press conference came first. Afterward he came up to us and talked a lot about witnesses and things, but then the FBI came and took me away. They arrested me, Rubin. You didn't tell me the right day." Kathy's voice became tense.

"No. Don't start thinking like that or you'll begin to believe you're trapped in jail, Kathy," said Rubin.

So the evil one was after them, Rubin realized. He had to tell Beatrice. He had to warn her.

But Beatrice did not care about the evil one. Beatrice had discovered a colossal foul-up in the President's plane plot.

"I know a Powie is turning evidence against us," said Rubin. "I'm sorry, Beatrice, I should have taken greater precautions when I set up the colonel. But I'm at my limit for Motrin, Valium, and Percodan. I can't take the pressure anymore."

"Well, you will. Because this foul-up is the end all of foul-ups. This one is unforgivable. I will never forgive. One I can't forgive."

Rubin did not think of his ears as some positive rung on a ladder of happiness. He thought of their needing to be covered by his palms. But Beatrice slapped his hands away.

Rubin dropped to the floor and curled into a ball.

Beatrice fell on him. She grabbed an ear in her teeth.

"Rubin, you pathetic imbecile. Do you know what you did to me?" she said through teeth clenched on Rubin's ear.

"No, dear," said Rubin, very careful not to move his head quickly lest he leave a piece of himself in Beatrice's mouth.

"You missed."

"Missed what?" begged Rubin Dolomo.

"Missed what!" screamed Beatrice, spitting the ear out of her mouth and pushing his head away so she could get up on her feet and deliver a more satisfying kick. "Missed what! Missed what? he asks. Missed him!"

"Who, dear?" begged Rubin, trying to find a stronger part of his body to receive the kicks.

"Who? he asks! Who? he asks! And I married this . . . this failure. You missed our main enemy. You failed in a Beatrice Dolomo threat."

"But we've threatened everyone."

"This one I really wanted," said Beatrice. "This one is behind everything, every one of our problems."

The President's Oval Office was clear of everyone else when Harold W. Smith entered. He had not been listed on the guest sheet; this time was in the official records as a period of rest for the President.

The first thing the President said was:

"I am not giving in to crooks and frauds."

Smith nodded and sat down without waiting to be invited to do so.

"You're here because America is not for sale. I am not for sale. I will not give in. They may get me. There's a good chance of that. But if the President of the United States caves in to this petty blackmail, then the entire country is for sale."

"I couldn't agree more, sir," said Smith. "Apparently they already are pretty familiar with your security system. Though I agree you can't give up, you also can't do business as usual."

The President took off his jacket and dropped it on his chair. He looked out into the protected garden just outside the Oval Office. No one could see in, a precaution quite necessary in the age of the sniper rifle.

He was not a young man but he had a young spirit, and stamina that would shame men forty years his junior. Ordinarily he was smiling. Now he was mad, but not mad that an attempt had been made on his life. That was part of the job.

The President of the United States was mad because American servicemen had been killed, a senator to whom he had lent his plane so that the man could fly home to his seriously ill wife was dead, and the people he was sure were behind the crash were still playing legal games with him.

"This court system we have is precious, and I wouldn't tamper with it for the world. But sometimes . . . sometimes . . ." said the President.

"What makes you sure it was the Dolomos?" asked Smith. "I am aware of the threats made by Kathy Bowen, aware also that she had to know of the plan to destroy you and *Air Force One* because she announced it ahead of time. I am also aware that a young woman, a Powie, was used to set up Colonel Armbruster. But do you have the clinching evidence that it was the Dolomos themselves?"

"We have the black box," said the President, referring to the tape recording of the entire flight. "The man who flew that plane into the ground had the mind of a nine-year-old. His mature memory had been wiped out."

"Like the mailroom people who forget what they were working on."

"Like the Secret Service men."

"And this Powie gave Armbruster a letter in a Ziploc bag."

"Exactly."

"A letter in the mailroom. A letter to the pilot," said Smith.

The President nodded.

"So this substance can be transferred on paper. By touch, I imagine. Weren't some of the people who attacked you stricken also by loss of memory?"

The President nodded again.

"What a wonderful way to cover up a trail. Have your

hired guns forget everything about who ordered them to do the dirty work."

"All of these people had Poweressence backgrounds, we found out through investigations."

"They forgot, of course," said Smith. "But what about the girl who turned state's evidence?"

"The problem with her was she didn't see the person who gave her the orders."

"How can that be?"

"Poweressence may be all hustle but it is part religious cult. And they have ceremonies. Have you ever read Dolomo's books?" asked the President.

"No," said Smith.

"Neither have I. But the Secret Service is beginning to. Almost all of the nonsense is in his books. Part of the cult is hearing voices in darknesses, among other things including being able to cure yourself through finding pieces of your body that don't hurt. I don't know how it works, but you are going to have to look into it."

"We have, somewhat," said Smith. "We are on their trail, but for another reason. We're after them on this witness program. They have been able to turn witnesses, also by getting them to forget. It's clear now they didn't bribe or threaten. They are using this substance, and this substance, whatever it is, is the danger. I think you have got to change the way you work, Mr. President. That's the first order of business."

"I am not going to change a damned thing for those two frauds. I won't give in."

"I am not asking surrender. Just protect yourself while we nail them."

"I don't know," said the President. "I hate to give even a change in schedule to those two murderous hustlers. I represent the American people and, dammit, Smith, the American people deserve something better than to have two of those . . . those whatever they are change the presidency. No."

"Mr. President, not only can I not guarantee your safety if you don't change things, I can virtually guarantee you are going to lose to those two. Just for a little while, sir, just for a little while. I think you should make it a definite rule that you do not touch any paper, because that seems to be the device they transfer the substance on. I would also suggest you do not allow yourself to shake hands or get close to anyone but your wife," said Smith. He held up a hand because the President wanted to interrupt.

"Also, sir, I would suggest that you do not use any office cleaned by regular staff. They could leave something around you might touch. I will personally do the cleaning. And if I lose my memory, have someone else you trust do it. Touch nothing. Your touch can destroy you."

"What about you? What happens if you lose your memory, Smith? Who will run your organization?"

"No one, sir. It was designed that way. It will automatically shut down."

"And those two, those specialists you use?"

"The Oriental will happily leave this country. He has always wanted to work for an emperor and doesn't understand what we are doing or why we are doing it. I think he is embarrassed that he works for us. So he won't talk. As for the American, he won't talk out of loyalty to the country."

"Might they sell out? Might they go to some magazine and for money say what they have been doing in the country's name?"

"You mean, can we stop them?"

"Yes. If we have to."

"The answer is no. We can't. But I know we won't have to. Remo loves this country. I don't know exactly how he thinks anymore, but he loves his country. He's a patriot, sir."

"Like you, Smith."

"Thank you, sir. I remember a man we lost a long time ago once said, 'America is worth a life.' I still think so."

"Good. I've got so much on my mind. I will leave it all to you, Smith. It's your baby. Now, where were we?"

"The connection to the Dolomos."

"What connection?" said the President.

"Don't move. Don't touch a thing," said Smith.

"I just momentarily forgot," said the President.

"Maybe," said Smith. "You're under my care now. I want you to go to the door to your living quarters. Don't touch it. I will open it. On the other side, slip out of all your clothes. Can you walk to your living quarters in your underwear? Will anyone see you?"

"I hope not. I feel sort of foolish doing this."

Smith got up from his seat and followed the President's nod to a door. He opened it. The substance might be on the handles. At every step Smith was acutely aware of his mental activity, exactly what he remembered and where he was. Even so, he did not touch the doorknob any more than he had to.

"Use another office while we have this one cleaned. We'll monitor everyone who works in the office. I am going to call the Oriental back from assignment. We were after the Dolomos for other reasons."

"Don't call off your efforts against them," said the President.

"I won't. But I want Chiun here. He can sense things routine examinations would miss. I don't know how he does it, but it works."

"The older one?" asked the President.

"Yes," said Smith.

"I like him," said the President.

"He can stop things we can only imagine."

"We'll have to give him a suit. He can't be around me wearing a kimono without attracting attention."

"I don't think we could get him to change his clothes, sir," said Smith. "He really doesn't change much. He probably won't change anything. He doesn't even understand our form of government. He won't accept the fact that some emperor doesn't run the place."

"Hell," said the President of the United States, unbuttoning his shirt. "Nobody runs the place. We all hang on for dear life."

He left his clothes in the Oval Office and walked with as

much dignity as he could muster in his underwear through the passage to the presidential apartments.

Smith made sure the Secret Service examined all the clothes and all the objects in them. Then he made sure everyone who touched anything in the office was given an immediate test for memory. Everyone passed.

Still, the only real test was to have human hands run over everything in the office. It might have been that a minute amount was secreted on something, so minute that it might have been entirely rubbed off by the President. But on what? And how would they deliver it?

Smith sighed as he looked around the office, wondering who or what had entered it to deliver the substance. He looked at the American flag and the presidential flag. He looked at the office he had known of since childhood. He had always been taught such respect for it and he had always treated it with that respect.

It struck Harold W. Smith hard that he had told his first lie to a president of the United States right in this office.

Chiun was not going to be brought in here solely to protect him. Because if the President could not be protected, Harold Smith had a duty to his country and the human race to assassinate his President as quickly and as surely as possible.

If a person regressed to childhood, as the plane's black box indicated, then what would happen to America if the President succumbed to that? What would happen to the ship of state with a child running it, one who could trigger a nuclear holocaust in one angry fit?

Smith resolved that at the first sure sign of childish behavior, the President would have to die. Smith could not take chances. He looked at the Oval Office one last time, shook his head, and left.

It had been so long since he had been ordered to start the organization by a now-dead president, so long and so many deaths ago. It had not been planned as a permanent thing. He was to help America get through the chaos an analyst saw coming. That was in the early sixties. The chaos came. It went, somewhat, and the organization was still here, now adding the President of the United States to its hit list.

Harold W. Smith said a silent prayer as he prepared to set up his own office out of the way of normal traffic and very close to the President, a man of exceptional integrity and courage. But that had nothing to do with whether he would die. He was going to die if he should appear to be stricken by that substance. Thereafter when Harold W. Smith asked the President how he felt, he really would be asking if he was going to have to kill the President that day.

In California, Remo got a strange response when he reached Smith. He knew immediately that Smith was in danger.

"One, I am not at normal home base now, Remo. Two, I want you to get some things straight before you put Chiun on."

Remo had found a street phone that worked after six failed to respond to quarters, nickels, or dimes. He knew Smith preferred street phones, because while they appeared more public, they gave less of a stationary target to anyone for bugging purposes. And Smith's own electronics could clean the line, as he called the process, from his end.

So here was Remo watching skateboarders zip through palm trees and Rolls-Royces form caravans as he made an absolutely safe phone call on Rodeo Drive. Chiun stood nearby, glancing every now and then at a jewelry display in a window. He had been on the alert for movie stars ever since he thought he saw one of the actresses from the soap operas he used to watch so faithfully. Chiun had stopped watching when violence replaced the romance. He did not approve of violence in shows.

He placed his delicate hands inside his kimono and surveyed the passing Hollywood scene. It did not, of course, get his approval. Remo watched him out of the corner of his eye.

"What's the problem?" asked Remo.

"We might be close to end game."

"We've been compromised?" asked Remo. He knew that if there should be any chance of exposure of the organization, it could be ruinous for the nation it hoped to serve. So everything was planned to self-destruct. This included Smith's taking of his own life. Smith would do it, too. Once it had been arranged for Remo to die, but Smith gave that up early on when it began to seem impossible to kill him. Instead, he trusted in Remo's lasting good feelings for his country, and a promise just to leave. Remo did not tell this to Chiun because he knew Chiun might do something to take down the organization. The only thing holding Chiun in America was Remo, whom he called his investment and the future of Sinanju.

Remo knew that with all the new dictators and tyrants in the world, Chiun was thirsting for an opportunity to align Sinanju with one of them.

"Remo. It's the new Dark Age coming. Let's not miss it," he had said.

"I am against Dark Ages," Remo had answered. "Just to kill someone for a few more bars of gold to be held in a house somewhere for centuries doesn't make sense to me. I love my country. I love America."

Chiun had almost wept at that remark.

"You work. You train. You give the very best of yourself, and look. Look at what you get in return. Lunacy. Disrespect. Nonsense. A despot is the best employer an assassin can have. Someday you will appreciate that."

Sometimes, but not often and not for long, Remo began to think Chiun might be right. But not really. It remained the one great difference between them. And as Remo listened to Smith, he reminded himself to remind Smith where Chiun stood.

"If we are not compromised, why is it end game?" asked Remo.

"I can't explain that now. But you will know why if it should happen. I want a promise from you, Remo. I want you to agree that if it is all over, you and Chiun will never work in America again. Can I get that promise?"

"I don't want to leave America," said Remo.

"You must. It's almost been a full-time job, covering for you, making sure people don't put together all those strange deaths you and Chiun have left behind."

"Why should I have to leave if I served the country so well?"

"Because you're like me. You love it, Remo. That's why."

"You mean I'll be an exile?"

"Yes," said Smith.

"I don't know."

"Yes you do, I think."

"All right. But don't end the game for a silly reason."

"Did you think I would?" asked Smith.

"No," said Remo.

"All right. I am going to speak to Chiun. I want him with me at the White House. Now, I don't want any grand entrances with fourteen steamer trunks or pages announcing the arrival of the emperor's assassin. I want it sub-rosa. I want it secret. You are going to have to tell him how to enter. Tell him just to ask for Route Officer Nine. It's part of a system of clearances for entrance to the White House."

"It's the one that isn't cleared, isn't it?" asked Remo.

"Exactly. I want no one to see him enter."

"You seem especially interested that no one sees him this time."

"Not especially," said Smith. "It's just that I get the drift from Chiun that he feels he doesn't get proper attention."

"But he's always felt like that. Why is it special now?" asked Remo.

"You'll find out."

"I think I know. And I hope I won't," said Remo. "Are you not using me because you think I am not at peak?"

"No," said Smith.

"Then why not?"

"Because you might not be able to go through with it. You are a patriot, for all your Sinanju presence. That's what you are. Chiun would have no trouble with this particular assignment."

Chiun watched Hollywood go by, occasionally glancing at the price of a mere string of diamonds in the window. It was an exorbitant price, but the diamonds were nothing compared to the treasure of Sinanju which was stolen while Remo was foolishly trying to save his country. Gold lasted. Countries did not.

But of course, try reasoning with someone whom whites had brought up.

"Smitty wants to talk to you," said Remo.

"More nonsense?"

"No," said Remo. And when Chiun was close enough to hear a whisper, he said:

"He wants you at the White House. He's there. I'll tell you how to enter."

"At last, he makes his move toward the throne," said Chiun. Smith had tried even Chiun's patience, he had been so slow at taking the proper course toward being recognized as the true emperor of this land.

"Hail, O gracious Emperor, your servant stands here to glorify your name," said Chiun.

"Is Remo all right? Can he function at moving on the target people I've set out for him?"

"He is attuned to the very wind, O gracious Majesty."

"Well, you said a few days ago that he was not up to what you considered correct. Has he recovered?"

"Your voice heals the ill."

"Then I can count on him without you?"

"More important, you can count on me without him," said Chiun. "Your reign will be the glory of your nation, the star by which future generations guide their very hopes."

"Level with me. What can't Remo do?" asked Smith.

"He cannot do what the Master does, but he can do everything else. Anything you need him for he can do."

"All right. Put on Remo."

Chiun returned the phone to Remo with a glowing report.

"The emperor has come to his senses."

And then Remo was sure. For some reason the President was going to die.

"Is it definite, what you're calling Chiun in for?"

"No. Not definite in the least. Not definite, Remo. We're facing something far more difficult to deal with than anything in the past. I believe the Dolomos are behind it. It's what is making those witnesses forget. They really did forget."

"Then it wasn't that I had lost something."

"No. There is a substance that creates forms of amnesia. It regresses people. I think it can be transferred through the skin. There are drugs that can do that. I want you to get it from the Dolomos. I am sure those petty little hucksters are behind it."

"What should I do when I get it?"

"Be very careful with it. Make sure it doesn't touch you."

"Not a problem with me or Chiun. Things can't touch us if we don't want," said Remo.

"Good," said Smith.

Remo hung up. Chiun was beaming.

"Well, I can't say I wish you luck, because I think I know what you are going to do."

"At last Smith is going to make his move on the emperor. I must admit, Remo. I had misjudged him. I had thought he was insane."

"You've got to enter quietly. With no fanfare, through a special route."

"I will be the stealth of yesterday's midnight. Don't look so glum. Don't look so sad. We will help Smith reign in glory, or if he proves to be as truly insane as I have thought, we will help his successor reign in glory."

"I thought Sinanju never betrayed an employer."

"No one has ever complained about how we do business."

"No one's been left, little father. The histories are lies."

"A man without history is not a man. All histories do

not have to be true, but they have to be histories. You will
see. I am right here, as I have been right before.''

Remo did not tell Chiun that when he killed the
President Smith would not take his job, but take his own
life. And then they would both have to leave the country.
Nor did Chiun bother to tell either Smith or Remo the one
thing Remo had not regained in training: the ability to
control the outer layers of his skin.

10

Beatrice took charge of the packing. This meant she abused whoever was really doing the job. Rubin, despite the hectoring, got the two things they would need to continue their fight for freedom.

Three suitcases of cash, and the formula.

Then he called together his Warriors of Zor. They gathered in the basement of his estate. The basement was dark. They wouldn't see a wheezing pill-popper, only hear the powerful voice of their master.

"Warriors of Zor. Your leaders are making a strategic retreat. But know this. The forces of goodness can never be defeated. You can never be defeated. We shall conquer and give the world a new day, a new age, a new order. May the power of the universe be with you, and with your kin forever. Alarkin sings your praise."

"Alarkin?" asked an insurance adjuster who had joined Poweressence to cure his headaches.

"Chapter seventeen in *Return of the Alarkin Drumoids.*"

"I don't read that crap."

"It can inspire you," said Rubin. "Prepare for my return. Prepare to receive word from our new home, a safe place, a more decent place where enlightenment is loved, not fought. Where honor is respected, and the good walk humbly with their gods forever in peace."

"The planet Alarkin?" asked one woman.

"No. I think the Bahamas," said Rubin. "Be gone, and bless the very essence of your spirit."

That done, he rolled Beatrice's lingerie, folded her favorite blouses, wrapped her pumps, high heels, and slippers in several layers of tissue paper, and then called his press conference.

With Kathy Bowen not with them, only one reporter from a local weekly showed up. Rubin had built an auditorium for just such an occasion.

The reporter sat alone in the twentieth row.

"You can come up front," said Rubin.

"I feel uncomfortable up front," said the reporter.

"You're up front wherever you sit. You're alone."

"I'll stay here," she said. She was a mousy sort with very large eyeglasses. Rubin wondered if bad eyesight could be cured by projecting a nonmousy essence. He would have to add that to a Poweressence course. As you think, so you see, he thought. It would be a good course. They could sell it for the cost of a hundred pair of eyeglasses, saying that with the proper use of the course they would never need eyeglasses again. There were lots of things he could do with vision. But these things were not on his mind this day as he read his statement.

"This is a message to the world about religious freedom. Today we face the slings and arrows of an oppressive government. Little do you heed. Today Poweressence, which has brought so much love and freedom to the world, suffers persecution. And why, you may ask," read Rubin.

"Because we can cure insomnia without making the drug companies rich. Because we can make people happier and more secure without making the officially approved psychiatrist richer. Because we can help people without the government demanding more money. Today your government attempts to suppress people reintegrating with their essence, claiming it is some sort of mail fraud. How will they treat the Mass tomorrow? Can the Catholics prove the Eucharist is the body and blood of their Lord? Can the Jews prove their Passover really commemorates the flight from Egypt? Can Protestants prove the laying-on of hands heals? Yes, we have been indicted for promising and giving cures for headaches, unhappiness, depression, a poor love life, and the ever-popular and soon-to-be released seeing through your eyes instead of eyeglasses."

On the last one, Rubin lifted his gaze from the printed page. He had just made that one up.

"Do not ask for whom the bell tolls," he rang out. "It tolls for me."

He liked that even better. The lone reporter from the county weekly finally came up for a press release. She had a small question.

"We certainly want to run your story, but we have an advertising problem."

"Not enough space in the paper."

"Not enough advertising. I also sell advertising space. My boss said to tell you it would be a wonderful story if we could run your large advertisement right beside it."

"How much?"

"A hundred dollars."

"A free press is vital to a free nation," said Rubin, stuffing a wad of bills into her hands. "Don't forget to mention seeing through your eyes, not your eyeglasses. It's a new program."

"Really, you can help me to see without eyeglasses?"

"Only if you want to help yourself," said Rubin.

"I do."

"Fill out an application for Poweressence. You've got to start at the beginning. I'll take back the entrance fee," he said. Fortunately it came just to the cost of the advertising. And thus the last testament of Poweressence in America was given to the *Bruce County Register*, which Rubin noted would become famous just as the *Virginia Pilot* of Norfolk, Virginia, became famous for being the only newspaper to carry the first flight of man at Kitty Hawk, North Carolina.

"I never heard of the *Virginia Pilot,*" said the reporter-advertising salesperson.

"They'll hear of the *Bruce County Register,*" said Rubin.

Upstairs Beatrice was now fully realizing she was going

to have to leave the estate. Rubin knew this because anything she wasn't taking she was breaking.

Glass littered the floor. Mirrors hung precariously on walls. Windows looked like a war had been fought through them.

"Rubin. No more playing around. We're hardball now. Do you know why we have to run?"

"We're going to go to jail if we don't," said Rubin. "The forces of negativity are after us."

"We have to run because we haven't been tough enough. We've played by their rules, not ours. Our problem is we've been too nicey-nice and not tough enough. No more games. We're going for it all. We're going for our own country. Then let them try to convict us. If you run the country, you can't violate laws. You make the laws."

One of the young bodyguards Beatrice favored ran into the room.

"There's something at the front gate. He didn't take no for an answer."

"What do you mean, 'something'?" asked Rubin.

"What do you mean he didn't take 'no'?" asked Beatrice.

"Well, we have Bruno and the dogs at the front gate. And you know how tough they are," said the bodyguard.

"I do," said Beatrice with a pleased smile.

"A guy came up to them, had a Powie with him. The Powie kept pointing toward here, saying you and Beatrice lived here. Said it was the spiritual home of the world."

"What was her name?" asked Rubin.

"I don't know, they're all alike. All that trust and stupidity. Anything you tell them, they go and figure out how it makes sense. You know."

"Who cares," said Beatrice.

"Well, Bruno says they can't come in, and this guy throws the dogs halfway up the lawn like footballs with everything but a spiral and then tells Bruno he'll do the same thing to him. Well, Bruno panics. I know this because he's pressing the alarm and I'm listening in to this gate outpost and he's promising everything to the guy if he will just ask for it nicely.''

"Did the negative intruder have thick wrists?" asked Rubin.

"Wrists? Who cares about wrists?" Beatrice laughed. "What can you do with a wrist?"

"You saw the monitor. Did he have thick wrists?"

"I think so," said the bodyguard. "Dark eyes. High cheekbones."

"The negative force, Beatrice," said Rubin. "The ultimate negative force has come after us. I've said it a thousand times. If you're good, they'll attack you. The better you are, the more they'll attack you. And if you're representing ultimate good, then ultimate evil will find you out."

"Well then, kill him! Is that such a problem? What's the problem here?" said Beatrice. "Is there any reason that man has to live? Do I hear a reason? Do I see a hand?" Beatrice looked around the room, as though expecting to find an answer. "Thank you. Please shoot the trespasser."

"Well, Bruno tried that," said the bodyguard.

"And?" asked Beatrice.

"Bruno sailed past the dogs up the lawn. He isn't moving too much."

"Bruno never moved too much," said Beatrice.

"I could have told you guns wouldn't stop him. We've already tried guns. Our faithful Mr. Muscamente had many guns himself, and succumbed to the negative force. I have tracked this man across America. I have seen what he can do."

"We're packed, let's go," said Beatrice.

"No. I want to cover our retreat. I want to end this evil person now."

"Rubin, I like that in you," said Beatrice. "I'll go through the back way, and you can join me."

"No. I'll set up everything and we'll both go."

"How long will that take?"

"Three seconds. I have been expecting this. Miami airport proved that bullets cannot stop the man. And given

that people cannot escape him, I came to the conclusion
that the only way to destroy such a force—''

"Just do it, Rubin," said Beatrice, and to the
bodyguard added:

"If it weren't for me he would still be wasting reams of
bond paper putting his silly ideas on them."

"This will not miss," said Rubin, and he went to the
basement to activate the system he had arranged. Since it
took twenty more seconds than the three he had promised,
he found himself alone in the mansion, and had to run to
catch up to the car the bodyguard was packing in the rear
of the house.

"Don't drive away. Don't let him see us escaping. If he
goes after us, my trap won't work."

"I wouldn't mind being caught by him," Beatrice
laughed. She tickled the bodyguard's thigh. He was at the
wheel.

"Yes you would," said Rubin. "He obviously works for
the President."

"That bastard," said Beatrice.

"Just wait. Let him get into the house. Turn off the
motor and let the trap work."

Remo slowed his walk to keep pace with Daphne. It was
a good half-mile from the gate to the mansion and they
had only gone a hundred and fifty yards when they passed
the gate attendant named Bruno lying very still on the
rolling lawns of the grand estate.

"You sure you can identify him? You sure he doesn't
look like any of his pictures?" asked Remo.

"Yes. It was his inner light that remained constant. He
could have stayed younger than I am, but he chose to allow
himself to experience the suffering of aging. However, he
is going to start getting younger when he chooses."

"Do you believe that?"

"Do you believe Sinanju?"

"Sinanju works," said Remo.

"Before Poweressence I was a desperate young woman
seeking any solution that would work. But now I have
found what works, what I have been looking for. You

should try it. You wouldn't have to be so negative."

"Have you ever heard of being able to make people forget things?"

"No," said Daphne. "You have to remember your hurts and past life injuries so that you can deal with them, and release your problems into the universe instead of harboring them."

"I like to harbor," said Remo. "And I feel fine."

"Why do you argue with your sweet father?"

"Because he's argumentative," said Remo. He looked up at the house. It had that sense of defense, that quietness of danger, of the moment before things would spring out. With the vast green lawns, the sun sparkling off windows, the air so filled with warm life, it reminded Remo most of all of some especially beautiful and deadly insect. The deadly ones, Chiun had said, advertised their power by having attractive colors.

When he thought of Chiun, he was sad. He did not know why the President might have to die, but he trusted Smith. Over the years he had learned that the one thing that could not be questioned was Smith's loyalty to the country. Remo was loyal to the country. He could never explain to Chiun what that meant. More and more as he became Sinanju he understood why. Yet even though he understood how Chiun felt, he did not feel the same way. He was caught between two worlds, and both of them were inside him.

He knew that quite soon he might be leaving the country he loved and had served so long. He wondered if he could ever adjust to serving some dictator or tyrant. He needed to serve what he felt was right. Chiun felt only Sinanju was right, and in the sense of how the human body worked, he was right. But not for governments. Not for people.

"A penny for your thoughts," said Daphne.

Remo pushed her to the side of the road. Metallic objects were secreted under the pathway. The soft green lawn was safer.

"I was thinking about Sinanju," said Remo.

"Does it give you the absolute freedom of power that Poweressence does?"

"No. Frankly, little lady, it confuses me," said Remo.

"If it confuses you, how can it work?" asked Daphne.

She found herself in the air turning over and over, seeing Remo beneath her, way beneath her, perhaps twenty feet beneath her. Then she started coming down again. Apparently he had flipped her like he had the man at the gate, but she had hardly felt it, and most certainly did not see his hands. She only realized they were touching her when she was already in the air. Now she was coming down again. She screamed.

But the hands caught her again, quite softly. She landed with no more force than if she had just taken another step.

"That's how Sinanju works," said Remo.

"It's beautiful," said Daphne. "It's what I've been looking for all my life. It's dynamic. It's forceful. It's alive."

"It's a pain in the neck," said Remo. "Don't step there!"

"Where?"

"Just move over to the right a bit."

"Why?"

"There was something that could go off under the ground."

"You knew it was there?"

"It's not a big thing."

"It's magnificent. Teach me."

"You'd have to change your whole life."

"I'd love to," said Daphne Bloom. "I've been doing that all my life. I changed from est to Scientology, to Sedona, to Universal Reunification. My father was a Reform Jew."

"How long did you give Judaism?"

"A half-hour," said Daphne. "I found it wanting. I want Sinanju. I think it's what I need. What I've been missing. What does it cost to join?"

"You don't join, it joins you."

"That's beautiful."

Remo realized that Daphne probably joined these organizations to find people to listen to her life. He found it extremely tiring after a few minutes. He also found that if he just said "uh-huh" every few minutes she would keep on talking happily. By the time they reached the entrance to the mansion Remo had said "uh-huh" seventy-three times and Daphne was sure that he was the wisest man in the world.

"You have an understanding that surpasses even my first five therapists," said Daphne, ringing the doorbell. "You have a—"

Remo found himself suddenly enjoying Daphne's silence. She was smiling. Then she collapsed by the door, but she was uninjured. She curled up into a ball on the doorstep, at first cooing and then stopping completely. Her eyes shut, and she looked as though she were floating somewhere.

Daphne Bloom had returned to the womb.

And Remo had found the substance. He looked at the doorbell. There was a thin coating of an oily substance. He could always take the doorbell, but if they could smear it on the bell, there probably was a larger amount inside.

Remo focused on the door, sensing the wood and brass as much as seeing it. Nothing there. He pushed it open. As he did, a spray mist filled the room. He backed out, letting it settle, and walked to the corner. As Chiun had said, never enter a building through the front. He couldn't dodge the mist, but he wouldn't have had to. If it were the same substance, he could keep it on his outer layer of skin until it could be removed.

The skin breathed like every other part of the body, and since he had controlled his breathing through lungs, he naturally could move it to the outer layer also. It was not something that was done but something that came about through the proper breathing in the first place.

But it was that breathing, the refinement of it up to Sinanju standards, that he was still having some trouble bringing into correctness.

And the second floor had to be safer. He put one foot on the windowsill and propelled himself easily to the second floor, where the window was locked and reinforced. He pressured the frame to crumbs and entered. The room looked like a child had thrown a fit, with glass scattered about and fine furniture broken.

Clothes had been thrown on the bed as though someone were hastily packing.

He heard voices downstairs, strange voices. They were grown-up voices but saying baby things, crying out for their parents. There was desperation in those voices. Remo moved downstairs quickly and found that off the main entranceway was a series of rooms. One man in a diaper was drowning inside a large white tub.

It was not water that filled the tub, but an oil substance. He had found it. The man was wriggling like a sperm and not bothering to breathe. Remo had to reach in to save him.

He let the air become one with his breathing, let his breathing try to find itself and its own center, then quickly plunged his hands into the solution, lifting the man in the diaper out of the tub and then pressing the substance from the man's lungs, pressing down, trying to get the breathing apparatus to work. But strangely, it didn't. The eyes didn't focus. The body did not respond; it was dead. And not from drowning.

Remo felt the substance work in through his pores and he used the unity of his breathing to let his skin shrug it off. He sensed the room and the softness of the air, saw the stillness of the dead man in diapers beneath him. There was a strange sense of onions in the air, as though he had eaten them a long time ago and now they were coming back.

The droplets made ever-so-delicate kisses on the floor as they fell and became small pools beneath him.

The scent of the solution was in the air also. He could not breathe it. He had to stop. Everything in his body began working against it and yet somehow it had entered through his skin. But he was not without resources because the greatest thing the body could do in Sinanju was what it did by itself. He saw Chiun in front of him giving him those first lectures. He heard the voice telling him about the powers he would have if he were good enough. He knew Chiun was not there in person. He knew Chiun was in him in the spirit.

He could see himself taking that police oath when he was a young man in his twenties, just out of the Marines, thinking he was tough because his muscles were tough. He used to punch with those muscles. He had once thought he had power because he had knocked someone out with a fist.

The room seemed to close in on him, but he didn't allow his body to accept that. He forced himself to work even as he fought the invasion of the substance into his skin, fought the further invasion into his bloodstream, fought the invasion in his mind and his breathing and the last bastion of a person's power, that which was nothing but himself.

Outside, Rubin Dolomo looked at his watch.

"I guess the doorbell didn't work. There are seven other traps," he said.

"Do you think he's stealing things?" asked Beatrice. She found the car uncomfortable. She was in the front seat with the bodyguard. Rubin sat in the back with his papers on the formula.

"You know he might not even be able to make it out of the house," said Rubin. "When I worked with the witnesses I used only fresh solution because that was the only reliable kind. The traps were set with stored solution. Incredibly volatile. Could send a person back to a past life."

"If you believe in them," said Beatrice. "Go inside and see what he is doing."

"I wouldn't survive. Nothing can survive in there. Plants are going to forget how to grow. Nothing. I have unleashed the ultimate power."

"Put out that cigarette."

"I can't. I'm not finished. I need it," said Rubin.

"The secondmost-ultimate power," said Beatrice.

"Uh-oh. Look what's coming," said the bodyguard.

A thin man with thick wrists and dark eyes was coming out of the rear entrance toward the car. He walked easily. He had a smile.

"He should be back in the womb," said Rubin.

"Start the car," said Beatrice.

"The powers that negative force must have!" gasped Rubin. "How can he still walk? How can he breathe? How can he do anything?"

"He's going to kill us," said Beatrice.

In the panic the bodyguard had shifted into reverse, then forward, then reverse again, all while pressing the accelerator to the fullest. The gears clashed, ground, and crashed.

The man made it to the car.

"We pay more than your employer," said Beatrice.

"I will abandon the force of Yes for the force of No," said Rubin.

"Damned car," said the bodyguard.

"Hello," said Remo.

"Hi, sweetheart," said Beatrice.

"Hail to your negative influence," said Rubin.

"Look," said Remo. "I've got a little problem."

"We'll solve it with you," said Rubin.

"Not a big deal," said Remo. He was forcing the breath now. "I keep seeing things. Faces."

"We have three of them," said Rubin.

"No. Not real faces. A face. Chinese or something. With a wisp of a beard and wisps of hair. He is talking to me. Even now he's talking to me. And I don't know what he's saying."

"He's not telling you to harm someone?" asked Rubin. "Those are the voices you cannot trust."

"No. He's just telling me I am going to be all right. Well, I don't know what it is. I guess I'll just have to give you a ticket. Where's the ticket book? Where's my gun? Where's my uniform? Am I on vacation?"

"You're on vacation. Go back inside and enjoy yourself."

"No. The old guy is telling me not to go back in there. He's like a mirage. Have you ever seen a mirage?"

The bodyguard stepped out of the car and took the man by the hand and in so doing got some of the substance on his own palm. It felt oily. He liked oil. He liked it when his mommy put oil on his bottom after a bath. His mommy was not here. So he cried.

Rubin saw the bodyguard cry.

"That proves it. What power the man has. You are the agent of No."

"Is that my name?" said Remo. "I remember it as Remo."

"Hail, No. Good-bye, No," said Rubin Dolomo, and transferred the suitcases of money to another car, this one unfortunately with license plates that belonged to them. He had planned this escape even before the first trial began. He had the proper phony passports and a car to drive them to the airport that would not be spotted as theirs. No matter, he would have to use the large white sedan with the lettering "Power Is What Power Does."

It was usually used to pick up franchise owners from the airport. Maybe it wouldn't be noticed at all, now that the forces of negativity were in abeyance. Maybe they could just park it at the airport and not be noticed.

Remo saw the man and woman loading a long white car with luggage. He offered to help but they didn't want him to touch anything. When he grabbed one suitcase they simply left it there and drove off without it. This was surprising because when he opened it he found bundles of hundred-dollar bills. He would have to turn it in to police headquarters. He wondered where it was. He looked around. He saw the bright sun and the rolling lawn and the palm trees. Palm trees?

Palm trees in Newark, New Jersey? He didn't remember ever seeing palm trees there. The Oriental face was in front of him now, telling him how to breathe. Breathe? He knew how to breathe. He'd known how since he was a baby. If he didn't know how, he would have been dead.

Was he dying? He walked around to the front of the house. He felt an oily substance on his hands and he tried to wipe it off. It didn't seem to come off too well. He knew his body was fighting it, but why he knew that he did not know.

An attractive young woman lay on the ground in front of the house. She wasn't moving except for an occasional kick. Her hands were curled up near her chin. She didn't seem to be in much trouble, other than being dead drunk. Her breath had that awful oniony garlic smell that was all around him.

Apparently it was a new form of liquor. Two dogs seemed quite afraid of him as he walked to the gate with the suitcase full of money.

He liked that, especially since they were Doberman pinschers. A man with a crewcut lay unconscious on the lawn. This place was crazy, he thought. The whole place had to be investigated. He wondered if he should call in for detectives. He would have done that but he forgot the number of the station house.

One telephone number kept repeating itself to him. A lemony-faced man kept repeating it. Apparently he was somewhat upset with Remo because Remo kept using it wrong. Finally he repeated the number. Every time Remo thought of telephone numbers he thought of that number. He remembered trying a trick to remember it. The trick was told to him in a funny language. Chinese or something. It was a thing to indelibly engrave something into the memory.

Now how could he know what to do if he didn't know the language? The Oriental was calling him stupid and ungrateful. But the strange thing about it was the man did not dislike him. The Oriental loved him. He loved him as no one had ever loved him. And he loved the Oriental. And what was strange was that he had no reason why. There was no romance involved whatsoever. When he thought of romance he thought of women. Well, that was good. He was straight at least.

Outside the gates of the estate Remo got a lift. He asked to be taken to the downtown police station. He was told there was no downtown. This was a rich residential community in California.

California? What was he doing in California?

"Let me off near a public phone, would you?"

That phone number was still with him.

"Make sure you shut the door tight," the driver said as Remo got out of the car in a small town with clean streets and elegant little shops.

"Sure," said Remo, and shut the door so hard two of the wheels came off.

"Hey, what did you do that for?"

"I didn't do anything," said Remo. "I think."

He offered to pay for the damage. While he would never steal from evidence in a normal police case, he certainly was not on some normal case. He didn't even know where he was. He took two thousand dollars in hundreds from the suitcase and paid for the damage.

"You some kind of crook?" asked the driver.

"I don't think so," said Remo. "I hope not," he said.

He found some change in his pocket. He dialed the only telephone number he knew.

"How's everything going, Remo?" came back the voice.

So the man knew him. Maybe it was headquarters.

"Where are you?" asked Remo. Maybe he was reaching downtown Newark.

"Why do you ask?"

"I just wanted to know if I reached headquarters."

"Headquarters is where I am. You know that."

"Sure," said Remo. "Just where is it now?"

"Are you all right?"

"I'm fine. Where are you now?"

"You knew earlier today. Why are you asking now?"

"Because I want to know."

"Remo, have you touched anything today?"

"That's a stupid question. Of course I touched things. You can't live in the world without touching things."

"All right. You sound all right."

"I'm great. I never felt better. I almost put a car door through its frame, I feel so good."

"That's not extraordinary for you. Why did you do it? Never mind. Did you find the substance?"

"I've got a suitcase full of it."

"Good. And the Dolomos?"

"I didn't arrest them. Did you want me to arrest them?"

"You don't arrest people, Remo. I think you are under the influence."

"I havn't had a drink for a week."

"Remo. You haven't had a drink for a decade."

"Bulldocky. I had a ball and a beer last night in a downtown bar."

"Remo, alcohol would destroy your system now."

"I don't believe that stuff."

"Remo, this is Smith. Do you know me?"

"Sure. Lots of guys named Smith. But you don't sound Negro."

"Remo. I am white and no one has used that term in the last fifteen years. It's 'black.' "

"I wouldn't want to call any Negro that."

"Blacks don't like to be called Negroes anymore. Remo, answer this. How is the Vietnam war going?"

"Good. We have them on the ropes."

"Remo," came the voice from the telephone. "We lost that war ten years ago."

"You're a damned liar," said Remo. "America has never lost a war and never will. Who the hell are you?"

"Remo, you obviously remember the contact number. I don't know why and I don't know how. But find out where you are and I will try to help you."

"I don't want your help. You're a damned liar. America couldn't lose that war. The Vietcong are tough, but we don't lose wars. I fought in that war last year. And we were winning."

"We won the battles, Remo. We lost the war."

"Liar," said Remo, and hung up.

How could America lose to a bunch of guerrillas in wicker hats? America didn't lose to Japan in the Second World War, why should it lose a little advisory action when it even had a client state fighting for it?

Had things changed? Had time passed? Had someone done something to his memory? And who was that Oriental telling him to breathe?

He found a place to buy a newspaper. He didn't bother reading the headlines. He went right to the date. He couldn't believe it. He was almost twenty years older. But he didn't feel twenty years older. He felt fine. He felt great. He felt better than he had ever felt in his life, and when he looked in the mirror he saw something even stranger. The face he looked at hadn't changed one iota since the late 1960's. Now, how could he have spent so much time and not aged?

The Oriental was talking to him again. As soon as he thought about age he heard the Oriental talk about age. It was strange. The man wasn't in front of him, but appeared to be in front of him. Remo actually saw the sawtooth leaves of the palm trees, smelled the exhaust fumes of cars, and felt the solid sidewalk beneath him, yet there was that vision. And it was saying:

"You will be as old as you wish. The body ages because it is rushed."

"Well, how old are you?"

"I am the perfect age because I chose it," answered the vision. A woman with shopping bags was looking strangely at Remo.

"Am I talking to myself?" asked Remo.

"No. No. You're fine. Fine. Thank you. Good-bye," she said with enough fear to let him know he most certainly was talking to himself.

He looked at his hands. He looked back at the telephone booth. He tried shutting the door hard. All the glass in the booth shattered and he jumped back to avoid it, but as he jumped he felt his body take off, and at the height of the jump, he panicked, thinking he would break a leg as he landed.

But the body took over in a splendid way. It did not try to stop the fall or cushion it, but made him part of that which he landed on. He liked it. He liked it so much he tried it several times.

"Hey, look at me, I'm superman."

But then the vision came back to him, scolding him for showing off.

"You are Sinanju," said the old man. "Sinanju is not for showing off, not for games, not to make bystanders like you. Otherwise we would have gone into the Roman arenas centuries ago. Sinanju is Sinanju."

"What the hell is that?"

"That, you ungrateful piece of a pale pig's ear, is what you are and shall always be. Before you were born you were destined to be Sinanju. Before you breathed you were destined to be Sinanju. You are Sinanju and will be beyond the very bones of your death, which if you don't stop being so ungrateful will happen sooner than it should."

Thus spoke the vision, and Remo still didn't know what Sinanju was other than it was supposed to be part of him, or was him, and was something that went on before he was born.

That, too, he seemed to remember now, but his body was fighting it. He wondered if he should make it stop. He wondered if he should make the visions stop. He wondered if he could.

But all he heard was the Oriental's voice repeating that he should breathe. That he was in the greatest danger of his life. And that he would come for him and save him if only Remo would hang on.

11

Remo was lost. Smith had to make that realization. There was still Chiun and therefore the best chance to protect the President. The workers who cleaned the President's office were all examined for memory. Apparently none suffered noticeable memory loss. But the substance was not the major problem. Somehow the Dolomos had gotten to the President. And if they had gotten to him once, they could do it again.

And if he became like Colonel Dale Armbruster, the pilot of *Air Force One,* he could, with one childish decision, destroy mankind. Smith had hoped that with Chiun protecting the President he could send Remo against the Dolomos. But having in all practical respects lost Remo, Smith decided to use Chiun in the White House while having the President send normal agencies against the pair.

How effective the solution was and how long it lasted were key elements of the battle. So far none of the people afflicted had regained their memory. The damage seemed permanent. Even if it weren't, the President would have to die, Smith had decided, because there was no way to make him harmless while under the influence of that solution.

As for the solution itself, how long it stayed potent was a question that had to be answered. They had to know what they were up against. Could a small dose poison a city? Could a large dose create a wider swath of mental destruction?

And what were its potential delivery systems? What the

world was facing now was something that could change the very nature of human beings. It could make man a helpless animal, because without his mind he was little more than meat for the predators.

It would be like creating cats without claws or balance.

Smith put these thoughts out of his mind while taking control of the investigation at the Dolomo estate. He got the Agriculture Department to exercise control over the area and moved scientists in with warnings about what they were looking for. Then he put a Secret Service seal around the area, with special instructions. No one could leave and no one was allowed to touch anyone who had entered. Whatever was needed would be sent into the estate. But nothing could come out.

He even ordered the sewer lines plugged up so that nothing could be washed into the water supply. The first news was horrendous. The entire first wave and part of the second wave of Agriculture Department scientists were lost by the time they figured out a surefire way to handle the substance. When the Dolomos had left the estate, Smith hesitated to put a missing persons alert out for them through the police department. He would wait until they failed to appear in court.

Their lawyer, Barry Glidden, had also disappeared, but it was thought that one of the afflicted found in the estate might be him.

Smith stayed just outside the President's new office so that every half-hour he could come in on some pretext or other to see how the President was doing. He was introduced as a new personal secretary. He stayed out of the office when an old OSS buddy of his had a meeting with the President. The old friend now owned his own company.

Chiun arrived near midnight without fanfare.

"Our hour is near," he told Smith. "I salute you and give you exaltations."

"Uh, thank you, I suppose," said Smith. "I think you realize what we are up against. But let me be frank."

"Your subtlety over the years is now appreciated, your

genius evident," said Chiun, who for a while had given up all hope that Smith was going to make himself emperor of this nation. Consequently Chiun had seen no hope in America for Sinanju, and the moment he could get Remo to leave, he planned to be gone.

But now fate, as ever the curious wonder of the universe, had exposed Harold W. Smith, the silly-looking peculiar man with the strange meaningless missions, as actually far more cunning than Chiun had even imagined. He had shown inordinate impatience, a rarity in a white man.

Now with Smith about to become emperor of the richest nation in the world, with Sinanju at his side, his loyal and faithful assassins, the oblivion suffered by Sinanju since the first of the Western world wars was about to come to an end.

With America acknowledging Sinanju, and Sinanju performing as no amateurs could, there would be a demand again for the professional assassin. And of course the greatest demand for Sinanju. It would be an age to rival the reigns of the Borgias, or Ivan the Prompt, who paid the very day a head was delivered to him in Russia, a man curiously known by other whites as Ivan the Terrible, but a person whose word to his assassin was his bond.

All these things did Chiun think about as he joyously hailed Harold W. Smith on the threshold of their shared greatness.

But Smith only seemed worried.

Chiun assured him that it was normal to be worried.

"A first for you, an age-old mission for us," said Chiun.

"The first thing I want you to do is to examine the Oval Office."

"We will remove him there," said Chiun.

"Not necessarily," said Smith.

"We will use a more secluded place. When he sleeps."

"Perhaps," said Smith. "First I want to protect him from something."

"Of course, but may I suggest something that has worked well through the ages?" said Chiun. He noticed

Smith's office was sparse and small. But it had always been like that. He hoped that Smith would not be one of those emperors who insanely denied themselves the glory of the throne, living frugal and bare lives. Genghis Khan, who ruled from the saddle, was impossible to work for, and when the fine civilization of Baghdad fell before his barbaric sword, it was a sad day for Sinanju.

But one could never tell with Smith. He was inscrutable.

"No. What I want is this. We will attempt to protect the President from a certain substance. If we cannot, then and only then will I possibly order that you do what you have to do. But I don't want to put this country through another assassination. I want it to appear like a heart attack. Can you do that?"

"A heart attack is one thing, a seizure is another. We do a wonderful fall with just the right bones broken, leaving the face untouched for a state funeral. I would recommend that," said Chiun. "We have a prepared speech that could be translated into English. You assure everyone you are going to carry on his wise policies, except make them more lenient while enforcing safety even more. People like to hear that. It goes over so well. It is a good way to start a reign."

"You don't quite understand. Let's just look at the Oval Office for now. I'm looking for a substance that can take away memory. I believe a small amount has affected the President. It occurred in that office. I'm afraid of what would happen if you touch it, so touch nothing."

"You mean the sort of poisons that move through the skin? Do not worry about us."

"You mean Remo is safe from that too?"

"At peak, the skin is as controllable as the lungs," said Chiun.

"I see," said Smith, "but Remo was not at peak."

"Is he all right?" asked Chiun.

"Yes," said Smith. It was the first time he had ever lied to either Remo or Chiun. "He's fine."

Smith did not want Chiun distracted.

"I wonder if around the White House you might wear

something less flamboyant than a gold-and-red robe. I know it's your greeting robe to the ruler, but I would prefer you go unnoticed."

"Until the time is right?" said Chiun.

"If we must eliminate the President, I want you to take Remo away from here."

"But how will you rule?"

"You will understand everything at the right time," said Smith.

"A great emperor is a mysterious emperor, for who knows what wonders he performs," said Chiun. Actually emperors who acted mysteriously did very well for a very short time until their empires collapsed around them, because no one knew what to do.

Chiun examined the Oval Office for any strange substance. He found forty of them, from the synthetic material in the flags to the plastic on the desk.

"We are looking for something oily that makes people forget."

"Olive-flavored gin," said Chiun.

"Not drunk, steals the mind."

"A living death," said Chiun. "You wish to put this emperor out of his misery?"

"No. They are happy when they forget. I guess pain is a learned thing."

"Pain and happiness are both illusions, O great Emperor Smith," said Chiun. Whites liked that sort of thing nowadays. It made them feel as though they were getting something wise.

Even Rubin had to admit that Beatrice's plan was brilliant and the only way out.

"He wanted war, he's got war. Our only problem is we weren't fighting a war."

"You're right. You're right. When you are right, you are right," said Rubin. He wheezed under the weight of the bags at Nassau airport. They had gotten out of America easily. They simply used two phony passports and carried the money on board.

Just before their bags went through the X-ray check he coated the money with a fiberglass that made it all look like loose sweaters.

But at Nassau they had to open their bags entering the Bahamas. The airport was hot, with signs for rum and entertainment on the walls. The light was Caribbean bright, like rhinestones under fluorescence, a bit too bright to feel natural for Americans.

The customs inspector saw the fiberglass coating and politely inquired what it was. He had to be on the lookout for anyone bringing in narcotics or weapons.

Rubin explained it was a gift for his good friends on the island, a new sort of material to make building houses easier.

"A technology from outer space," said Rubin.

"Lay off that planet-Alarkin stuff or we'll both be in the slammer," said Beatrice. She asked the customs inspector where they could buy suntan lotion and because he did such a good job with directions, gave him ten crisp hundred-dollar bills.

"You are welcome with your invention from outer space to the Bahamas," said the inspector.

But Beatrice and Rubin did not stay on Nassau. They took a small charter aircraft to the island of Eleuthera, a long strip of coral and sand dotted by occasional beaches and many small villages with no more than two stores apiece. There could not be more than ten thousand people on the island, and a closer guess would have put it at three thousand.

"Too many for the plan," said Beatrice. "Too big. The people can make trouble."

Rubin looked over the map. He pointed to an even smaller island ten minutes by boat from Eleuthera. It was called Harbor Island, and it was famous for two miles of pink beaches and a "decency of people rare anywhere in the world."

"Good," said Beatrice. "We can push them around."

"Or buy them," said Rubin.

"Why buy what you can bully?" said Beatrice.

"It's easier on my nerves," said Rubin.

"Try another Percodan."

"I'm running low."

At Harbor Island the first part of the plan went into effect immediately. They purchased all the available hotel rooms. Then the call went out by phone, along the squeaky radiophone system, to all the Warriors of Zor.

"We are safe. We are here. Join us."

And the call went out to all the franchises.

"Send us Powies. The moment of truth is at hand. Profits about to go through the roof. We have all been in the wrong business. About to make you all rich beyond your wildest dreams."

Of course the reply was: what level Powies did the Dolomos want from their franchises? No one was going to give up the big spenders.

"I don't want money. I want believers. We'll pay the way down. Believers."

"Believers mean money," was the general answer.

"Then poor believers," said Rubin.

"You mean the kids, the ones who want the future and try to sell Poweressence on the street corners?"

"Yes. Them. Anyone. We are ready to strike back. Beatrice says we're not taking it anymore."

"That's why you had to leave the country in the first place, isn't it?" asked one of the franchise owners.

"We're going to have a place very shortly that we'll never have to leave. Have you ever wondered why Presidents don't go to jail and citizens do?"

"No," said the franchise owner, who was more interested in a "Be Free from Eyeglasses" promotion Rubin had mentioned as an aside.

"Then," said Rubin, "you will be bound by your pettiness forever. Do you want to play with sight enhancers all your life?"

"Rubin, if we can sell 'see without glasses' we can devastate the eyeglass market and put contacts out of business forever. Forever. Millions. I'm talking millions.

How many people are embarrassed to wear eyeglasses? We will own the geriatric market."

"I don't know if it will work," said Rubin.

"Doesn't matter. We just need people to believe it will work. Lots of diets don't work, Rubin, but people still belong to clubs and buy books."

"Small change," said Rubin. "You don't know how big we're going to be. As Beatrice says, we're not taking it anymore."

Within two days the Warriors of Zor had arrived at Harbor Island, and Rubin, with his suitcases of cash, was able to put them all in a fine little resort that straddled the island in the middle, each with small bungalow cottages and central dining room.

"It's like a vacation," said one man who sold insurance. To him Rubin entrusted the mission to the banking commission of the Bahamas.

"I want to open a bank," said Rubin. He gave the man twelve inches of hundred-dollar bills to establish the proper credentials. Rubin Dolomo had his bank before sunset. But there were other things he was doing.

The Warriors of Zor would lead other Powies. With his own bank he could receive or give loans. The first thing he did was put the paper into it, and through a tangle of financial maneuvering got himself credit around the world.

The native population being open, honest, and friendly, he immediately established himself as ruler, with Beatrice as queen. Those who went along received a large, friendly stipend. Those who did not were threatened successfully.

Within three days of landing, the Dolomos had turned Harbor Island into their own preserve and announced independence from the Bahamas.

The Prime Minister of the Bahamas was quite rightly infuriated. Since the Bahamians had the good sense to avoid enemies and even the better luck to have an ocean between them and any neighbor, they had never needed an army. They sent their police force, a finely trained, disciplined, and polite constabulary, still retaining many

British officers as well as equally competent natives, to subdue the rebellion.

The first wave got to the beach and were met with smiling, friendly people wearing rubber gloves and carrying cotton swabs. The first wave never reported back. The second wave went in with orders to let no one near. But by this time the Powies had the guns of the first waves. There was a slaughter on the beach.

And here Rubin showed his true skills. Instead of hunkering down, Rubin prepared an announcement for his new Secretary of State, a pleasant man who ran a souvenir shop featuring tall cups with bug eyes that stared back at the drinker.

"We are the Revolutionary People's Army of Harbor Island seeking to redress age-old oppression by Nassau, Eleuthera, and Great Britain, which made all these islands colonies. Our struggle will not stop until total freedom, total liberty, and total independence are achieved."

Since Rubin had carefully kept himself and Beatrice out of sight and since it seemed as though these were truly natives conducting the rebellion, fourteen Third World countries offered them recognition immediately, and Russia sent a trade delegation to give them arms.

Just off the pink beach Rubin enlarged a crude factory into an underground bunker that could produce the memory formula. The Warriors of Zor trained the Powies who made it. Men of the Bahamian constabulary were allowed to play in the sand. No more tourists were allowed.

Rubin felt so good he was down to one Percodan an hour, and it was then that he told Beatrice:

"Your Majesty, we are ready."

Beatrice chortled. She confided to her new minister, Oscar, the souvenir man:

"We're not taking it anymore."

And then on a phone system as mysterious as the far reaches of the planet Neptune and sometimes just as inaccessible, she telephoned the State Department of the

United States of America and told them she wanted to speak to the President on a matter of utmost urgency.

"And who is this?"

"This is Beatrice of Alarkin. We are a newly independent state and we can go either way. There already is a Russian delegation here willing to sell us all the weapons we might need."

The President was on the phone in a half-hour.

"We certainly wish to extend the greetings of the American people to your new nation. However, we also have relations with the Bahamas and with Great Britain and I do believe that to be recognized, you must clear up the question of your legitimacy first."

Thus spoke the President of the United States from his new office, with the State Department brief in front of him. Intelligence had reported a takeover of the small Bahamian island.

Under the new setup he touched nothing. No paper came to him, rather all material came through a computer screen. He was a healthy man for his seventy-odd years, and his mind was sharp. He didn't want to get America entangled in a revolution, especially one against nations that were friends. On the other hand, he wanted to keep communications open.

The name Alarkin struck a bell with him. But his two aides, now restricted to only entering the outer edge of the office, just shook their heads when he asked them what Alarkin reminded them of.

"Nothing, sir," said the aides.

A door opened and a lemony-faced man in a gray three-piece suit stood in the doorway.

"I'm fine," said the President.

And Smith left, shutting the door.

The aides had seen the man in the gray suit do that several times. One of them thought the man might be a personal physician but the other had been told he was a new private secretary. There were even rumors about an old Oriental who seemed to vanish when anyone saw him.

And even stranger, the President refused to enter the Oval Office anymore.

The President put his hand over the phone.

"Alarkin. I've heard that name somewhere."

"Might be one of the old native gods."

"She sounds white. She sounds American," said the President.

Both aides shrugged.

"They're in a revolutionary secession from the Bahamas," said one aide.

"Right," said the President, and taking his hand off the phone, spoke into the receiver.

"Can we possibly help you resolve your differences with the main islands?" the President asked.

"What we want is freedom of religion," said the Queen of Alarkin.

"We too want that, and we support it," said the President. He turned up the speaker so that the aides could hear. He shrugged. They shrugged.

"The Bahamas have never been known for religious intolerance," said the President, signaling that he wanted all of this recorded.

"No, but you have," said the woman who called herself Queen of Alarkin.

"I beg to differ, ma'am. America from its very founding has promised and given freedom of religion. We are proud of it."

"Religious freedom for some. For the large, for the wealthy, for the powerful. But what about the small and oppressed?"

"Are you talking about small black churches? They do very well here, your Majesty."

"I am talking about those churches that dare to tell the truth. Those churches that dare to risk new and startling ideas."

"The fact is, your Majesty, America has more and different churches than any other country in the world."

"Yes, and what about Poweressence?"

"Ma'am, the people who run that are not facing charges because of teaching new religious doctrines. You may or may not be aware of it, but they put an alligator into the pool of a columnist who was exposing them. The post office has a good case for mail fraud, and we believe they are behind the murder—and I call it murder—of an Air Force colonel, a United States senator, and an entire plane crew. Those poor people died when the rulers of Poweressence tried to kill me."

"There is no need for death," said the Queen of Alarkin.

"I'd like to believe that," said the President.

"If you dropped your cases against them, no one would have to die."

"I would not interfere with our judicial system for anyone, but least of all for that pair of con artists and murderers," said the President, his voice rising in anger. He remembered Colonel Armbruster, remembered how he would ask if the landing was just right sometimes, remembered the man had a family.

"I want you to know," continued the President, "we are not giving in to terrorism of any kind."

"I am speaking of your life. I can not guarantee the safety of your life as long as the thousands of devoted followers of Poweressence see their leaders persecuted."

"Is that a threat?" asked the President.

"It is a friendly warning for you to be evenhanded in the matter of the Dolomos. Why do you act friendly to the Catholics, Protestants, and Jews, and feel nothing for the Poweressence devotees, beautiful people, beautiful people all?"

"I will tell you how I will be evenhanded. I am going to suggest Congress deliver me an antifraud-cult bill today. And we are going to put bums like that out of business. Because that's all they are, Queen of Alarkin. Bums."

"Well, I can only say, Mr. President, you have only yourself to blame. Because we are not taking it anymore."

"I don't understand."

"You're not picking on a couple of defenseless citizens anymore. We are a nation. And we have a right to defend ourselves from oppression in any way possible. I warn you. Look to the sea. Look to the skies. Look to the land. We're not taking it anymore. We're going to get you."

"Who is this?"

"The beautiful wife of Rubin Dolomo herself."

"He doesn't have a beautiful wife."

"That has to be against the Geneva Convention. That's low. For that you will pay. I've warned you. We're not taking it anymore."

The aides saw the President hang up and then dismiss them.

"Smith, come in here please," he said into an intercom that worked off a button under the rug beneath his desk.

"Are you feeling all right?" asked Smith as he entered. Chiun, the Oriental who worked with Smith's organization, was with him.

"I'm feeling fine," said the President.

The Oriental bowed and left the room.

"The Dolomos have taken over a small island in the Bahamas. They have declared themselves independent. They are now foreign leaders, and they have heaven knows what at their disposal. They are totally ruthless and unscrupulous. I suggest we use the other one to go at them now."

"He's been lost," said Smith.

"No," said the President, shaking his head. "If they got him, they can get anyone."

"Probably, but Chiun is better, I believe. Remo was not in top shape."

"Then why did you send him?"

"We didn't have anyone else, sir."

"Send the Oriental then."

"I'd like to keep him here."

"Look, if we get them, then I won't be in danger," said the President.

"And if they get him?"

"Then they'll get me. They offered terms, you know.

Just now. Let them off the hook in the courts, and they will let me off."

"Are you going to take it?"

"No."

"I wonder if this once we shouldn't back down, and get them at an easier time."

"I am not selling out to two hustling bums."

"We may be talking about your life, sir."

"Then I'll die in office, dammit. I am President of the United States, not some courthouse politician. I will not desecrate this office by compromising with two patent frauds who have turned to murder."

"That's your decision then?" said Smith.

"That is my decision," said the President. "Today I am going to have introduced into Congress a tough antifraud bill, a bill that would make hustles like Poweressence illegal. And even if those two should somehow beat this rap, then they will never be able to practice their chicanery again."

"If you say so, sir. May I suggest your sending military assistance to the Bahamas and hope more soldiers will be able to take them."

"I'd rather use the Oriental."

"Sir, he stays here. That's part of the safety built into my organization. No president can order me. He can only suggest. I have a choice of doing what he says or disbanding."

"And you will disband?"

"I will not order Chiun from your presence, sir," said Smith.

"You're going to kill me if I get infected with that substance, aren't you?"

Smith hesitated. He liked the President. He respected the President, but even more he respected the office.

"Yessir," he said. "That is just what I'm going to do."

"Because acting without a memory, acting like that pilot, I can get everyone killed, is that it?"

Smith nodded. He swallowed.

"Yeah. I suppose that's the right move. They told me

when I took over this office you always made the right move. That's what my predecessor said. Well, let me suggest this. You send Chiun after those two, and if I show any signs of being afflicted, you shoot me. Right in the head. Don't let me do to this country what the pilot did to that plane."

"Can't do that, sir."

"Why not?"

"Because I couldn't pull the trigger, sir. And since it is all out, let me say that Chiun can kill you in a way no one would know wasn't an accident or even a heart seizure."

"Okay," said the President. "You and Chiun stay here. But how do you know when you come in again I won't lie and say I'm feeling fine just so he won't kill me?"

"You'd have to remember for that," said Smith.

"You certainly do make the right moves, Mr. Smith."

"Yessir," said Smith, and disappeared behind a door, only to come out a half-hour later while the President was speaking to several senators about his bill to put greater penalties on frauds in religious cults.

"Absolutely fine," said the President with a courageous smile.

"Yessir," said Smith, and shut the door.

"Who was that?" asked a senator.

"Just a new secretary," said the President.

12

It was the largest oil tanker ever built. Her hold could keep a city lighted and warm for a winter. The belly in the *Persia-Saud Maru* was so vast it would be cleaned by specially designed tractor scrubbers that would start at the bow and not finish until a half-month later.

The oil disgorged while cleaning her tanks could tar fifteen miles of modern highway. So dangerous would a spill be that international law prescribed her route, and both American and Russian submarines would break radio silence to identify and chart icebergs that might be in her way.

She was built by an Arab prince at the height of Arab oil power, despite warnings from advisers that so much oil in one place would be a danger to the entire world. In its full belly was more wealth than most Third World nations possessed, and its construction cost more than the gross national product of all but three African nations.

When she was done, only three ports in the world could handle her, and despite the danger of her spills or threats from one nation or another, no one could afford not to use her anymore. Too much money had gone into building her to have her be idle. Dockage cost two million dollars a day. Her insurance premiums were so vast that her government underwrote them.

When she lumbered across the Atlantic, crewmen competed in long-distance runs across her deck. It took her fifteen minutes to build up cruising speed and thirty miles to stop.

Only one pilot was allowed to guide her in, and he was flown out to the ship with his crew ten days before the vast island prepared to dock.

"So you're back. I thought you went down to the Bahamas for some crazy religious convention," said the harbor pilot as his junior mate climbed aboard the seaplane at their Bayonne dock.

"It's not crazy," said the junior mate. "It's a way of life. It's a religion. Like any other religion."

The harbor pilot was in his early sixties, with light gray hair and alert blue eyes. He was in better shape physically than his junior mate, who was in his twenties.

The harbor pilot, Cal Peters, strapped his seat belt and glanced over to the junior mate to do the same to his. Peters knew the lad was a good boy, always a hard worker, but he tended to worry too much. He had often told the boy to "care about what you do, but don't worry about it. Worry won't help you do spit."

He thought the boy was taking his advice when he seemed to be worrying less. Of course the junior mate also seemed to be without enough money for lunch at the time, and Peters asked him what was wrong. If anyone on his harbor crew had problems he wanted to know about it before they cropped up while guiding some city-size tanker into dock.

He found out then about Poweressence.

"Son," said Peters, "I don't interfere with any man's religion. How he comes to God is his business. But those people are frauds."

"They called Jesus a fraud too, in his time," said the junior mate. His name was Arthur, and he had graduated from the Coast Guard Academy, served his time, and come to work for the harbor commission right after.

"But Jesus didn't have a moneymaking operation."

"What do you call the Vatican, the poorhouse?"

"But the Catholic Church provides hospitals and schools. Poweressence only seems to be more expensive for every class you go to."

"They aren't classes. They're levels. If you joined, you

would see. Your life would enhance itself. You would be happy all the time," said Arthur.

"Son," Peters told Arthur, "the day I am happy all the time is the day I commit myself to a sanitarium."

"Happiness is what we are supposed to have. The negative forces have convinced you to be this way."

No matter how Cal Peters tried to reason with the young man, Arthur always seemed to have an answer. And then one day he disappeared, saying he was following his better self, and then just as mysteriously he returned. Cal almost refused to let him back on the harbor crew. Except that Peters liked the boy. And against what he thought at the time was his better judgment, he took him back on.

"Don't go running off again unless you give me plenty of warning. We run a harbor-pilot service here, not some street-corner pencil stand. We have major ships coming in. And the *Persia-Saud* is the most major."

"That was the last time," Arthur promised.

It was a small plane, but Cal Peters liked small planes. It gave him a better sense of the wind and the sea as they flew out to the *Persia-Saud*.

"What did they have to do down there in the Bahamas anyway? I hear there's trouble down there. A rebellion, sort of."

"It's always called trouble when people want to be free," said Arthur. "When people are tired of taking it anymore. When people are ready to fight to preserve what is holy and good."

"So you're a revolutionary now, is that it?" asked Peters.

"The only revolution I want is within myself."

"Just what did you do down there?"

"I learned to love what was good and hate what was bad."

"And who was doing the deciding what was good and what was bad?"

"It was obvious," said Arthur. He kept his eyes fixed ahead of him, into the clouds. In the small plane they could see right over the pilot's shoulder at the front windshield. They could feel the vibrations of the engines in their seats.

"Well then, you're one step up on me, son, because the older I get, the less obvious things seem."

"If you get rid of your negative impulses, everything will be obvious."

"What a damned dull world that would be," said Peters. The aircraft pilot laughed. The rest of the crew laughed. Only when the great *Persia-Saud Maru* came into view ahead of them did they stop laughing at poor Arthur, who could withstand their laughter. He felt he could withstand anything. He knew the one right, true way and they did not. Besides, many of them would be dead within a few days and he would not.

It was not murder. Murder was when you harmed an innocent. But he had learned in the Bahamas at an absolutely free course, raising him up to where he could control his own destiny, that people were not innocent just because they seemed to be doing nothing harmful.

You were only innocent when you were helping the positive forces of the world. When evil abounded and you worked within an evil system, you were as guilty as the President of the United States.

The aircraft pilot circled the *Persia-Saud Maru* looking for a piece of sea that would not be subject to her massive wake with the undertow force of a whirlpool. In some seas he would have to circle for an hour until explorer boats, now being let down from her building-high decks, could find safe landing for a light seaplane.

This day on the calm seas they found it rather readily, and the plane put down easily. The power boats, smaller than destroyers but larger than PT boats, anchored the seaplane, and the harbor pilot and his crew went aboard. Arthur went with Cal Peters.

Before the power boats were allowed near the *Persia-Saud,* the harbor crew had to be frisked and their baggage searched. This was in accordance with the safety protocols which allowed no uncleared person or vessel within range of the massive ship.

Cal Peters' bag contained four days of clothing changes and a picture of his wife, along with his charts.

Arthur Daniels' bag contained twelve course-level books from Poweressence, four days of clothes, and a red plastic water pistol, filled.

"It's mine," said Arthur, stopping the ship's inspector from touching it.

"Fine, so long as it doesn't shoot bullets," said the inspector.

"Well, glad to see you're having some fun in your life at least," said Cal. But he also noticed Arthur had a package of headache capsules, and he had never seen that before. He was relieved to see it apparently had only one capsule inside. At least Arthur hadn't become addicted to anything chemical.

Addicts, whether alcohol or otherwise, always made sure they had good supplies available. This was a thing Cal Peters had learned to watch out for early on. When you brought in the *Persia-Saud* you could no more call something this massive back than you could redirect a bullet. What the *Persia* lacked in speed she made up in size, and Cal could afford no problems.

Elevator cranks lifted the power boats up her sides. But it was a short lift this day. The *Persia-Saud*'s holds were laden with Arabian light. She had come out of the Arabian Gulf a month ago with enough oil that if it were sold on the spot market immediately it would have shot the skids out from under the already shaky prices. But this load had been sold years before in an agreement with a major oil firm that had been emptying its Bayonne, New Jersey, tanks for months.

An entire depot was waiting for her cargo.

Cal Peters liked the *Persia-Saud*. Most ships had a pitch to their decks; the *Persia* had a roll little more noticeable than a sidewalk in Missouri.

Cal didn't take over immediately. He first held the meeting of the habor crew. There were the navigator, engineer, junior mates, and the rest, all preparing the schedule of entrance. To stop the ship they had to start slowing down by morning, and take very careful readings every hour as to speed and distance to shore. If the *Persia-Saud* sighted land going faster than a crawling two knots an hour, no force on earth could stop her from crashing into the dock. But if she went too slowly and the tides caught her, it could mean a day before they got her back in control. She was as touchy as she was massive.

Arthur Daniels volunteered for the first day, and Cal Peters was glad to see him do it. It showed that despite his eccentricities the boy still cared about the job. And that was the bottom line with Cal Peters and always had been.

Peters felt good about his decision to accept the boy back despite the unauthorized vacation, right up until Arthur Daniels brought the water pistol onto the captain's desk.

"Arthur, if the ship's captain ever saw us playing with those things he'd head right back to the Arabian Gulf," said Peters.

He saw the little red plastic gun point at him. He saw Arthur pull the trigger. He saw the stream come right at his face. That was it. He was going to fire Arthur, if the nice man wasn't so nice to him, and hadn't given him a shiny silver dollar to play with. He could even put it in his mouth if he wanted. That was very nice. Cal's mommy never let him put things in his mouth like this nice man. All Cal had to do was stay in the room and anytime anyone came in he was to nod.

"Just nod," said Arthur. "Good boy. You're a very good boy. That's nice."

In that first moment, seeing Mr. Peters responding like a baby, Arthur Daniels had his first doubts about what he was doing. But such was the wisdom of Poweressence that they had prepared him.

"When you feel guilty, that is an old habit pattern," he had been told. "You were always made to feel guilty to keep you in line. Guilt is the old way of doing things. We are the new, positive way of doing things."

But still, no matter how he focused on his positive essence, he could not dispel the guilt. And there were five days ahead of them. On the fourth day the relief pilot asked why they hadn't started to slow. On the third day he demanded to know and accused Arthur of being insane for trying to shoot him with a water pistol. Now Arthur had two grown men in his hands, neither of whom knew enough not to soil their pants. On the final day, even the captain became aware of problems and seized the bridge. By then it was too late.

"Why on earth did you do it? Why did you do such a thing?" said the captain.

Arthur Daniels only smiled. He had taken the pill Mr. Dolomo himself, the finest mind in the world, had personally given him even as the Warriors of Zor stood to salute his sacred mission.

But unlike Arthur Daniels, the captain of the *Persia-Saud Maru* did not worry about grown men whose pants smelled, didn't even bother to worry that he would soon have Arthur's undies to worry about. He had a ship headed for Bayonne, New Jersey, and no way to stop it, no time to turn it, and only an hour before an entire city went under a flood of oil.

In Washington, D.C., the President called Smith in to listen, adding that the Oriental was not needed at this moment.

"We have that . . . that Beatrice on the line again," said the President. His hand covered the speaker.

"What is she saying?"

"Says it's all our fault," said the President, nodding to another line. Smith picked it up.

"I never like to hurt innocent people. I have nothing against Americans, Mr. President. I am an American. But what will happen in Bayonne, New Jersey, today is all your fault."

"What will happen, your Majesty?" asked the President.

"Your fault it will happen. Stop the anticult bill in Congress before more harm is done."

"If I stop it, your Majesty, what will you stop?"

"I can't stop it now and neither can you. That's why I

am telling you. When you think of hurting a beautiful, charming, decent woman again, think of Bayonne, New Jersey. I would advise you to evacuate now."

Then the line went dead.

"Are the advisers ready to invade Harbor Island?" asked Smith.

"Just about," said the President. "We've got to get them into protective suits first. That's what's slowing them up. What are the science boys up to?"

"Nothing yet. They won't even touch it with rubber suits. Experimenting on animals, but it doesn't seem to affect them the same way. Chiun says—and in his own strange ways he often understands things about the body we don't—it possibly only attacks learned memory, intellectually learned memory."

"Is there another kind? Instinct isn't memory."

"There is, but we had better order Bayonne to evacuate right now."

"Where the hell can they evacuate to, Jersey City?" asked the President.

The *Persia-Saud Maru* moved slowly into Bayonne, New Jersey, so slow it could make an onlooker, if there were any left, believe that the slightest nudge would stop it. But that was because it was moving at fifteen knots, the speed of a good jogger.

The thing about the *Persia-Saud* was it just kept going. It crumpled the offshore rocks, and the force of its lake of oil continued to move at the same speed, taking the upper prow with it as the lower hull stayed behind, dismantling itself on the shore.

It was as though someone had driven a large lake into Bayonne, New Jersey. The lake was black and sticky and became a tidal wave that swept up the narrow city into Jersey City. There at the ebbing of its powerful thrust it subsided, looking to hovering aircraft like a plateau of liquid black that suddenly lots its energy and widened into the largest parking lot in history, fouling both the neighboring ports of Elizabeth and New York City.

It was the greatest natural and commercial disaster in history.

Alone in his new White House office, the President of the United States counted the seconds before the advisers, assisted now by scientists, would invade Harbor Island.

It was a crazy world. Remo heard about the disaster in Bayonne and wondered if Newark policemen were going to be called up to assist. When he was a Newark policeman the Vietnam war was going on. It was a lot of years since then. He was afraid to pick up a newspaper. Everything had changed so much. There had been so many presidents.

And the Oriental face was still in front of him. It was telling him there was no such thing as a president. Didn't he realize that there were only kings using different titles? Remo should know that. Remo should breathe properly. Remo should let his body fight for him. ⌐mo should return to the Oriental. Remo should return ₋o that funny-sounding place, Sinanju.

But Remo had never been in Sinanju. And stranger, still, when he got to the ticket window of the airline he would use to take him back to Newark, he noticed two Orientals having difficulty explaining what they needed. They were from Seoul, South Korea, and they wanted to fly to Phoenix, Arizona, where they had a daughter.

They had difficulty making themselves clear. Remo translated for them. He asked them in Korean where they were going and then he explained to the counter person what they wanted.

"You speak an old formal sort of Korean. In some parts of the north they speak that," said the man in Korean.

And then Remo realized he knew Korean, knew it like English. The thing was, no one had ever taught him Korean. He didn't remember ever learning it. And then he realized that was the language the vision used.

And he also didn't like the couple's Korean. It was less precise than the language he knew. And for some incredibly strange reason he was thinking of them as foreigners because they spoke that bad Korean.

Koreans were better than others, but not all Koreans. One was only home in Sinanju, he thought. Sinanju? There was that place again.

"Do you know where Sinanju is?" he asked them.

"Sinanju, yes. Way north. No one goes there. No one."

"Why?"

"We don't know. No one goes there."

"But why?"

"It's the place no one goes," said the man. The woman thought her grandfather knew.

"He said it was the place everyone was afraid of."

"Afraid? They're the nicest people in the world," said Remo. How did he know that?

"You've been there?"

"No," said Remo. "Never."

"Then how do you know?"

"I don't know," said Remo. "I don't know lots of things. I was born in Newark, I think. I was raised in an orphanage. I went to high school. I played linebacker. I went to Vietnam as a marine. I came back. And then boom. I am in California and I don't know what's going on."

"Yes, that is how we got here too. Life moves so quickly, yes? We were born in Seoul, Korea, raised, moved to California, boom. Now we see our daughter in Phoenix."

On the plane back to Newark, Remo heard people talking about the great Bayonne disaster. They said no one knew whether to rebuild the city or scrap it entirely and use it and Jersey City as expanded parking lots for New York.

Someone said it was a terrorist act. Another said they didn't know which terrorist group had done it because a half-dozen had taken credit for it.

"Of course we'll blow them out of the world," said Remo. "Crazy bastards, admitting something like that, admitting doing something like that to America. They'll never get away with it."

"They all do," said another passenger.

"I don't believe it. You're lying."

Remo wanted to punch the passenger in the mouth. Someone else behind him was saying how America deserved it.

The first thing Remo did when he got to Newark was go into a bar that had a television set. The disaster in Bayonne was a major news story and announcers were breaking into every program for it.

Remo ordered a whiskey and a beer. Since he had a suit-case full of cash, he ordered the best brand, the one he savored for special occasions. When he lifted the glass the fumes almost made him throw up. He put it back down. He loved that whiskey. Why was his body revolted by it?

And then the vision was talking to him again, about how a body set on the road to perfection rejected all that did not enhance it. Remo found himself ordering rice and water.

The bartender said he didn't serve rice and water and that Remo should shut up and finish his drink or get out of there. The bartender did not bother Remo long because he had a great deal of difficulty prying a whiskey shot glass out of his left nostril.

Remo still didn't know how he had done that, but he was glad he had.

He got control of the television knob and turned it to the station which concentrated on the disaster. A panel of television newscasters was discussing the disaster. And Remo couldn't believe what he heard.

Of the five newsmen, four were talking about what America had done to deserve losing a city. America had sent military advisers into South America. Therefore, because American soldiers fought guerrillas it was only logical that an American city might be destroyed with entire families buried under oil.

America supplied arms to Israel. America supplied arms to Arab governments. Therefore, anyone who didn't like Israel or those governments had a right to kill any American anywhere. Arab experts were brought in. They decried violence against Arabs in America on the one hand, but on the other they told the American viewing audience to expect more of the same evil violence until it provided a more evenhanded approach to the Middle East.

Then there was a discussion of how America should change its foreign policy to avoid such incidents in the future. The newscasters then talked about themselves, saying they knew they might face unpopularity because they were bearers of bad news.

"Bearers of bad news—they *are* the bad news," said Remo. "Do the networks know about those guys?"

"Know about them? They employ them. Those guys make seven figures apiece," said a man nursing a beer.

"A million dollars a year to trash America?"

"If the agent is doing his job."

"Aren't they reporters? I didn't think newsmen made that much money. I remember reporters from the Newark *Evening News*. They didn't make that much."

"Hey, buddy," said the barfly in the Newark airport lounge. "Newark *Evening News* has been dead for years. Where you been?"

There were two notes of relief in the abysmal picture coming from the television screen. The President got on to announce emergency aid to the victims, and then he said while there were many groups taking credit for this act of horror, it was still an act of horror. And his message was simply this:

"They may get away with it today. They may get away with it tomorrow. But there will be a day of reckoning, as surely as the sun rises and justice beats in the hearts of Americans."

As soon as the President was off the air, the television reporters came back on to discuss how irresponsible he was, and what little likelihood there was of success, and besides, one man's terrorist was another man's freedom fighter.

But one commentator, his red hair neatly parted, a cowlick in the back, with precise metal-rimmed glasses and a bow tie, disagreed.

"No. Freedom fighters and terrorists are not the same thing, and it is not just a point of view, any more than saying a surgeon and Jack the Ripper are the same thing because they both use a knife. When the purpose is to harm innocent civilians, then you are a terrorist. It's that simple."

Remo found himself applauding. The whole bar was applauding. Black and white. An announcer immediately stated these were the private views of the commentator and not those of the network and immediately put on someone else with a balancing view. The balancing view was that until all hunger and all injustice everywhere was overcome, Americans should expect with a certain justification to be kidnapped, bombed, burned, drowned in oil, and shot in their sleep.

This man was a professor of international relations. His name was Waldo Hunnicut. He had once been an ambassador to an Arab country where he used his ambassadorship to attack America's policy in the Middle East, so therefore, according to the announcer, he spoke from a respected position.

Remo threw the beer glass at the face of Hunnicut and the bar exploded in applause. The television just exploded.

'How can these guys get away with that crap?" he asked.

"What can you do? They're all like that on television. You don't have a choice," said the man next to Remo.

The vision now told Remo that everything changed but Sinanju.

"No," said Remo to the vision. "I love my country."

To this the vision got quite angry, said it had given the best years of its life to Remo and Remo was unappreciative, ungrateful, and totally undeserving of all that the vision had given him.

"What have you given me?"

"More than I should," came back the voice, and then the vision wasn't talking to him anymore. The vision was insulted.

Remo didn't know how one insulted a vision. But then

again, he never had a vision before. He was close to where he was raised, close to the orphanage in Newark.

He took a cab there, and was surprised to see no white people around. He had remembered a mix of everyone, but now there was no mix.

"How long has Newark been black?" asked Remo.

"Where you been, boy?" asked the black driver.

"Away."

"Then let me give you some friendly advice. And I do mean friendly. You don't want your ass around here too long."

"I'll be all right," said Remo. How did he know he would be all right? He didn't have a gun. Yet he knew he wasn't in danger, no matter who came after him.

He smelled the odor of garlic and onions, felt the nauseating oily mixture move out across his pores. Somehow he knew he was now able to hold on, perhaps even get better.

The orphanage was gone. The block was gone. The neighborhood was gone. It was as though someone had bombed it.

Windows were smashed. Pipes were left hanging out of buildings where someone had tried to remove them. Graffiti littered the walls. Rats and garbage covered alleys.

Four black toughs ambled up to him, all wearing jackets indicating they were from some organization called the Righteous Skulls. They demanded tribute from him for standing on their sidewalk. They wanted to know what was in the briefcase.

Remo did not attempt to reach a dialogue of understanding. He slapped the teeth out of the one closest to him, sending the slash of white across the ebony countenance, sailing like Chiclets clattering lightly across the sidewalk. The smile was gone.

"I don't like to be threatened," said Remo.

Three swore they weren't threatening, and the fourth was nodding as he looked for his teeth. He had heard they could be replaced by modern medicine.

"What happened to the orphanage here?"

"Gone, man, can't you see?"

"And Sister Mary Elizabeth. Any of you heard of her? Or Coach Walsh at Weequaic High School? Any of you heard of them?"

They hadn't.

"Okay. Sorry about the teeth. I didn't know I hit that hard," said Remo, opening the suitcase and giving each young hood a hundred dollars.

"That's a lot of bread there, man. You'd better watch out. You want some muscle to wear?"

"I don't need muscles," said Remo. Now, that was absurd. Of course he needed his muscles. But then there was the vision again telling him muscles weren't man's strength. It was his mind that made power.

"I thought you weren't talking to me," Remo said to the vision. The toughs stared at the crazy man talking to himself.

"I want to keep you alive, not company," said the vision. And then the vision went on about bad habits, a lifetime of bad habits Remo had acquired growing up with whites.

Whites, thought Remo. That was funny, he could have sworn he was white.

He did not know it, but he was heading for the one place that might force Harold W. Smith to disband the organization, the one place he had always avoided when he had his full memory. If Harold W. Smith had known about Remo's direction, he might have taken the little cyanide capsule he always carried with him, and before swallowing it, put all the organization's vast computer network into self-destruct. Because Remo, without a memory, was going to open up the secret of his own murder.

13

Harold W. Smith, who dealt with disasters daily, had a formula. He would have been dead by now if he didn't know how to handle them, and the organization would have collapsed in the first week.

The secret to handling a disaster was not to run from it or wildly run to it. The way to handle the enormity was to first number it. A number gave a sense of proportion. If you were going to die in a week, that was a tragedy. But if the entire world was going to be destroyed in an afternoon, that was a greater tragedy.

Harold W. Smith had placed the President's viability as number one, just because he had such power under his control. But the danger of the amnesia formula was a close second. An entire city was gone, undoubtedly because of the Dolomos and the formula. The scientific reports got worse every day, it seemed. Sometimes the formula for some strange reason would lose power. Other times it would increase in potency.

And then came Remo, and the destruction of the organization if he, and it, should be compromised. The question that presented itself to Harold W. Smith at this time was that if the country were in danger of being destroyed, what difference would it make if the knowledge of its secret organization were exposed? Wouldn't it be better for Smith to stay alive and help?

It was a time to search his own motives. The desire to live was always there, no matter how old a person got. If he and the organization were gone, then the idea that a constitutional democracy could work would still exist. The President could always surrender to the Dolomos to buy time. But he could not surrender the idea of a constitutional democracy. If that were gone, it would be gone forever. There would be calls for a police state when things got too chaotic, a return to the force employed by Remo and Chiun, but this time openly.

It was a hard decision, but Harold W. Smith was used to making hard decisions. If they were compromised, he decided, he would still take his own life and destroy his computer network, which made the organization.

As he was labeling the disasters, it struck him that if Remo remembered the phone number, what else did he remember? Did he remember being framed so that he could be publicly executed, thus removing his fingerprints from any files anywhere, removing the idea of the man? Did he remember getting that plastic surgery on his face? Did he remember he was once a Newark cop? And if he were to return to his old precinct, would anyone recognize a dead man?

What if they began to look into a state execution that failed? And would this dead man with the new face be recognized in hundreds of places where he had operated in his extraordinary manner? The whole disaster was ready to go the moment Remo returned to where he used to work. If he returned there. Only Chiun might know what Remo's mind and body would do now. Smith had to find out. He went to the small room provided for him in the White House.

Smith never knew when Chiun slept. He never slept at the same hour, and he had seen him and Remo stay awake for longer periods than the human mind was supposed to be able to tolerate.

He knocked on Chiun's door.

"Is it time?"

"No, Master of Sinanju. I would like to speak to you."

"Enter."

Chiun sat in a lotus position in dark gray robes, his long fingernails concealed under the folds of the cloth.

"May I sit down?"

"An emperor need not ask," said Chiun.

"I want to know how much of Remo's training is in his mind."

"O gracious one, you have never asked about training in Remo before. Is something wrong?"

"You had said he was not up to peak."

"He is more than adequate for the minor tasks he has been assigned."

"I am curious," said Smith. He sat down. "If, as you say, I am an emperor, then I show an emperor's curiosity in my most valued servant, the great Master of Sinanju."

"The President hasn't died by accident?" asked Chiun, suddenly horrified.

"No," said Smith. "I wish to know how much training is in the mind."

"It is all in the mind," said Chiun.

"Then if a substance reaches the brain, Remo could forget everything."

"I did not say his training was in the brain."

"You said mind."

"The brain is part of the mind. But the mind is what the body knows and remembers, the mind is the receptacle for the person, and the person is beyond it. Even the first breath of an infant is the mind."

"What are you saying?"

"I couldn't be clearer," said Chiun.

"Suppose Remo were to succumb to this potion we are seeking that takes away memory. How much of your training would remain?"

"That which is not in the brain, but in the mind is the receptacle for what is him. Do you understand?" said Chiun. He had spoken slowly so Smith could not miss the obvious.

"No. Let me be more specific. Before you started to train Remo, he was a policeman in Newark, New Jersey. Might he forget that? What would he remember?"

"He would remember everything he needs, but he would not know all he remembers," said Chiun. "Now, is it time for you to become rightful emperor, and for Sinanju to embark publicly upon your glory?''

"No. Not yet. Is there any chance that Remo would return to his old neighborhood if he were afflicted with this memory loss?''

"That depends upon what neighborhood he was raised in.''

"Why?''

"Because some meridians of the universe affect his mind more strongly than others. He is Sinanju.''

"Newark, New Jersey.''

"The one afterward is the state, yes?''

"New Jersey is the state.''

"And he was a form of constabulary there?''

"Yes, he was a policeman. Would that matter?''

"Everything matters," said Chiun, which was not a lie. But he was counting on Smith hearing it wrong, like most Westerners heard things wrong.

Everything did matter. But that Remo had been a policeman in this Newark, New Jersey, did not matter to his mind at all. Smith had told Chiun all he had to for Chiun to know what was really going on.

And what Chiun knew, and Smith did not, was that the world was always filled with emperors and tyrants and kings and what the Americans called presidents. They were everywhere. But there was only one Remo. And he was Chiun's. And Chiun would never let him go.

Captain Edwin Polishuk was two weeks away from retirement, and counting the days and minutes as he had once counted the years and months and days and minutes, when a nightmare happened to him. It happened when he went into Tullio's, a restaurant-bar that featured extra-thick roast-beef sandwiches. Captain Polishuk not only never paid his bill, but the owner left him a tip.

The owner left the tip in a white envelope every week as he had been doing since Polishuk had taken over the precinct. Then Captain Polishuk would normally move on to other establishments in his precinct and at the end of the day meet his own payroll to his own men who did his special favors. Perhaps it was really disguised self-hatred, but Captain Ed Polishuk took enormous pleasure in turning young police recruits into bagmen like himself.

The honest cops were given the worst assignments. Polishuk was as notorious in Newark, New Jersey, as he was safe. Ed Polishuk knew where to spread the money, and if he didn't, he always managed to buy the right information to keep himself safe. He had been up on charges three times and gotten off three times, despite the roaring anger of the mayor and half the City Council. Ed Polishuk was the cop no one could get.

But on this Friday, with the roast beef dripping rich brown gravy on the crisp white Italian bread, he was to pay for it all. He didn't even get a chance to take the first bite.

"Ed? Is that you? Ed?"

A young man in his late twenties, thirty at most, with thick wrists, was holding back Polishuk's hands. There were few things more enjoyable in the world than Tullio's roast beef.

"My name is Captain Polishuk."

"Yeah. Ed. Ed. That's you. Hey, you shouldn't be eating at Tullio's. It's a numbers drop. They're going to raid it next week. No. Not next week. I got trouble with time, Ed. Is that really you? I can't believe it. You put on thirty pounds. Your face is sagging, but that's you, Ed Polishuk."

"Son, I don't know who you are, but if you don't let go of my hands, I'm going to put you through the wall."

"You can't do that. Your arteries are clogged. You can't move well enough."

Ed Polishuk took his two hundred and thirty pounds of muscle and flesh and yanked down his hands.

They didn't yank. The sandwich went into his lap, but his hands didn't yank. For all practical purposes he had done a chin-up on someone's outstretched hands across a table, and only Ed Polishuk's shoulders moved. They moved with great strain. He had wrenched them.

"Who are you?" asked Captain Polishuk.

"Ed. We were on the same beat. Remember? We walked. Foot patrolmen. You always called me 'Straighto Dum Dum.'"

"I called a lot of guys 'Straighto Dum Dum,'" said Polishuk.

"Yeah, but remember the psych tests everyone was taking and I scored a 'compulsive patriot' or something? Remember that? You said you would have thought Dum Dum would have been the best in the country. I wouldn't even take a free pack of cigarettes."

Ed Polishuk looked at the guy in front of him. There was something about the face he remembered. The dark eyes and high cheekbones reminded him of someone. But the rest of the face was that of a stranger.

"I think I remember you. I think I do."

"Remo. Remo Williams."

"Right. Yeah. I think. Right. Remo." And then Ed Polishuk jumped back in his seat.

"Remo, you're dead," he said. "And what happened to your face? You got a different kind of a nose and mouth. You're dead, Remo. No, you're not dead. You're not Remo."

"Remember the newsstand you tried to shake down for cigarettes and I threatened to report you, Ed?"

"The dumb-dumbest straighto. Remo. Remo Williams," yelled Polishuk. And everyone in the bar and grill turned to look. Ed Polishuk hushed his voice.

"What the hell has happened to you, Remo?"

"I don't know. Crazy things. I see this old Oriental in front of me. I speak Korean fluently. I can do things with my body like you wouldn't believe. And you, Ed, you're twenty years older."

"And you're not. That's the strange part."

"I know."

"Remo," whispered Polishuk, "you died about twenty years ago."

Remo let go of Polishuk's wrists. He pinched his own arm. He felt it. He knew even more certainly in his breath that he was alive.

"I'm not dead, Ed."

"I can see that. I see that. Something's going on here."

"What?"

"I don't know, Remo. I don't know. I remember they electrocuted you. You shot some punk. I thought: Serves him right for being such a straighto. It doesn't pay to be straight, Remo. You never learned that lesson."

"I don't know what I learned. Have you ever heard of Sinanju?"

"No. But let's get out of here. Hey, you lost weight. And you look younger. You look friggin' younger. How did you do it?"

"I don't know."

"You were electrocuted, you know. Do you remember the trial? It was," said Ed, lowering his voice, "the niggers. They run everything now. Newark's gone to hell. Everything's for sale. Niggers."

"But you were always for sale, Ed. What do you mean, Negroes? You were always for sale. What's that fat envelope in your pocket? So it's not cigarettes now. It's cash."

"I'm trying to be friendly. I forgot you can't be friendly with a dum dum. So lay off. Niggers steal. I, on the other hand, protect my future retirement. It don't do no good to be honest. What for? For niggers?"

"You weren't even honest when Newark was mostly white."

"So, look at you, Remo. Look at you. You got shanghaied and railroaded. I knew you didn't shoot that guy in the alley. But they had witnesses up the kazoo. And then the pressure from above. That's what everyone said. The pressure from above. They had to show a white cop could be electrocuted for shooting a black. That's what they had to show."

"How do you know I didn't do it?"

"Because you never used your gun against regulations. You were impossible as a buddy. I can't believe how young you look. You're dead. I know you're dead."

Outside on the street, Remo picked up a can from the gutter.

"If I'm dead, how can I do this?" asked Remo, crushing the can.

"Hey, cans are light nowadays. Anyone can crush cans, Remo."

Remo opened his hand and showed Ed Polishuk a small shining ball.

"You fused the damned thing."

"I know. I can do that. I found it out on the plane when I tried to fit an ashtray back into its holder. That's nothing. You know the kind of money I could make throwing baseballs for a living?"

In an alley, Remo picked up a rock and threw it at a square marked off for stickball. The rock crunched into the softer red brick like an explosion, making a hole through the wall into a warehouse. They knew it was a warehouse because they saw men looking around inside, startled. The hole was big enough.

"Sheeet," said Captain Ed Polishuk. "Where did you learn that? Where have you been?"

"I think Sinanju," said Remo.

"Where's that?"

"I don't know, but I come from there too. Now, how can that be?"

Ed Polishuk told his desk sergeant that he would be busy for the rest of the afternoon. He did not make his normal pickups, partly out of shock but partly because he suspected that indeed this was crazy Straighto Remo Williams, and he would turn in the entire bag route, from whorehouses to bookie joints.

So this day Ed Polishuk was not going to let him out of his sight. In his office, he sent requests to the public-relations division for all newspaper clippings on the police force during the years following Remo's execution.

"I don't remember those," said Remo.

"Of course you don't. You were dead."

Remo read the comments about himself. The one that

touched him most was from Sister Mary Elizabeth, who remembered Remo as "a good boy."

He saw that he maintained that he was innocent until the end. But he didn't remember the trial. Was there something that should make his memory stop on one night? Because the last thing he remembered was looking up at the stars. And Polishuk was with him. Patrolman Ed Polishuk was with him.

"I remember thinking I was a star as I looked up. Something really crazy about eternity and who I was," said Remo.

"You were always crazy, but not like this," said Polishuk. "You had no feel for poetry, music, taking a little bit of the action which a patrolman deserves on his salary. Nothing."

"Now, why should my memory end there? Do you see that?"

"What?"

"That Oriental guy. He's speaking Korean."

"Remo, you're really crazy."

"Maybe," said Remo.

"You returned to that one night," said the Oriental in the language Remo now knew, "because that was the one night you understood, if ever so briefly, who you were, and that was who you were going to be."

And then the name Shiva came to Remo. He kept hearing how Shiva was the destroyer of worlds, and that one had to die to live as something else. Captain Ed Polishuk thought it sounded like some born-again-Christian group. He also did some detective work for Remo, who wouldn't leave his office.

Sinanju was a town in North Korea on the West Korea Bay. Historically it had a lot to do with the courts of Europe and the Mediterranean and Asia for some reason. They provided advisers of some sort to kings. Remo couldn't remember who or what he would advise. He didn't know how to advise anyone. Yet Sinanju somehow seemed just as strong in him as the orphanage.

Shiva, as it turned out, was some Asian god. So that left

him nowhere. But there was something Captain Ed Polishuk could do to help them all get to the bottom of this. He could prove once and for all to the satisfaction of anyone, especially the FBI and the news media which he was ready to call in, that Remo Williams indeed was the same Remo Williams who had been electrocuted in Trenton State Prison. If he could do that, then both the glare of publicity and the good work of the FBI would find out what kind of phony execution went on in Trenton State Prison.

"How are you going to do that?"

"We're cops, right?"

"I thought so," said Remo.

"Then it's simple. Give me your fingerprints. Do you remember how? Roll the pads over the ink. You can do it with stamp-pad ink," said Polishuk, pushing a white piece of paper and a pad across his desk. Then he phoned headquarters to get fingerprints.

"I want the fingerprints of Patrolman Remo Williams."

"We ain't got no Williams, Remo, Captain," said the fingerprints clerk.

"He'd dead," said Captain Polishuk.

"What do you want with a dead man's prints?"

"I want 'em," said Polishuk.

The fingerprints clerk took twenty minutes to find the card. It was from the days when people actually typed out names and identification on typewriters and then stored them on cards, way before computers. Someone had actually written the information in ink. There was no way you could press keys and find this information. It was even dusty.

A patrolman delivered the fingerprints from main headquarters to Polishuk's precinct. Polishuk took them himself at the door, then shut it behind him. He laid them out on his desk and then had Remo make his own print in front of him with the stamp-pad ink on paper.

Captain Polishuk examined the swirls and marks, even the little cut on the forefinger.

"Holy shit. It is you, Remo. It is. It's you."

"Call the press?"

"Call everyone. Somebody somewhere has really pulled a fast one on this country, and you too, Remo. Welcome back, I guess."

"Yeah, I guess," said Remo.

In the White House no one was certain what had gone wrong at Harbor Island, but it had gone wrong in the worst possible way.

The military adviser had hit the mainland shore south of the hotels, with the scientists safely behind them. They carried M-16 automatic rifles and hand grenades and were told that if they had any difficulty, an aircraft carrier would supply fighter bomber support. Their mission was first to capture two American fugitives, then secure permanently a liquid. The formula for it, the scientists would identify.

The advisers sweated heavily in the Bermuda sun, almost suffocating in their waterproof rubber suits. Their air had to pass through three filters before it reached their mouths. They moved slowly, like space walkers.

They secured the main harbor beach and the hotels by 0900. By 1200 they had seized the humpback ridge central to the island and were moving on the resort said to contain the Dolomos.

Each step of the way was reported. The last told the dismal tale.

Half-nude girls shouting "All power to the positives" ran laughing at them. They certainly didn't seem dangerous. The only weapons they had were knitting needles in their hair, and the men weren't looking at their hair.

Then, as if on signal, they all slipped the harmless needles into the rubber suits. No one was reported injured in the invading party, but then, no one bothered to report anything after that. The aircraft carrier made several quick overflights but saw no shooting. There was nothing.

"The needles contained the solution," said Smith. "That's obvious."

"You know the power these cult leaders exercise over their followers is enormous," said the President. "To think girls would get undressed and go out to injure someone just for a spiritual leader. A leader who is a damned fraud, Smith. A fraud. No, we will not give in to him. Now, I know you want to save Chiun for me if you have to. I can live with that. But can we work out something to send him after the Dolomos? Armed soliders don't even seem to work. We're lost, Smith. You have got to come up with something."

"Mr. President," said Smith, taking a small thumbnail-sized box from his gray vest. "I have saved this pill for myself. As you know, if the organization is compromised, I have vowed to destroy the system and take my own life. This I intend to do. There can be no evidence left that our nation once admitted the Constitution could not work on its own."

"I am aware of that," said the President.

"The pill is strong enough to kill twenty men instantly. I can cut it in two."

"You mean you are trusting me to take it on my own if my memory fails? There's a problem there, Smith. I won't remember."

"No. You won't have to. Write me a note in your own hand reminding me to give you your pill. Address it to me on your stationery. You will in all likelihood not remember what this is all about if the Dolomos get to you with their solution. And if they get to me too, then the note will take care of it."

"You'll give me the pill then?"

"Yes," said Smith. He felt his stomach tighten.

"I thought you couldn't kill me. That's why you had to use the older one, the Oriental."

"I couldn't shoot you. This is different."

The President called for White House stationery and a pen. Then he dismissed the secretary who brought it.

" 'Dear Harold,' " said Harold W. Smith as the President wrote on the stationery.

" 'Please do not forget to give me my pill. I always seem

to forget it lately and I do need it so much. Thanks.' And then sign it.''

"Here you are. May I see what it looks like?"

"Better not. You'll think about it too much."

"How do you know?"

"I made the mistake of looking at it once. It sits there in my mind like my grave, sir."

"Well, now, get the Oriental after them. Tell him he has total freedom."

"He always does, sir," said Smith, taking the paper and folding it carefully before he put it in his jacket pocket.

Smith was back in fifteen minutes.

"Sir. I have bad news."

"Not him. He can't fail. He does things no one else can do."

"I don't think he's failed in that way, sir. Three hours ago he left. Someone, I think it may have been a secretary, reported that he mentioned something about New Jersey. He wanted to see New Jersey. He has done this only once before, when the treasure of his ancestral house disappeared."

"Promise him we'll double that treasure."

"That's how I got him back the first time. I don't know why he has left this time."

"We're hostage. The whole nation is hostage. We've lost."

"As of now, sir."

"We have lost to two petty swindlers. We have been brought to our knees."

"That's the right place to rise from, sir."

"Do you have any suggestions?"

"Cut off all access to Harbor Island, now the nation of Alarkin. Make sure no one leaves by ship. It isn't big enough for airplanes. Quarantine the place."

"Like the plague," said the President of the United States.

"I think I know where Chiun went. We just might luck out."

"How?"

"They are strange creatures, the two of them," said Smith.

Remo prepared himself for facing the television cameras. So did Captain Polishuk. He had the sample of Remo's old fingerprints and the new ones. He would take Remo's prints again when the television crews arrived and demonstrate both were the same. Then Remo would face the cameras and tell his story.

"But look, don't be crazy. Don't mention you remember me trying to shake down someone for a pack of cigarettes, okay, Remo?"

Remo nodded.

Polishuk phoned the FBI office in Newark.

"Look, I got a crazy thing here. A guy who was supposed to have been executed just walked into my office. And no, he didn't escape from jail. He didn't escape from execution. He was executed. Everyone swore to it, right down to the coroner. I want you to look into it. All right? Oh, by the way, I may say something to a few reporters and such. I'll send over the prints now," said Polishuk, and hung up.

"They got their own prints in Washington. We'll just send him a set of your new ones."

The captain had the proper ink, glass, and roller brought up to his office. Remo gave him his right hand. He felt like a criminal doing this. He could feel the ink fill his pores. Strange that he could feel such things, but then, everything was strange. All he remembered from the first time was that the ink felt oily. But now every ridge and pore had its own sense.

Captain Polishuk gave Remo a cloth to clean his hands, but he dropped his mouth and the cloth in amazement. Remo's hands were cleaning themselves. It was as though the skin was alive and collecting the black ink into a stream where it just poured off the fingers.

"Better than cloth. Cloth rubs things into the skin," said Remo.

Before the television reporters arrived, the desk sergeant

said there was a crazy old gook on his way up to see the captain. He had been asking around about someone who sounded like Remo, and the desk sergeant had sent him up.

When the door opened Polishuk saw a frail, old-looking Oriental with wisps of hair and parchment-frail skin.

"I'm busy," he said.

"No," said Remo. "The vision."

"I have come for you," said Chiun. "I told you I would never leave you."

"Ed, how can you see the vision?"

"He's no vision," said Polishuk.

"What's your name?"

"What do you remember last?"

"The star."

"Of course," said Chiun. "Come with me. You are mine forever."

"I don't belong to anyone," said Remo.

"You belong to who you are. That is why you will come with me."

"Hey, hold on," said Polishuk. "I got television reporters coming. He's mine."

And when Chiun saw the grotesquely fat, meat-smelling man touch Remo's arm, and when he heard the man say such a sacrilege about Remo, who must be saved, he destroyed the man there in the office, breaking him in two, leaving him dead and done with.

"You killed Ed Polishuk," said Remo.

"Why do you always bother to learn their names?" asked Chiun, and Remo knew he was home. He didn't know who Emperor Smith was or why they had to make amends. He knew there was something he belonged to and that belonged to him, and it was happening now. He left the station house with absolutely no regrets.

The television crew arrived to find Captain Polishuk in a bundle, his hands having smeared a great deal of ink in his last desperate moments.

The investigation would show two things. One, he varied from his normal routine that afternoon to lock himself in his office with a younger man. Second, he appeared to be

crazed because he ordered old prints of a dead buddy to be
brought to him.

At the FBI office, the prints arrived by messenger after
Captain Polishuk was dead.

A report was filed, but the word came back: Polishuk's
discovery of a dead man's prints was not so unusual in the
last twenty years. Similar prints had been discovered
elsewhere, but every time the case was investigated, it was
shown the real holder of the prints was dead and buried
many years ago.

Unless one was a practicing Christian, one had to admit
the dead did not rise again.

14

Beatrice Dolomo woke up to see an American aircraft carrier off the eastern side of her island, along with American patrol boats spitting white foam trails behind them, their guns trained on her island and on her.

This was too much. Especially when international terrorists had dared to take credit for obliterating Bayonne, New Jersey.

"We are surrounded, isolated, and ignored. Rubin, I have come to a conclusion," said Beatrice in the main house of Home Island Lodge, waiting for her breakfast of fried grouper and bananas.

Rubin coughed out the smoke of his first cigarette of the day. It was noon. He had just woken up and taken the cotton out of his ears. He needed the cotton here because the place was filled with Powies now, and one of the ways they showed they had overcome their negativity was by greeting the sun. Since many of them had paid for the course that got them away from "lazy body syndrome," none of them wanted to show they hadn't overcome that negativity.

Which left Rubin with an island full of chirpy six-A.M. lunatics.

Cotton out, phlegm making its way around his lungs, Rubin listened to Beatrice.

"Rubin, I have come to the decision that we are not taking it anymore."

Rubin nodded. The phlegm came out like a tidal wave. Beatrice turned away in disgust.

"No more nice guys for us. Our only problem is that we've been too soft."

"Dearest dove," said Rubin, "I guarantee we will not be ignored after today."

"Don't play softy."

"You'll be happy, dear."

"Can you imagine an entire city destroyed and not a word about the persecution of our beliefs, about poor Kathy Bowen, about us, about me? Me, Rubin. Not a word about me."

"By tomorrow there won't be a household in America unaware of how you have been mistreated."

"Television?"

"I promise."

"A chance to trash that bum President who won't make a deal?"

"You'll have help."

"You're not just getting my hopes up, are you?"

"The Warriors of Zor are ready."

"And I'm the queen."

"Right," said Rubin.

"But that doesn't make you king."

"Right, dear."

"Don't fail me, Rubin," said Beatrice. "Don't fail our marriage."

"You said you wanted us to be heard. You didn't say sex, dear," said Rubin, worried. He looked at his watch. His plan was beginning. He walked down to Pink Beach with his commanders, one of whom fortunately happened to be an engineer.

The beach had a faint pink tinge because of the crushed red coral mingled with the sand. It was most noticeable as the sun broke, coming up from the European side of the world, making the Caribbean blue into a delicate pastel mirror.

A few Bahamians had private homes on the beach. These had been commandeered by his Powies. A rumor had gone around among them that the decripit middle-aged man with the smoker's hack was Rubin Dolomo himself, which caused some of those who had purchased the "Be Free of Nicotine" course to feel some doubts. This was quickly squashed by the informers, who reported the doubters to the counselors.

Ordinarily the counselors would work out the negative feelings of Powies, but now there was an easier way than tracing back through one's life to find where the negativity deposits were. Several strong men threw those in need of retraining into a small cabin with bars and beat them until they apologized for thinking such thoughts.

The cabin was hot, and in the Caribbean sun it smelled rancid. Even without the beatings the Powies who dared think such seditious thoughts would have changed their minds about the man with the cigarette cough.

Rubin asked the engineer if he thought Pink Beach would do for the landing.

"It depends how fast they'll be going. You might be able to bring it in. But what about them?" asked the engineer, nodding to the patrol boats cruising on the Atlantic side of Harbor Island. Above them Navy tomcat fighters flew close formations, letting the island know that whenever they wished they could bomb and strike, but that they chose not to do so at this moment.

This little island was in the palm of the American Navy and was being reminded of it constantly. Rubin had shrewdly ordered more consciousness sessions to remind Powies the aircraft were only an illusion of power. They themselves, in themselves, were the real power. They had to have a lot of sessions because Navy jets breaking the sound barrier every twenty minutes were hard to call an illusion.

"Don't worry about the planes or the ships or the guns. They won't matter."

"I hope you're right," said the engineer, who had been having headaches until he joined Poweressence and had learned that keeping his eyes closed a half-hour a day while concentrating on his power source would relieve him of the pain. His own doctor had said this was a standard way of relieving some minor forms of headaches. But ever since he had joined, he felt better about everything, especially when counselors would listen to his problems and help him trace them, reminding him that he was good in himself.

Like a true Powie he refused to listen to those who said it was just amateur therapy and group mind control.

It was the one thing in his life that seemed free of everything, free of all the constraints of his entire life. But looking now at the two-mile strip of beach and the naval power all around them, he had doubts whether the man who had made him a Warrior of Zor could pull it off. Even this man, this great mind in a poor frail body hacking up the results of four packs a day of unfiltered cigarettes, could not make the beach larger, or the U.S. Navy disappear.

"Don't worry," said Rubin. "It'll work. It'll work like it's always worked. It works all the time. That's not the problem."

"If that's not the problem, what is?"

"What I'm going to have to do if it doesn't."

The engineer shuddered. No matter how frail this man looked, he was a genius of organization. Whether it came from his thoughts about planets the engineer did not know. But the man understood what great generals knew about reinforcing and contingency plans. What bothered him was that there was nothing that semed to bother Rubin Dolomo, since he came out from behind the screen and told the engineer that now he and other Warriors of Zor could know his true identity.

He kept telling himself that his fear was the negative voice from the past. He saw that his partner, too, was trying to get in contact with his positive self.

Perhaps because he had been a classics scholar, Robert Kranz felt especially nervous this day. Athens, Greece, had once been the center of Western intellectual thought. But that was twenty-five hundred years ago.

Now it was home to revolutionary groups and had an airport that was, to hijackers, what an engraved invitation was to a dinner guest.

Robert Kranz and his fellow warrior in the cause of
Poweressence had a choice of either bringing the weapons
on board the plane and stashing them, or buying them
outside the open gate from a dissident group of Pales-
tinians who had seized the concession from the Red Army
Brigades of Revolution.

More hijackings had originated in Athens, the Arab
assured Kranz and his companion, than any other airport
in the world.

"And for good reason. Not only do they not care,
you've got people in power here who hate America. And
who hijacks planes? The British? The Israelis? The
French? No. So why should they change things? My
friend, you have come to the right place."

"I don't know," said Robert Kranz. "I couldn't bring
my weapons in on an American plane so I had to buy them
here in Athens. I just don't know if I should pay premium
price at the airport sale."

The Arab pulled Robert Kranz closer to him so the noise
from the jet engines would not drown out what he was
about to say. They were just outside the perimeter gate,
which was a loose connection of links that could be walked
through.

"Friend," said the Arab. "You look like a smart boy.
You wouldn't come here if you didn't know what you were
doing. Right?"

"Actually, we were sent," said Robert. His partner still
had his eyes closed, working on his fear.

"Smart people. They know the business. If you're going
to do your business, Athens is the place to do it. Now you
can put your bombs and guns in a valise, wrap them up in
fiberglass, and walk right through their metal detectors.
You could make them look like other things."

"We had thought of that," said Robert.

"Or you could have your friend here walk through the
gate and give some ground-crew guy a hundred dollars and
maybe the weapons will be left where you want them. And
maybe not. Maybe he'll take your money and keep your
weapons and sell them again."

"That's possible," said Robert.

"But with me you have a guaranteed weapons placement you can count on. I take credit cards. If the weapons aren't there, you can cancel payment."

Robert thought about that for a moment. But he remembered what Mr. Dolomo said:

"In an operation like this, the more people involved, the more chances for it not to work. Get your guns and grenades there, but test them. Test them anywhere you won't get arrested, but test them. There are certain places on the plane where you can stash them. Here is a list drawn up by our engineer."

Robert looked at the list. He looked at the Arab. He decided against letting the Arab place the weapons.

"I'll pay cash, but I've got to have weapons that work."

"Actually they don't have to work, you know. The pilot only has to think they work."

So that was why Mr. Dolomo had told him where to fire the guns so the plane would not be disabled in flight, thought Robert. He was not to kill anyone, but to make the crew think they were capable of killing someone.

"I want real working weapons."

"That'll cost more. But don't be crazy. Don't take a real hand grenade. Those things can go off and take down the whole plane with you. You really want the dummy in a grenade. I can give you the American pin-pull and lever-release or the popular Russian. I don't like the Russian myself, because once you pull the pin it really is all over. It reflects their national character. On the other hand, with the American grenade you can even put the pin back. I would go American for your grenade," said the Arab.

"American for the grenade, without the powder in it," said Robert. He tried to keep his stomach from jumping around by remembering a positive part of his body that would put it all back into calm control. It wasn't working. But brilliant Mr. Dolomo had an answer for that too. In his wisdom he had said:

"Never mind that shit, Robert. Just get on board the

plane with the weapons. It'll work fine. If you're scared, to hell with it.''

The Arab had a nice assortment of handguns and field guns.

"There is nothing like the Kalishnikov rifle, except in airplane aisles the barrel can get in the way. And a passenger can grab it, although I must say, if you are dealing with American passengers you often have help. We had a fine hijacking to Beirut recently where an American actually reminded one of us that we had forgotten a gun in the lavatory. You just can't beat that in passenger cooperation.''

"You're talking pistols," said Robert.

"I definitely am," said the Arab. "And let me recommend a heavy butt. You don't want to go onto an aircraft with a flimsy butt that can only be used to hold. You want heft because you are going to have to be beating people over their heads with it. It's your crowd control.''

"We already knew that.''

"So you've done this before?''

"No. First time.''

"Well then, you know you need at least two guns apiece, one for the belt and another for the hand. You can always use one in each hand. You've got to appear somewhat hysterical so they will think you're really going to go through with any insane thing, like killing yourselves too.''

"But you see, we will if we have to," said Robert, who, after he had paid an exorbitant price for the guns and dummy grenades, offered to clean a bit of dirt from the salesman's hand with a cotton swab that he held in a rubber glove. The Arab gun salesman never looked happier as Robert Kranz took back the money for Dr. Dolomo, who had explained that they were all at war and that money was the main ingredient for that war.

As ordered, Robert dropped the swab away from himself and carefully removed the rubber glove. Then with four pistols and an American grenade apiece, Robert and the other Powie, who was still working on his fear, went into the terminal and bought tickets for a flight filled with American passengers headed back to an American airport. According to plan, they returned to the outside perimeter and walked through an open spot in the linked fence.

The biggest danger was getting run over by one of the planes taking off. Once they found their plane, however, Athens security, already scorched by the world press for laxness, moved in.

Two burly guards surrounded them.

"You two. You just walk through fence?"

"No," said Robert.

"You got guns?"

"No," said Robert.

"Okay. You good guys. Go ahead."

Athens security having been breached, Robert Kranz and the other Powie entered the plane.

Five miles above the Atlantic, as prescribed, they screamed hysterically that it was a hijacking, ran up and down the aisles hitting people with the butts of their guns, and then told the captain of the aircraft that he would either fly to Harbor Island or they would all be dead. A real shot into a real aircraft seat with a person's thigh in between convinced the pilot they were all going to die unless he did what Robert Kranz said.

"There's no airport at Harbor Island," said the captain, looking at his charts. "We've got to land at Nassau. It's the only one big enough for us."

"Look at your map. You will land here," said Robert, pointing to the Atlantic side of Harbor Island.

"That's a beach. How the hell can we take off from a beach?"

"I don't know. Do what you're told and you won't be hurt. We don't want to hurt you. We won't hurt anyone if you cooperate."

Before they got to Harbor Island the pilot was met by naval aircraft warning him to veer away from the quarantined airspace.

"I can't. A lunatic has got a gun at my head and I can lose all my passengers."

"Veer."

"Sorry, no," said the pilot, whose first responsibility was for the safety of those aboard.

"Veer," came the order again from the naval aircraft.

"No," said the pilot.

Below on Harbor Island the engineer watched the Navy tomcats backing away from the passenger jet.

Rubin Dolomo coughed and didn't even bother to look up.

"They've backed down," said the engineer.

"Of course," said Rubin. He knew the Navy world. It would have to. He had figured out what made hijackings against America so successful. It wasn't who the hijackers were, it was who the Americans were. They were people who cared enough to protect human life. In the real world that made them very vulnerable.

Could anyone imagine a Russian plane being hijacked?

Rubin Dolomo watched the large Boeing 707 come down on Pink Beach. That was a show. With surgical precision, the pilot skillfully brought the center of the plane down on the hard-packed sand at the edge of the water, palm trees on one side and open sea on the other, and the belly met the sand as gently as a soap bubble.

It was a bright morning on Harbor Island as Powie guards moved in to relieve Robert Kranz and his quaking partner. The crew was kept on the plane while the passengers were taken to prearranged spots around the island so that if any part of the island were bombed, the passengers would be hit. They were, as Rubin had figured out, "our living sandbags."

It was noon before the news media arrived by boat from Eleuthera Island, having used political clout to break through the naval quarantine. As soon as it was learned that the Navy was blockading Harbor Island, almost every major commentator was accusing the Navy of suppressing news. Was America at war with a Bahamian island? If so, why wasn't it declared?

The American government did not have a right to hamper the freedom of the press, and the Navy patrol boats were ordered to give way to the throngs of cameramen and reporters.

Rubin was ready for them. He put the television cameramen in old cattle pens and the newspaper reporters in lamb pastures, with the news photographers assigned to goat pens. Anyone leaving the prescribed route was whipped by Powie guards.

One reporter, in an effort to establish the humanity of the Poweressence movement, was lacerated so severely that he passed out. Another Powie threw a glass of water in his face, bringing him to, and immediately it became a story of Powie medical care for the wounded.

When he was ready, Rubin Dolomo called Beatrice.

"It's all yours, precious dove," he said. "They're going to give you the world."

In the White House the President and Smith watched as Beatrice Dolomo spoke live to the American people. Almost every station across the country broke into programming to broadcast the live announcement of the Harbor Island hijacking.

"Good people of America," said Beatrice Dolomo, her face in even heavier makeup for the cameras. "I have never had anything against the American people. In fact, I am an American. I do not wish to harm the innocent passengers, because we like the passengers. What I seek, and what we all seek, is religious freedom. Today, languishing in American jails are people whose only crime was that they dared to be positive instead of negative. I refer to one who is dear to our hearts. Our good friend Kathy Bowen from *Amazing Humanity*. What is her crime? What is our crime? We seek only peace and comfort for all of us."

Beatrice finished reading the prepared statement, smiled especially broadly at a very handsome reporter, and then nodded to Rubin.

Rubin assured everyone that the passengers were safe and feeling better than ever before because some initial Poweressence was being given to them.

"This amazing new form of reaching our ancient power roots has given help to millions, solved sleeping problems, cured eye defects, made success out of failure, and given people a new lease on life. For your free character test that will tell you who you are and how you can be stress-free forever, all you have to do is contact the Poweressence temple in your neighborhood."

The President turned from the set.

"They're murderers and crooks, and I'm going to tell that to the country," he said. "Dammit. They're getting millions of dollars' worth of free advertising. And we're helpless. I'm more afraid of their formula than I am for those poor passengers. This just complicates things."

This time when the Queen of Alarkin phoned she wasn't kept waiting by State Department channels for a half-hour. She was put right through.

Her demands were simple. Drop the mail-fraud, conspiracy-to-commit-murder, accessory-to-murder-before-the-fact, extortion, and embezzlement charges against Rubin and herself, and the President could be hailed as a peacemaker to the world. Fail, and he would be trashed throughout the nation.

"Honey," said the President, "I wasn't elected to make deals with petty con men. You go ahead and trash. No deal. America is not for sale."

By evening it seemed as though almost every station had a program on religious intolerance in America. Persecution of Catholics, Jews, Mormons, and Quakers was now made to seem like a mere prelude to the latest in religious intolerance.

Professor Waldo Hunnicut was on the air again. It was he, after President Sadat was shot, who blamed America and not the fundamentalist Muslims who did the shooting. He blamed America for the massacres by the Khmer Rouge, whom America had once fought, and he now blamed America for the hijacking.

"I have yet to speak to one president in America who really understands religious freedom."

When he tried the same trick with Congress the next day,

two representatives cut him short, explaining that he was just another "blame-America-first-for-everything" nut.

But the media did not investigate his background. Instead they interviewed beautiful Kathy Bowen in jail. Her tones were professionally sweet, her eyes even more innocent than the time she played a saint in an Easter television production.

"I know that I am in jail because I believe people are good. I wish no harm to come to any innocent person. But is the President innocent when he quarantines the blameless nation of Alarkin because they dare to think people are good? Is the President innocent when powerful American aircraft daily fly over the tiny island, when nuclear warships patrol its beaches? Who is the President that he thinks he has a right to stop goodness with his nuclear evil?"

No one mentioned Ms. Bowen was in jail on a charge of conspiracy to murder, that she had been caught just the week before in an announcement of the President's death even before his plane went down, and that she undoubtedly was implicated in the murder of an American Air Force colonel and everyone on the plane.

And alligators in swimming pools were considered past history and not worth mentioning as the story became American arms in support of intolerance.

One network and newspaper did a combined poll.

The question was: Should American nuclear weapons support religious intolerance?

When the answer came in negative, everyone announced the President was slipping.

One of the hijacked passengers who had been elected spokesman told Americans on breakfast and supper news programs that many of the hostages had devoped "a profound sense of empathy with the Poweressence cause."

The President called a press conference and outlined the petty and major crimes of the Dolomos, exactly how Poweressence extracted money from people under false pretenses.

The press conference was followed immediately by commentators pointing out that calling names never helped anyone. The President was labeled reckless and irresponsible, especially when he said the Dolomos were not going to get away with it.

"I certainly would not want him as my negotiator," said one commentator who had been released from the cow pens of Harbor Island, now called Alarkin.

He was the one who led the others in calling Beatrice Dolomo "your Majesty," saying America had to get over the arrogance of thinking it could decide how people would live.

"I personally find Poweressence spiritually and emotionally uplifting in ways that Christianity has never been."

There were also many interviews at Poweressence temples to explain how Poweressence devotees were suffering for the handful of actions of a few faithful.

"I do not support hijacking. I support freedom of religion," said one franchise owner, who also slyly warned that as long as America kept persecuting its religious minorities it should become used to hijackings and oil spills like the Bayonne disaster.

"Yes, I do believe the Bayonne diaster just as much as the hijacking was the result of America's persecution of religion."

In the Oval Office the President gave a single order to Smith.

"I want your two specialists. I don't care how you go about getting them. Get them."

"The organization's system located them in Newark, sir, but after that I don't know where they're going to be. I believe that Remo was the one who kept both of them here, but we can't count on that now."

"Why the hell not?"

"Because I don't know if he knows anymore that he's working for us."

Remo felt it was great to finally meet the image that had been talking to him.

"All I wanted to do, little father, was to go home, but I never knew where that was. Now I know. Sinanju, right?"

"The most perfect village in the world, where your ancestors came from," said Chiun.

They were in an airline terminal, and Chiun had placed his long fingernails under Remo's shirt just under the breastbone to synchronize his breathing, to make his lungs and the pores of his body work in unison so that his bloodstream would reverse the process of absorbing substances and now eject them.

But Chiun did not think of it in terms of bloodstream, rather as the poetry of the body, as he had learned from the Master before him and as the Master learned from the Master before him, from those first days when Sinanju learned the true powers of the human body and became the sun source of all the martial arts, only to be copied by others over the centuries.

Remo felt the fingernails and tried to concentrate, but the clank of coin machines and the smell of passing perfumes bothered him. It was then that he realized the coin machines were at the other end of the airport and his hearing was coming back. The perfumes were faint scents, which meant his smell was coming back.

His memory came only in pieces, though. He remembered looking at the star, and then he realized it was at that moment in the universe when it was decided what he would become, and his mind remembered it even if he couldn't.

He remembered Chiun. He remembered the lessons. He remembered thinking so many times that he would die. He remembered hating Chiun, and remembered learning respect, and later knowing and loving the man as the father he never knew.

He remembered Sinanju, the muddy little village from which came the greatest house of assassins of all time. He remembered to breathe. He tasted the onion-and-garlic essence of the liquid he had touched back in California. He remembered reaching into a tub to save a grown man, acting like a child, who was drowning. He remembered losing control of his skin.

He was not up to peak. And this had set him back a little farther.

Some things were still spotty. He knew Sinanju was the village, but his home was not in the place itself but in its teaching. He was raised in the orphanage in Newark. He got that right.

"Yes, you are Sinanju, Remo," said Chiun, who was now not a vision anymore. And Remo knew why he could see him when he had forgotten everything else. He could see him because Chiun was within him like any good teacher. And Remo thought Chiun was the greatest teacher the world had ever known.

"I remember. I am not Korean at all," said Remo.

Chiun's fingers stopped. "Don't go that far. You are. Your father was Korean."

"Really? I didn't know that. How did you know that?"

"I will explain it later, but you will see the histories of Sinanju, our histories, and you will understand how you have been able to know so much."

"It's because of your great teaching, little father. I think you are the greatest teacher the world has ever known," Remo said.

"That too," said Chiun.

"Hey, I forgot. I've got to check in. The people I was after got away."

"Everyone gets away in America. We don't belong here."

"I do, little father. That's the problem," said Remo, who still remembered the contact number for Smith.

15

Remo was apologetic and Chiun was outraged.

"Never admit to an emperor you have done wrong," Chiun said in Korean. But Remo ignored him.

"What are we all doing in the White House? Isn't this the worst possible contact point? Talk of risking exposure."

"Somehow the Dolomos have gotten through to the President. I am afraid they will again. If the President turns into a hostile three-year-old, the whole world can go up. I brought Chiun here for that reason."

"Ah, so. That is the excuse he will use to seize the throne," Chiun said to Remo in Korean, and to Smith in English, "Most wise."

"He's not going to take any throne," Remo answered. "He had you here because he couldn't kill the President himself. He wanted you to do it. Then he would demolish the organization and kill himself."

"On the eve of his enthronement?" asked Chiun, so incredulous that he forgot to speak in Korean.

"I've told you this, you just don't want to know, little father," said Remo.

"I have since worked out a way to defend against an intrusion of that sort," said Smith. "The question is, how fit are you?"

"I'd be vulnerable to that solution."

"You stay here. Can you do what is necessary if the President is stricken by the Dolomos?"

"You mean can I kill him?"

"Yes."

"Sure," said Remo.

"No problem there?"

"It's the right move, Smitty."

"Yes. I suppose so," said Smith. "Maybe I'm getting old. I couldn't do it."

"He couldn't do anything, the crazy lunatic," Chiun said in Korean, and in English added, "Benovolence is of course the signal character of a great ruler."

"Chiun, with Remo here we can send you. We need to free a group of passengers being held prisoner on an island, and make sure, above all make sure we get control of a formula created by two people, Rubin and Beatrice Dolomo. Get them too while you're at it."

"Another stupid shopping list from the lunatic in residence," Chiun said to Remo in Korean, and in English told Smith, "We fly with the speed of your very words."

"No. Remo has to stay here."

"Then we shall guard your honor with our lives."

"No. I want one to do one thing and the other to do another."

"Both shall do both simultaneously and add to your glory in greater power than a single leaf on a single branch."

"We have got to have Remo here to do what must be done and you in Harbor Island to do what you must do."

"Ah," said Chiun. "I understand. Remo and I will be off to Harbor Island immediately."

"Smitty, he's not going to let me be anywhere alone in my condition. So give up on that plan of splitting us," said Remo.

"Why did you say such a thing to Smith?" asked Chiun in Korean, and in the same language Remo answered:

"Because it's true."

"So?"

"So if we all know what we are doing we don't have to play games."

"Treating an emperor properly is not a game. Woe be to the assassin who always tells his emperor the truth."

And in English Remo said to Smith:

"You've got to choose."

"All right. I have something worked out here if the President is stricken. Go to Harbor Island. But stay in contact. The phone system there is shaky. We'll give you a communications device that links you with a satellite. This whole thing is going to be tricky. I want control from here. I care about the hostages, I want to get the Dolomos, but that stuff is a nightmare."

"What is it exactly?" asked Remo.

"They're finding out now. The real problem is that some of it won't break down with time."

"So bury it."

"In what place that won't be near a water system? We've got the situation at the Dolomo estate contained, but it is a nightmare if ever they start mass-producing the stuff."

"So we should get the stuff first?"

"I don't know. That's why we want you with the communicator," said Smith.

Before they left, Smith wanted to see the President and personally assure him they were going through with this.

"He's been attacked all over the country. Only the people are with him. He's a stand-up guy and he should know that he's got help."

"And of course, while we are there, if he should fall and suffer an accident . . . ?" suggested Chiun.

"No," said Smith.

"Not now, then," said Chiun.

In the Oval Office, Remo Williams promised his President that nothing would stop him.

"I'm an American," said Remo. "And I don't like to see my country trashed."

"No. Just the Dolomos. Don't do anything to the press," said the President.

The President kept avoiding Chiun's eyes. Remo guessed that he knew it had been Chiun who was supposed to kill him.

Chiun saw the President's reaction. This could mean

that the lunatic Smith had actually told the current emperor of his plans. Nothing was beyond the insanity of these whites whom Remo continued beyond all reason to serve.

"For the first time I feel like we are in control of the situation," said the President.

"Whites are never in control of the situation. They are the situation." This, of course, in Korean.

Remo and Chiun entered Harbor Island, now being openly talked of as Alarkin or Free Alarkin or Liberated Alarkin. The people doing the talking were newsmen. Some of them were reporting right from the boat. Remo and Chiun avoided the cameras.

One announcer talked of how weak Alarkin had made America, how it had exposed not only America's weakness but also America's intolerance of religious minorities to the world.

"The feeling of many of the hijacked passengers is that while they disagree with hijacking, they have come to learn the pain and persecution suffered by the Powies. They have seen American ships and American guns surround the tiny nation of Alarkin, once Harbor Island. They understand how Poweressence devotees can find themselves in American jails, and they have no wonder that America is a target for those who do not have aircraft carriers or nuclear bombs, but only their own lives. These lives the Powies used in what some in the West might call terrorism. But to the weak and oppressed it is a chance to risk everything against the powerful for the sake of loved ones in American jails. After all, they ask, why not trade one innocent captive for another, and they refer to Kathy Bowen, seized by armed American law-enforcement officers and put behind bars."

When the announcer finished, he took off his makeup and looked around for applause.

Remo looked to Chiun. "That's not reporting, that's propaganda."

"Why do you care? I don't understand anything about the crazy whites of your country."

"Somebody is supposed to try to tell the truth. These guys color everything."

"Who doesn't?" asked Chiun. "If you are dissatisfied with these, hire your own."

Even before they reached the dock, two other reporters gave reports to their television cameras on whether the press was a factor in the story. Their conclusion was that the press, considering its handicaps, was doing as well as it could. There was a reporter on the boat who was doing a story for a jouralism magazine on criticism of the media, and he was coming to a conclusion that the critics were biased and narrow-minded and that the press had done an outstanding job.

"Am I wrong?" he asked the television newsmen and the reporters.

They all thought he was basically right.

"Good, because I am going back with the boat. I don't have to actually go onto the island to get the story if I have it now."

"Why are you bothered by such silly things?" asked Chiun. "What is this thing about truth? That you know what is so is the only matter of importance."

"But these guys are heard by millions."

"Then it is the problem of the millions. You may not remember, but I once told you that to know the truth is enough for any one person. What another knows is his problem."

"I don't like to see my country get trashed by its own," said Remo.

"I do," said Chiun. "Your country deserves it. Now, if they were to defame Sinanju, the glorious gem of civilization on the West Korea Bay, then we might take proper action."

"Forget it, little father. I am well enough that I remember Sinanju. It's a mudhole of a fishing village. I remember now. We had a big fight there once."

"You had a fight, I had a glorious homecoming," said Chiun.

The boat landed and about twenty young men and women with whips met the American newsmen. Some were herded to the old cow barns. Others were taken to the sheep pasture before they were allowed to interview the hijackers.

Remo turned on his communicator.

It was half the size of a loaf of bread and had been designed for absolute simplicity. There were only two buttons to push. Somehow Remo managed to push them four times in combinations that failed to work. He thought that should be impossible. He banged it once. He banged it twice, gently.

"Working," came Smith's voice.

"What do you want first?"

"Locate that liquid but keep Chiun with you. You know what happened to you last time."

"When do I do that, what should I do then?"

"Probably move on the Dolomos and then on the Powies, and that should take care of the hijacked passengers. Let the Marines rescue them."

"How does this thing work? I got it going by accident."

"You press the button on the right to turn it on and the one on the left to turn if off."

"Oh," said Remo, and was cut off when he pressed the wrong button.

Chiun was outraged again that they were following a typical Smith insanity. A professional assassin should remove great leaders, he pointed out, not go shopping for formulas. Let his chemist take care of that, not his assassins, Chiun said. None of this would happen if they worked for a legitimate emperor instead of the lunatic.

It was not easy getting out of the corrals set up for the reporters. Remo opened the gate using a Powie head as a battering ram. The reporters did not escape but waited for other Powie guards to return to tell them where to go and what to report.

At the harbor facing the neighboring Bahamian island

of Eleuthera, Remo saw that many of the houses were boarded shut. These were pleasant houses, many with pink shutters and pastel walls, with red and yellow flowers growing in abundance over white picket fences. The British had been here and left their influence.

There was a sense of civility about these houses that surpassed anything in Great Britain, however. The homes were warm, welcoming, and open. And yet all the doors were shut.

"Now," said Chiun, "in an occupied land, to whom do you go to find out what the occupants are doing?"

"I remember that one, little father," said Remo. "You go to the occupiers second."

"Because?"

"Because while only a top few of the occupiers know what they are doing, almost every one of the occupied knows," said Remo.

"Correct," said Chiun.

The thing that hit Remo hardest, while walking these pleasant stone streets amid pleasant bungalows and cottages, was the silence. No one was in the streets. The houses talked of liveliness and the streets talked ominously of silence.

"They're all inside," said Remo. He entered a pleasant pink bungalow with white shutters bordered by an expanse of bougainvillea over a manicured white picket fence. The air smelled of sea and flowers and it was good.

Remo knocked.

"We are inside as ordered," said a pleasant British voice.

"We're not the occupiers," said Remo.

"Then please leave. We don't want to be caught talking to you."

"You won't be caught."

"You can't assure us of that," replied the very British voice.

"Yes I can," said Remo.

The door opened and a black face appeared.

"Are you from the press?"

"No," Remo admitted.

"Please do come in, then," said the man with the British accent.

He shut the door behind Remo and Chiun. The parlor was pleasantly furnished with white wicker furniture. African designs covered the walls, and prominent over an artificial fireplace which never needed use was a lithograph of a very white, almost blond Jesus.

"I will not talk to another American reporter. They came around here asking if we wanted American planes to bomb our homes, and when we all said 'of course not,' they went on to report we were afraid of an American invasion. If we didn't know the British newspapers were worse, we would be outlandishly offended."

"We're here to get the bad guys."

"At last, somebody is capable of making a moral distinction. What I don't understand is how so many can say they are for these Powies but against the hijacking. They are the hijacking. They are putting alligators in people's swimming pools. They made the attempt on your President's life. That is who they are."

"Couldn't agree more," said Remo.

"And they have bad manners. And they pass out these ridiculous leaflets on their fake cult."

"Couldn't agree more," said Remo.

"Then let's have a spot of tea, and you let me know how I can help you. I am simply outraged that every time somebody takes over a place with force, your press calls it liberation and then blithely goes on to the next free country reporting its ills until it too is liberated. Do you know what 'liberated' has come to mean? Any country which will shoot you if you leave."

"Couldn't agree more," said Remo. "But I'm afraid we're going to pass on the tea. We're looking for something these people have. It's a formula, a liquid, they're making here. It makes people forget."

"I wish I could take some now," joked their host. "I don't know of such a thing, but my children might."

The man introduced Remo to a boy and girl about ten

years old. They were bright, intelligent, neat, and polite.

"I didn't know they made polite children anymore," said Remo.

"Certainly not in America," said Chiun, alluding to his problems with Remo.

Remo explained what he was looking for.

"I don't know if it will be any help, but these bad people are making some stuff, like water, that makes people forget. Even if you touch it, you can be affected just as if you drank it. It goes through the skin."

"Like interferon," said the boy.

"What?" said Remo.

"It's a drug. Many drugs can be transferred through the pores, you know. They do breathe."

"I know that," said Remo.

"That explains what they're doing under the north end of Pink Beach," said the boy.

"The big rubber bags," said the girl.

"The big rubber room."

"Rubber would do it. They'd have to seal it in something," said Remo.

"And to think the House of Sinanju used to serve czars," said Chiun. "By all means explain to us about rubber bags. That is what we are here for. Rubber bags for garbage."

"The first thing they did was to dig a giant hole in the north end of Pink Beach. They have those silly Americans working for nothing. They're part of the cult. Once it was dug, they built a concrete foundation with a concrete roof," said the boy.

"Yes, my friend Sally heard them saying an airplane would have to be able to land on it without disturbing it. That was before the hijacked plane arrived," said the girl.

"And then they built rubber rooms inside it, and I remember seeing them bring in rubber bags."

"How many?" asked Remo.

"We counted fifteen. We thought it was strange. Then they covered up everything with the sand."

"And then of course the plane landed."

Remo reported all of this to Smith and got the order he expected:

"Get the rubber bags."

He promised the family that he would personally remove the Powies from their island, even if the U.S. government didn't.

"I see that you've got an idiot box," said the boy.

"You mean the communicator?" asked Remo.

"I don't know what it does," said the boy. "But when you have to have something run by backward people you reduce it to two buttons. That way they have to be able to work it. It could be anything."

"Sometimes I have difficulty with mechanical objects," admitted Remo.

"They built it just for you, Remo," said Chiun.

The north end of Pink Beach was guarded by three Powies using their positive thoughts to ward off painful sunburn. They were in a great deal of pain from red, peeling skin.

One of them was talking about returning to group therapy instead of Poweressence. She was called a traitor.

Remo examined Pink Beach. They had done a good job of covering up the concrete. But it was easy to sense its location. The mass virtually breathed its presence under the pink sand.

The three Powie gaurds tried to stop Remo. With a flick of his wrist he caught their oncoming bodies and flung them into the sea. Just at the horizon was the American aircraft carrier sending off another flight of planes.

Chiun watched the wrist action as Remo propelled the charging Powies into the gently rolling waves off Pink Beach. It was hard for him to tell how much Remo was regaining of his functions by so simple a move. He could have done that while totally under the influence of the solution.

"You should have saved them to dig our way in," said Chiun.

But he knew moving through sand was only slightly

more difficult that moving through water and even people without Sinanju could do that.

They got into the room easily. Chiun pushed Remo back so that he would not step on an almost invisible spot of moisture on the rubber floor.

Remo recognized the onion-and-garlic smell. It was the formula.

Inside the room was a small glass chamber outfitted with rubber arms. A person could work with the material inside that capsule and then climb through the trapdoor underneath and come out at the entrance.

A spout and a conveyor belt were within easy reach of the arms. Apparently the rubber bags moved along the belt and were filled. A heating iron at the end of the belt probably sealed the bags.

And at the end were fifteen racks under shower heads. Apparently that was where the rubber bags were washed off and stored. But only one rubber bag remained.

"Chiun, you search for the rubber bags while I get away from here."

"I am not a treasure hunter, I am an assassin."

"Then I'll do it," said Remo.

"You know you don't have your breathing correct yet," said Chiun.

Remo went out through the sand to the fresh air and waited for Chiun. It was not a long wait.

"There is only one bag left," said Chiun.

Remo fumbled with the communicator and finally got Smith.

"Fourteen bags are missing."

"That's unfortunate. Move on the Dolomos now. Find out what they've done with the solution. Find out who has the formula. Find out everything."

"And the hostages?"

"Later. I'm sorry, but it's necessary."

"Maybe I can get to the Dolomos easiest by springing the hostages," said Remo.

"But remember, they are secondary," said Smith.

"Right," lied Remo.

Remo found the hostages were being kept at the hotels on the harbor and being moved to whichever news organization paid the highest price for an interview. As it turned out, the spokesman for the group who had such profound sympathy for their cause also sold printing to Poweressence. He had profound sympathy for them even when they put alligators into people's swimming pools.

He had manicured hair, a calm disposition, and was being lavished with praise from a reporter for his remarkable composure.

Remo gave the spokeman a light punch to the solar plexus, doubling him up to the applause of the rest of the hostages. Then he took the Powie whips and wrapped them tightly around Powie necks. He took the television camera cords and just as tightly wrapped them around the necks of the television reporters.

"You're free," he said to the hostages. "Just stay here till the Marines arrive."

Several Powies advanced on Remo and Chiun, firing machine guns taken from the American advisers. They stopped firing when Remo and Chiun mangled their hands and flung them and their weapons against the coral rocks.

When Rubin Dolomo heard the firing he ran to his command post atop the high ridge that divided Harbor Island, now his Kingdom of Alarkin.

He got reports immediately. It was the dark-eyed man with thick wrists.

"Absolute negativity has found us," he said.

"Launch the secondary plan?" asked the engineer.

"Not yet. We got him with the solution before, we can get him again."

Rubin Dolomo climbed up a little ladder atop the roof of his command post, and wheezing into a megaphone said:

"Here I am. Come after me, you negative force of evil. I am the leader of the Warriors of Zor, the light against darkness, the one truth that lives forever."

Hearing this, Beatrice Dolomo told her two handsome

Powie companions to put their clothes back on and rushed to the command post.

"Why are you telling him where we are?"

"Because I want him here, precious. We stalled him last time with just a little of the solution. This time we're going to send him back to the joining of his mother's egg and his father's sperm. I hope he likes the womb."

At the perimeter of the hotel a light mist emerged from the ground like a fog shooting upward. Remo smelled the garlic and onion and moved back.

He saw Rubin and Beatrice Dolomo peering down at him through binoculars from the roof of one of the resort cottages.

"You stay away from that mist. I will get them. At least it is a proper assassination, even if they are two nothings," Chiun said.

"Can't kill them. Got to find out where they secreted the formula and the rest of the solution," said Remo.

"Of course, I should have known," said Chiun. "This was too much like honorable work. I am still on a treasure hunt."

Some of the reporters had heard the firing and now were focusing on Chiun as he moved through the fine spray.

"Another devotee of the embattled religious faith now goes to pay homage to his spiritual leader, Rubin Dolomo, as powerful nuclear aircraft carriers surround their little stronghold," said the reporter into his microphone as Chiun moved on.

Rubin focused binoculars on the Oriental in the kimono.

"Saints have mercy, look at his skin," said Rubin.

"Let me see," said Beatrice.

"Look at the forehead. Look at the hands," said Rubin.

"They're moving. They're shedding the formula," gasped Beatrice.

"And the machine guns didn't work either."

"We're trapped."

"Not necessarily. Get the President on the phone, Beatrice. I want to speak to him."

"Why you?"

"Because I know the alternate plan."

Remo watched Chiun move through standard defenses: the guns, more formula (this time sprayed out of a cannon), iron bars, and flying darts, presumably coated with the formula. He knew Chiun was making slow work of it because he could have moved faster. But the flourishes of the arms and the kimono told Remo that Chiun was performing for the television cameras.

Suddenly his communicator started beeping as though the entire electronics had gone berserk.

Remo managed to press the correct button and got Smith's voice.

"Stop Chiun. Whatever you do, stop Chiun. Tell him not to advance on the Dolomos."

"We have them."

"Tell him to stop."

"But we have them."

"No. They have us. They have civilization. And they have no qualms about destroying it. Just tell Chiun to stop. I'll explain later."

Remo yelled out in Korean for Chiun not to close on the Dolomos.

"Why not?" asked Chiun. "Is it too much like honorable work?"

"Something has happened. We have to back down."

"In front of television reporters? In front of cameras? In front of the world?"

"Now. Yes. Now."

"I will not endure such indignity. It is my last straw."

"Then I am going to have to stop you, little father."

"What insolence!" Chiun said. "We are in front of the world, Remo. I cannot afford to be seen to lose."

"You mean you are going to have to kill me?"

"I cannot afford to be seen to lose," Chiun repeated.

"Then go ahead and kill me," said Remo. He skirted the area of the fine mist, looking for a dry spot inside the perimeter, and when he found it he did a forward tumble over the mist. He hoped it would not look too unusual to the cameras. He landed on the dry rock and advanced through the remnants of the defenses Chiun had already destroyed.

"Did you see that?" asked Rubin.

"Yes, can you imagine what he's like in bed?"

"I see now why he was able to get through bullets and everything."

"He's so sexy," said Beatrice.

"Do you think he'll take the older man?"

"He can take me," said Beatrice.

The Dolomos watched as the Oriental in the kimono turned to face the oncoming white with the dark eyes and thick wrists. The two spoke an Oriental language they didn't understand.

Then the white threw the first blow. It was so fast they did not see it, but the eddies from the stroke fluttered the reddish-purple flowers of the bougainvillea.

16

The reason for surrender was as simple as it was horrifying. The Dolomos had made a demonstration of a small American city.

"Before you have your minions of evil finish us off, check Culsark, Nebraska," Rubin had said.

"What's in Culsark?" asked the President.

And the President heard laughter.

"You check them now, because what happened to Culsark will happen to you. Will happen to Europe and Japan. We have devoted followers stationed at fourteen of the most vulnerable water supplies in the world. When you look at Culsark, look at the future of Paris, London, Tokyo, and Washington. Look at tomorrow, which doesn't remember yesterday."

Smith, listening in, immediately ordered Remo to back down. It was just what he was afraid of.

"We can at least check on Culsark first," suggested the President.

"No time. If my estimate of Rubin Dolomo is correct, he has his people set to go off without instruction. In other words, if they don't hear from him every so often, they unload the formula."

"Then it will be done with."

"Not if we don't know how long it lasts. Move it into a water supply and it might infect the world, for all we know. Imagine a world where no one knows how to read or can remember how to make bronze or steel. What we have here is something worse than nuclear weapons. We have the end of civilization."

"We can't keep surrendering to them."

"I'm sorry, sir," said Smith. "We just have."

The word from Culsark came quickly. State troopers found the population crying. They all were looking for someone else to bring them food and change their clothes.

Under orders to maintain secrecy so the entire country would not panic, state troopers wearing rubber suits moved the victims to a specially prepared hospital. The scientists Smith had recruited had found some success with flushing out the system immediately, although the long-term effects could not yet be determined.

He did not hear from Remo or Chiun for four hours. And when he did, the news was even more disastrous than he could imagine.

"Sorry, Smitty," said Remo. "Chiun's gone over to the Dolomos."

"But he can't leave without you. You're still working for us, aren't you?"

"I'm sorry. I just couldn't explain away your actions anymore to Chiun."

"You never could."

"I couldn't explain them to me is what I really mean, Smitty."

"Remo, if this is a maneuver, I will understand."

"Smitty, when you backed away from rescuing the hostages, you lost me."

"We had strategic concerns you didn't know about."

"I knew I was an American and I felt trashed by what was being done to the hostages. Besides, Smitty, I just threw a blow at Chiun that was so bad, he laughed at me. I can't live with that."

"Remo, remember everything you believe. Don't leave your country now."

"I'm sorry, Smitty. I learned something when I lost my memory. My country has left me. It isn't worth defending anymore. So long, sweetheart. It's been fun. But it's over."

Smith heard the communicator disconnect itself. Apparently Remo had destroyed it.

In Harbor Island Remo threw the last of the communicator into the Atlantic as the patrol boats veered away toward the horizon and the last of the naval aircraft landed on the carrier's desk for departure.

"We've won," said Beatrice. "We have won everything."

"Are you really the force of negative universe response?" Rubin asked the dark-eyed man who had given him so much trouble.

"He is," said Chiun. "I have labored against this negativity for years now, but only you have been able to spot it."

"I knew it," said Rubin. "The negative force coming after my positive force."

"I want him after me now," said Beatrice.

"Wait," said Chiun. "If I am to serve you properly I must admit that your forces are not worthy of such a gracious queen."

"That was Rubin's idea—calling me a queen. The press fell for it. But I rather liked it."

"You are a queen," said Chiun. "I have been working for these white lunatics lo these many years. You alone show the true nature of a queen. You appreciate revenge, I can see."

"Not revenge, justice," said Beatrice.

"The best kind," said Chiun. "Let me know your enemies so that they may grovel at your feet, begging your mercy."

"This man has a nice ring to him," said Beatrice.

"I don't know," said Rubin. "They've come a long way to surrender."

"It is not surrender," said Chiun, "when one leaves fools to join with those who understand the universe. We could kill, you know, but that would leave us without a monarch, and what is an assassin without his monarch?''

"Maybe you're playing along so that I won't ruin Western civilization," said Rubin.

"I never thought much of it anyhow," said Chiun.

Rubin wheezed and popped another sedative. It had been a long day.

"How do you do that stuff that you do?" asked Rubin.

"How do you do everything?" asked Beatrice.

"Your Majesties," said Chiun, "your way should not be burdened nor should your way be hard."

"I'm going to puke," said Remo in Korean.

"Shut up," Chiun answered in kind.

"You're mine, young man," said Beatrice, trying to put a hand on Remo's arm. The arm kept escaping her hand.

"Tell him to be still," said Beatrice. "If I'm queen I can have everyone in my kingdom."

"So much for your standards of being an assassin, little father. Do you know what they call this service?" asked Remo in Korean. He got a reply in the same tongue.

"She doesn't really care about your body. It's hers she is interested in. Satisfy her."

"I don't even like touching her."

"That's all you have to do, just touch."

"Then you do it," said Remo. "I'm your son. Is this what you would have your son do?"

"Oh viper, that you should use guilt on the aged, that you should turn morality against him who has given you everything you know and saved your life innumerable times," said Chiun, and he refused to discuss anything else privately with Remo.

The boy had much to learn.

"Gracious Queen, allow me to awaken you to the wonders of your body," said Chiun.

"Thanks," said Rubin, who knew he was off the hook for this afternoon at least.

But he was surprised to see the old Oriental stay right where he was on the roof of their command post and

merely rub Beatrice's inner wrists. Beatrice, Rubin could
tell, was enjoying one of her major orgasms.

"Seven. Seven. Eight. Nine, Ten ten ten, oooh, ten,"
shrieked Beatrice. "Ten, ten. Ten."

"I'm going to puke," said Remo.

"Was it good for you, you little sweetheart," laughed
Beatrice. She tried to tweak Chiun's cheek.

"And you, King, that you should suffer such breathing,
it is not right," said Chiun.

"That's okay. You just keep taking care of Beatrice, it'll
be fine with me."

"No," said Chiun. "You are to receive Sinanju."

And with that, he reached under the thin white blouse
Rubin wore, the one with the extra pockets for the pills.

Rubin jerked up straight. His eyes widened.

"What's that in the air?"

"You're breathing," said Chiun.

"That's right. A breath. A clean full breath. I had my
last one of those the day I snuck behind the barn for my
first cigarette," said Rubin.

Chiun bowed deeply. Remo turned to look at the ocean.
He wished the planes would turn turn around and bomb
everything. In the opening moves he had made earlier
against Chiun, moves of course never designed to harm, he
had agreed after he had obviously lost to go along with
Chiun.

Chiun had promised that everything would be all right.
Perhaps Remo should have known what "all right"
meant. Remo had said there was a world to save. And
Chiun had promised not to disgrace Remo. Now he was
courting these make-believe kings and queens.

And Remo knew how truly American he was at this
point. Because he suspected kings and queens were all
frauds. That's why they needed assassins, to keep their
relatives at bay and themselves in power. There had to be a
better way to select a ruler than some accident of birth, or
through fraud like the one Chiun was perpetrating now.

But Remo was not prepared for what he saw now. Rubin
wanted to know how Chiun had done that. Chiun

answered about forces of the body. Rubin said he knew a lot about those.

"Then you can learn Sinanju," Chiun said. "You must know it. Your soldiers must know it. Otherwise you will be trapped here forever."

"You can't teach Sinanju to a wreck," Remo said in Korean.

"What is that language? What are you talking about?" asked Beatrice.

"He said you were most beautiful," said Chiun.

"I didn't think he liked me. He was going to suffer for it, of course, but I didn't really think he liked me."

"Who cannot love such graciousness?" said Chiun.

"Rubin, give this man whatever he wants. We have got to have more Sinanju, whatever that is. More and better. And in the morning, too."

"You are trapped here," said Chiun.

"No we're not. The world is trapped. Have you ever heard of Culsark, Nebraska?"

"Of course not," said Chiun.

"I chose it because it had an open reservoir. Hit the whole town two days ago as a demonstration, but no one noticed because no one else bothers with Culsark, Nebraska. Worked beautifully. Better than the invasion of the Dromoids. Because when I told the President to check, they were already hit by the solution. Have I told you about the solution?"

"No," said Chiun.

Beatrice, realizing Rubin was going to enjoy himself recounting his victories, went downstairs out of the sun after telling the young white that he would be next.

Remo didn't know which was worse, being downstairs with Beatrice in her boudoir or up on the roof of the command post with Chiun telling Rubin how brilliant he was. The problem was that Rubin did have a good deal of cunning. The whole civilized world was vulnerable to him.

It was then that Chiun told him he didn't need the hostages. Rubin agreed. The hostages were a weak step. One must never use weaker when one had stronger.

Chiun told him he already knew elements of Sinanju. But when Chiun himself began teaching the first steps of breathing to Rubin, and then by some communication network to some nuts called the Warriors of Zor, Remo left the roof of the command post. He wandered over to the hostages, who were holding their final press conference.

"We have learned the other side at last," said the pilot.

"A deep spiritual communion with our fellowman," said the spokesman for the hostages.

Remo, now acknowledged as working for the Dolomos, was able to order Powies around. He told them to collect all the newsmen in one corral, print, television, and radio. Then he had all the film removed and destroyed. That took care of anyone recognizing him.

He put the hostages on boats back to Eleuthera and told the Powies to gather at the north corner of the island.

"I don't want anyone going into the homes of the island. Stay here."

"Is this part of Sinanju? Mr. Dolomo has been combining Sinanju with Poweressence. He has a new Warrior of Zor. His name is Chiun. We heard his voice on our radios. Are you Sinanju?"

This from a young girl who was indeed using the beginner's breathing technique.

"Yeah. I'm Sinanju."

"This breathing is wonderful. It's so powerful," said the young woman. "We want to know more. What shall we do?"

"Do push-ups," said Remo.

"Is that Sinanju?"

"Sure."

"After the push-ups what should we do?"

"Do more push-ups," said Remo. "But don't leave this spot."

"Because the breathing force will be lost?" asked the young woman.

"No, because I'll kill you all if you do," said Remo. He walked back through the harbor, past the pleasant pastel houses which were now opening their doors. Children played in the streets and old women set out their market baskets under the large trees where they had sold their goods for years. Fishermen, too, were taking off for the reefs to catch the spiny lobster and grouper.

The Bahamian air was pleasant on this island and Remo loathed every breath he took of it.

He caught Chiun and Rubin Dolomo at dockside. Rubin was beaming with new energy. He threw his pills into the harbor.

"I have Sinanju," he said. "I never need anything else again."

"Sure," said Remo. He saw that Chiun's hand was almost always on Rubin's spinal cord. It wasn't Rubin who was creating the energy within him but Chiun, manipulating the nervous system to send false signals of well-being to the brain. It was a form of drug. Rubin was not cured of anything.

"We are off, Remo," said Chiun. "We will be back shortly with His Majesty's defenses strengthened."

"He's a genius, your father. Did you know that?" said Rubin.

"Yeah, he's wonderful," said Remo.

"You know we could have all been wiped out if it weren't for him."

"Wouldn't want that to happen," said Remo.

"Do you know what would happen if the solution were released by accident? We could have America believing the war was on and they would hit us with everything they had."

"Awful," said Remo. He couldn't look at Chiun.

"Or what would happen if all the governments of the world started looking quietly for our people and were to strike only when they knew where all of them were? We would be defenseless. You see, they can't be allowed to find them. Your father is a genius, boy."

"Certainly does have smarts," said Remo. He looked down at the coral rocks of the harbor. The sea was the same. Maybe all this would pass someday, he thought. But he realized it would never pass from his mind.

"Aren't you going to wish him good luck?"

Remo turned from Chiun and walked up the hump of the island, and then down through a path to Pink Beach, where he dug his feet into the sand and very quietly said, "Shit."

In the White House Smith did not know that Chiun was already one step ahead of him.

"It's not hopeless, just colossally difficult," said Smith. "We know there are fourteen bags of the solution outside Harbor Island. We know there is one inside. There are therefore fourteen bags around the world we have to find."

"But if we burst one, the others will release their solutions into their respective cities. Civilization will still be gone."

"Of course," said Smith. "So what we do is back off, and we have already done that. We have the world on our side. We have every police force and intelligence agency on our side. It will not take long to locate all fourteen of those rubber bags and then strike simultaneously."

"Can we do it legally?"

"He's declared war on the world. He is a national power in that hocus-pocus country of Alarkin."

"It might work. It's got to work," said the President. He had forgotten where he had put his pen, but he didn't want to let Smith know that. He often forgot little things but now he was aware of them, acutely aware.

Within two days the worst possible news came from around the world. Indeed, the locations of the fourteen bags had been discovered. But they were all gone, hidden somewhere else by two men fitting the descriptions of Rubin Dolomo and Chiun.

In fact, one police force did catch up with the pair and arrested them with a special squad of combat-ready police. That squad was now recovering in a Brussels hospital. Most of them would, sometime in the future, be able to walk.

But the fourteen bags were gone without a trace.

Dolomo and his friend had positioned them so brilliantly that no neighborhood, no local precinct nor intelligence agency, no matter how ruthless and extensive, was able to find them. Because of Chiun, the world was more vulnerable than ever before.

Chiun returned with Rubin in triumph. Remo, who had spent that time on Pink Beach watching sunrises and sunsets, came back to see what Chiun had done.

Beatrice was delighted to see Remo again and asked where he had been hiding. She was even more delighted to see Chiun. Several of the Powies had succumbed to heat exhaustion because someone had told them to do push-ups and nothing else.

"We've got to restore order to the island," said Beatrice.

"Most certainly, your Majesty," said Chiun. "For I must keep a promise."

"He's brilliant. As brilliant as I am," said Rubin. "Do you know why we will never be exposed now?"

Beatrice shook her head.

"Because everyone is looking for something that doesn't exist. We brought the bags back here. It's all here."

"But what if they attack here? That was the point of putting them all in different places around the world."

"But they're not going to. Chiun understands the human mind even better than I do. What we had was not fourteen bags of solution ready to contaminate key water supplies of the world. What made us powerful was that the American government feared we did. They still do. And now they will never be able to find them."

"Going to hide them under Pink Beach in that room?" asked Remo.

"Of course," said Rubin. "You there, boy, carry the bags."

"Do as he says," said Chiun.

"I will not," said Remo.

"You would make me, your aged teacher, do the labors of servants?"

"You could carry the boat with them in it. Who are you kidding?" said Remo, glancing down into the boat and counting the fourteen black rubber bags.

"Are you sure we aren't trusting Chiun too much?" asked Beatrice.

"I'm sure. Do you know what he told me? He said I should be the only one with the formula, otherwise someone else would have my power."

And then with deep emotion Rubin Dolomo told Chiun:

"I have learned to appreciate hiring only the professional assassin. I realize now that I have made mistakes with amateurs. I will use only you, Master of Sinanju."

"See, Remo. Everything has ended happily."

Chiun, of course, did not carry the bags. Instead, several Powies managed to lug the rubber bags to the north end of the island, where they placed them neatly on their racks in the rubber-lined concrete bunker.

"Your Majesties should inspect your major weapon to see that it is perfectly placed," said Chiun, leading the Dolomos into the bunker.

"Enough," said Remo. "I'm leaving."

"Not yet."

"Good-bye, little father. I can't stomach this," said Remo.

"Would you wait one minute and let me walk you to the beach? Or is this how we say good-bye after these many years?" Chiun followed Remo.

From inside the rubber-lined concrete bunker came Rubin's voice:

"All here, Chiun. Now help us out."

Chiun looked at Remo and smiled.

"I say, Chiun," called out Beatrice. "We're down here and we need help to get out."

"We have a choice now, son who has little faith in his teacher-father. We can leave them there forever, as mindless babies without memories, or . . ."

"We can make them live with each other in a Bahamian jail," said Remo.

"Of course, let him live without his pills and her without her continuous boyfriends, only him."

"It's truly a just end," said Remo.

"Yes, but we would have to walk them across the island and then boat them to Eleuthera and then to Nassau," said Chiun.

"To hell with just ends," said Remo, who hopped down into the bunker, told the Dolomos what their fate was going to be so they could enjoy the horror of it for a moment, and then carefully emptied a bag of their own solution over them. He shut the door, covered the bunker with sand, and collected the Powies to help clean up the mess they had made on Harbor Island. The Bahamian police arrived to supervise arrests of the troublemakers, as the Powies were now called.

But in Washington, Harold W. Smith did not know things had gone quite this well.

When he entered the President's office for his half-hour check to see if any of the Dolomo's followers had somehow gotten through the defenses, the President asked him what he was doing there.

The President apparently was deep in discussion of a problem of nuclear disposal with his advisers.

"I'm here to give you your pill, sir, as you have requested by letter. You know how forgetful you are, sir," said Smith.

"What?" said the President, somewhat annoyed that he had been interrupted.

"Your pill. You wrote me a note. Here it is," said Smith, taking the small case from his pocket and removing the white pill from it. He placed it on the President's desk and divided it with a pocketknife.

"What are you doing with that?"

"Preparing it for you, sir. As you asked. Here's the note," said Smith. And he placed the note in the President's hand.

"That's for if I'm stricken. I was just overloaded now. I get like that sometimes."

"Often?"

"Sure. I have so much on my mind I forget some things. Every leader has that problem."

"I think we have just avoided a terrible mistake. I don't think the Powies ever got to you. I think we were so distraught over how they could do so much damage that we thought they had gotten through to you at the first lapse of memory."

"I think you're right," said the President.

"It explains why we found no traces of it in the Oval Office or anywhere else around you. I'd better get out of here. I don't belong here, sir," said Smith.

By the time he returned to headquarters at Folcroft Sanitarium in Rye, New York, Smith had a call waiting from Remo. They had taken care of the remaining formula. It was sealed forever with the Dolomos. And there was an even better report from Agriculture Department scientists, one that relieved Smith more than anything he had heard that day. While the formula did not break down easily in the bloodstream, which was unfortunate for those stricken, it did most certainly break down when left alone in the open air. It was so volatile that when it combined with the trace elements in the air over a long period, it became as harmless as salad dressing.

But when Smith tried to reach out to thank Chiun, Chiun was not available. He had taken with him from Harbor Island the most valuable item of any fraud cult: its mailing list.

And to those devotees who had been informed in one of the regular messages from the leader that they would now also learn Sinanju, there was a messsage from the Master of Sinanju.

It read:

"Dear followers: There are reasons you seek happiness, and intellectual power, and good feelings about yourself. This is not unnatural for you. There are very good reasons why you feel inadequate. You are. Do not pursue Sinanju, because you are definitely not good enough. And as a helpful hint, may I suggest you save your money on improvement programs. The world is made of many kinds of people. Some good. Some bad. Some adequate. And some like yourself, who will never be good enough for anything."

Chiun liked the letter. He thought it had a ring to it.

"It will never raise any money," said Remo.

"And I won't have to associate with these inferiors either," said Chiun. "Of course, they did show me more trust than you, who I have treated like a son lo these many years."

And Chiun said that all could be forgiven if Remo would sign the history scroll stating he had Korean ancestry.

It was the least Remo could do for Chiun, who had saved Western civilization. Remo said he would think about it.

ABOUT THE AUTHOR

WARREN MURPHY has written eighty books in the last twelve years. His novel *Trace* was nominated for the best book of the year by The Mystery Writers of America and twice for best book by The Private Eye Writers of America. *Grand Master,* co-written with his wife Molly Cochran, won the 1984 Edgar Award. He is a native and resident of New Jersey.

RICHARD SAPIR is a novelist with several book club selections. He is a graduate of Columbia University and lives with his wife in New Hampshire.